No one can resist a book by

DIANA PALMER

"Palmer knows how to make the sparks fly.... Heartwarming."
—*Publishers Weekly* on *Renegade*

"A compelling tale...[that packs] an emotional wallop."
—*Booklist* on *Renegade*

"Sensual and suspenseful."
—*Booklist* on *Lawless*

"Diana Palmer is a mesmerizing storyteller
who captures the essence of what a romance should be."
—*Affaire de Coeur*

"Nobody tops Diana Palmer when it comes to delivering pure,
undiluted romance. I love her stories."
—*New York Times* bestselling author Jayne Ann Krentz

"The dialogue is charming, the characters likable and the sex sizzling."
—*Publishers Weekly* on *Once in Paris*

Also available from
Diana Palmer

Wyoming Tough
Merciless
The Savage Heart
Lacy
Magnolia
Renegade
Lone Star Winter
Dangerous
Desperado
Heartless
Fearless
Her Kind of Hero
Nora
Big Sky Winter
Man of the Hour
Trilby
Lawman
Hard to Handle
Heart of Winter
Outsider
Night Fever
Before Sunrise
Noelle
Lawless
Diamond Spur
The Texas Ranger
Lord of the Desert
The Cowboy and the Lady
Most Wanted
Fit for a King
Paper Rose
Rage of Passion
Once in Paris
After the Music
Roomful of Roses
Champagne Girl
Passion Flower
Diamond Girl
Friends and Lovers
Cattleman's Choice
Lady Love
The Rawhide Man

DIANA PALMER

BEFORE SUNRISE

Recycling programs for this product may not exist in your area.

ISBN-13: 978-0-373-77649-8

BEFORE SUNRISE

This edition published by arrangement with Harlequin Books S.A.

For questions and comments about the quality of this book please contact us at Customer_eCare@Harlequin.ca.

www.Harlequin.com

Printed in U.S.A.

For Doris Hunter Samson
June 14, 1941–June 13, 2004
My friend

BEFORE SUNRISE

1

Knoxville, Tennessee, May 1994

THE CROWD WAS DENSE, but he stood out. He was taller than most of the other spectators and looked elegant in his expensive, tailored gray-vested suit. He had a lean, dark face, faintly scarred, with large, almond-shaped black eyes and short eyelashes. His mouth was wide and thin-lipped, his chin stubbornly jutted. His thick, jet-black hair was gathered into a neat ponytail that fell almost to his waist in back. Several other men in the stands wore their hair that way. But they were white. Cortez was Comanche. He had the background to wear the unconventional hairstyle. On him, it looked sensual and wild and even a little dangerous.

Another ponytailed man, a redhead with a receding hairline and thick glasses, grinned and gave him the victory sign. Cortez shrugged, unimpressed, and turned his attention toward the graduation ceremonies. He was here against his will and the last thing he felt like was being friendly. If he'd followed his instincts, he'd still be in Washington going over a backlog of federal cases he was due to prosecute in court.

The dean of the university was announcing the names of the graduates. He'd reached the *K*s, and on the program, Phoebe Margaret Keller was the second name under that heading.

It was a beautiful spring day at the University of Tennessee at Knoxville, so the commencement ceremony was being held outside. Phoebe was recognizable by the long platinum blond braid trailing the back of her dark gown as she accepted her diploma with one hand and shook hands with the dean with the other. She moved past the podium and switched her tassel to the other side of her cap. Cortez could see the grin from where he was standing.

He'd met Phoebe a year earlier, while he was investigating some environmental sabotage in Charleston, South Carolina. Phoebe, an anthropology major, had helped him track down a toxic waste site. He'd found her more than attractive, despite her tomboyish appearance, but time and work pressure had been against them. He'd promised to come and see her graduate, and here he was. But the age difference was still pretty formidable, because he was thirty-six and she was twenty-three. He did know Phoebe's aunt Derrie, from having worked with her during the Kane Lombard pollution case. If he needed a reason for showing up at the graduation, Phoebe was Derrie's late brother's child and he was almost a friend of the family.

The dean's voice droned on, and graduate after graduate accepted a diploma. In no time at all, the exercises were over and whoops of joy and congratulations rang in the clear Tennessee air.

No longer drawing attention as the exuberant crowd moved toward the graduates, Cortez hung back, watching. His black eyes narrowed as a thought occurred to him. Phoebe wasn't one for crowds. Like himself, she was a loner. If she was going to work her way around the people to find her aunt Derrie, she'd do it away from the crowd. So he started looking for alternate routes from the stadium to the parking lot. Minutes later, he found her, easing around the side of the building, almost losing her balance as she struggled with the too-long gown, muttering to herself about people who couldn't measure people properly for gowns.

"Still talking to yourself, I see," he mused, leaning against the wall with his arms folded across his chest.

She looked up and saw him. With no time to prepare, her delight swept over her even features with a radiance that took his breath. Her pale blue eyes sparkled and her mouth, devoid of lipstick, opened on a sharply indrawn breath.

"Cortez!" she exclaimed.

She looked as if she'd run straight into his arms with the least invitation, and he smiled indulgently as he gave it to her. He levered away from the wall and opened his arms.

She went into them without any hesitation whatsoever, nestling close as he enfolded her tightly.

"You came," she murmured happily into his shoulder.

"I said I would," he reminded her. He chuckled at her unbridled enthusiasm. One lean hand tilted up her chin so that he could search her eyes. "Four years of hard work paid off, I see."

"So it did. I'm a graduate," she said, grinning.

"Certifiable," he agreed. His gaze fell to her soft pink mouth and darkened. He wanted to bend those few inches and kiss her, but there were too many reasons why he shouldn't. His hand was on her upper arm and, because he was fighting his instincts so hard, his grip began to tighten.

She tugged against his hold. "You're crushing me," she protested gently.

"Sorry." He let her go with an apologetic smile. "That training at Quantico dies hard," he added on a light note, alluding to his service with the FBI.

"No kiss, huh?" she chided with a loud sigh, searching his dark eyes.

One eye narrowed amusedly. "You're an anthropology major. Tell me why I won't kiss you," he challenged.

"Native Americans," she began smugly, "especially Native American men, rarely show their feelings in public. Kissing me in a crowd would be as distasteful to you as undressing in front of it."

His eyes softened as they searched her face. "Whoever taught you anthropology did a very good job."

She sighed. "Too good. What am I going to use it for in Charleston? I'll end up teaching..."

"No, you won't," he corrected. "One of the reasons I came was to tell you about a job opportunity."

Her eyes widened, brightened. "A job?"

"In D.C.," he added. "Interested?"

"Am I ever!" A movement caught her eye. "Oh, there's Aunt Derrie!" she said, and called to her aunt. "Aunt Derrie! Look, I graduated, I have proof!" She held up her diploma as she ran to hug her aunt and then shake hands with U.S. Senator Clayton Seymour, who'd been her aunt's boss for years before they became engaged.

"We're both very happy for you," Derrie said warmly. "Hi, Cortez!" she beamed. "You know Clayton, don't you?"

"Not directly," Cortez said, but he shook hands anyway.

Clayton's firm lips tugged into a smile. "I've heard a lot about you from my brother-in-law, Kane Lombard. He and my sister Nikki wanted to come today, but their twins were sick. He won't forget what he owes you. Kane always pays his debts."

"I was doing my job," Cortez reminded him.

"What happened to Haralson?" Derrie asked curiously, referring to the petty criminal who'd planted toxic waste and in one fell swoop almost cost Clayton Seymour his congressional seat and Kane Lombard his business.

"Haralson got twenty years," he replied, sticking his hands deep in his pockets. He smiled coldly. "Some cases I enjoy prosecuting more than others."

"Prosecuting?" Derrie asked. "But you told me last year in Charleston that you were with the CIA."

"I was with the CIA and the FBI, briefly," he told her. "But for the past few years, I've been a federal prosecutor."

"Then how did you wind up tracking down people who plant toxic waste?" she persisted.

"Just lucky, I guess," he replied smoothly.

"That means he's through talking about it," Phoebe murmured dryly. "Give up, Aunt Derrie."

Clayton gave Phoebe a curious glance, which she intercepted with a smile. "Cortez and I are friends," she told him. "You can thank his investigative instincts for saving your congressional seat."

"I certainly do," Clayton replied, relaxing. "I almost made a hash of everything," he added, with a warm, tender glance toward Derrie, who beamed up at him. "If you're going to be in town tonight, we'd love to have you join us for supper," he told Cortez. "We're taking Phoebe out for a graduation celebration."

"I wish I had time," he said quietly. "I have to go back tonight."

"Of course. Then we'll see you again sometime, in D.C.," Derrie said, puzzled by the strong vibes she sensed between her niece and Cortez.

"I've got something to discuss with Phoebe," he said, turning to Derrie and Clayton. "I need to borrow her for an hour or so."

"Go right ahead," Derrie said. "We'll go back to the hotel and have coffee and pie and rest until about six. Then we'll pick you up for supper, Phoebe."

"Thanks," she said. "Oh, my cap and gown…!" She stripped it off, along with her hat, and handed them to Derrie.

"Wait, Phoebe, weren't the honor graduates invited to a luncheon at the dean's house?" Derrie protested suddenly.

Phoebe didn't hesitate. "They'll never miss me," she said, and waved as she joined Cortez.

"An honor graduate, too," he mused as they walked back through the crowd toward his rental car. "Why doesn't that surprise me?"

"Anthropology is my life," she said simply, pausing to exchange congratulations with one of her friends on the way. She was so happy that she was walking on air.

"Nice touch, Phoebe," the girl's companion murmured with a dry glance at Cortez as they moved along, "bringing your anthropology homework along to graduation."

"Bill!" the girl cried, hitting him.

Phoebe had to stifle a giggle. Cortez wasn't smiling. On the other hand, he didn't explode, either. He gave Phoebe a stern look.

"Sorry," she murmured. "It's sort of a squirrelly day."

He shrugged. "No need to apologize. I remember what it's like on graduation day."

"Your degree would be in law, right?"

He nodded.

"Did your family come to your graduation?" she asked curiously.

He didn't answer her. It was a deliberate snub, and it should have made her uncomfortable, but she never held back with him.

"Another case of instant foot-in-mouth disease," she said immediately. "And I thought I was cured!"

He chuckled reluctantly. "You're as incorrigible as I remember you."

"I'm amazed that you did remember me, or that you took the trouble to find out when and where I was graduating so that you could be here," she said. "I couldn't send you an invitation," she added sheepishly, "because I didn't have your address. I didn't really expect you, either. We only spent an hour or two together last year."

"They were memorable ones. I don't like women very much," he said as they reached the unobtrusive rental car, a gray American-made car of recent vintage. He turned and looked down at her solemnly. "In fact," he added evenly, "I don't like being in public display very much."

She lifted both eyebrows. "Then why are you here?"

He stuck his hands deep into his pockets. "Because I like you," he said. His dark eyes narrowed. "And I don't want to."

"Thanks a lot!" she said, exasperated.

He stared at her. "I like honesty in a relationship."

"Are we having one?" she asked innocently. "I didn't notice."

His mouth pulled down at one corner. "If we were, you'd know," he said softly. "But I came because I promised that I would. And the offer of the job opportunity is genuine. Although," he added, "it's rather an unorthodox one."

"I'm not being asked to take over the archives at the Smithsonian, then? What a disappointment!"

Laughter bubbled out of his throat. "Funny girl." He opened the passenger door with exaggerated patience.

"I really irritate you, don't I?" she asked as she got inside the car.

"Most people are savvy enough not to remind me of my heritage too often," he replied pointedly after he was inside with the door closed.

"Why?" she asked. "You're fortunate enough to live in an age where ethnicity is appreciated and not stereotyped."

"Ha!"

She lifted her hands. "Okay, okay, that isn't quite true, but you have to admit that it's a better society now than it was ninety years ago."

He started the engine and pulled away from the curb.

He drove as he seemed to do everything else, effortlessly. His hand went inside his jacket pocket and he grimaced.

"Looking for something?" she asked.

"Cigarettes," he said heavily. "I forgot. I've quit again."

"Your lungs and mine appreciate the sacrifice."

"My lungs don't talk."

"Mine do," she said smugly. "They say 'don't smoke, don't smoke...'"

He smiled faintly. "You bubble, don't you?" he remarked. "I've never known anyone so animated."

"Yes, well, that's because you're suffering from sensory deprivation resulting from too much time spent with your long nose stuck in law books. Dull, dry, boring things."

"The law is not boring," he returned.

"It depends which side you're sitting on." She frowned. "This job you're telling me about wouldn't have to do with anything legal, would it? Because I only had one course in government and a few hours of history, but..."

"I don't need a law clerk," he returned.

"Then what do you need?"

"You wouldn't be working for me," he corrected. "I have ties to a group that fights for sovereignty for the Native American tribes. They have a staff of attorneys. I thought you might fit in very well, with your background in anthropology. I've pulled some strings to get you an interview."

She didn't speak for a minute. Her eyes were on her hands. "I think you're forgetting something. My major is anthropology. Most of it is forensic anthropology. Bones."

He glanced at her. "You wouldn't be doing that for them."

She stared out the window. "What would I be doing?"

"It's a desk job," he admitted. "But a good one."

"I appreciate your thinking of me," she said carefully. "But I can't give up fieldwork. That's why I've applied at the Smithsonian for a position with the anthropology section."

He was quiet for a long moment. "Do you know how indigenous people feel about archaeology? We don't like having people dig up our sacred sites and our relatives, however old they are."

"I just graduated," she reminded him. "Of course I do. But there's a lot more to archaeology than digging up skeletons!"

He stopped for a traffic light and turned toward her. His eyes were cold. "And it doesn't stop you from wanting to get a job doing something that resembles grave-digging?"

She gasped. "It is not grave-digging! For heaven's sake..."

He held up a hand. "We can agree to disagree, Phoebe," he told her. "You won't change my mind any more than I'll change yours. I'm sorry about the job, though. You'd have been an asset to them."

She unbent a little. "Thanks for recommending me, but I don't want a desk job. Besides, I may go on to graduate school after I've had a few months to get over the past four years. They've been pretty hectic."

"Yes, I remember."

"Why did you recommend me for that job? There must be a line of people who'd love to have it—people better qualified than I am."

He turned his head and looked directly into her eyes. There was something that he wasn't telling her, something deep inside him.

"Maybe I'm lonely," he said shortly. "There aren't many people who aren't afraid to come close to me these days."

"Does that matter? You don't like people close," she said.

She searched his arrogant profile. There were new lines in that lean face, lines she hadn't seen last year, despite the solemnity of the time they'd spent together. "Something's upset you," she said out of the blue. "Or you're worried about something."

Both dark eyebrows went up. "I beg your pardon?" he asked curtly.

The hauteur went right over her head. "Not something to do with work, either," she continued, reasoning aloud. "It's something very personal..."

"Stop right there," he said shortly. "I invited you out to talk about a job, not about my private life."

"Ah. A closed door. Intriguing." She stared at him. "Not a woman?"

"You're the only woman in my life."

She laughed unexpectedly. "That's a good one."

"I'm not kidding. I don't have affairs or relationships." He glanced at her as he merged into traffic again and turned at the next corner. "I might make an exception for you, but don't get your hopes up. A man has his reputation to consider."

She grinned. "I'll remember that you said that."

He pulled the car into the parking lot of a well-known hotel restaurant and cut off the engine. "I hope you're hungry. I missed breakfast."

"So did I. Nerves," she added.

He escorted her into the sparsely occupied restaurant and they were seated near the window. When they finished looking at the menu and gave their orders, he leaned back in his chair and studied her across the width of the table with quiet interest.

"Is my nose upside down?" she asked after a minute.

He chuckled. "No. I was just thinking how young you are."

"In this day and age, nobody is that young," she corrected. She leaned forward with her chin on her elbows and watched him. "Don't fight it," she chided. "You might never run into anyone else who'd make you so uncomfortable."

"That's a selling point?" he asked, surprised.

"Of course it is. You live deep inside yourself. You won't let yourself feel anything, because it's a form of weakness to you. Something must have hurt you very badly when you were younger."

"Don't pry," he said gently, but the words warned.

"If I hang around with you very much, I'm going to pry a lot more than this," she informed him.

He considered that. He had cold feet where Phoebe was concerned. She wasn't the sort of person who'd settle for a shallow relationship. She'd want to go right to the bone, and she'd never let go. He was like that, too, but he'd been burned badly once, by a woman who liked him because he was a curiosity

"I've been collected already," he said quietly. "Do you understand?"

She saw the brief flash of pain in his eyes and nodded slowly. "I see. Did she want to show off her indigenous aborigine to all her friends?"

His jaw tautened and something dangerous flashed in his eyes.

"I thought so," she murmured, watching the faintest of expressions in his face. "Did she care at all?"

"I doubt it very much."

"And you found out in a very public way, no doubt."

His head inclined.

"I'm sorry," she said. "Life teaches painful lessons."

"Have you had any yet?" he returned bluntly.

"Not that sort," she admitted, toying with her fork. "I'm rather shy with men, as a rule. And boys I went to school with either saw me as one of them or somebody's sister. Digging isn't very glamorous."

"I thought you looked cute in mud-caked boots and a jacket three times your size."

She glared at him. "Don't start."

His dark eyes slid over her dress. It wasn't in the least revealing. It had a high lace collar and long sleeves gathered tight at the wrists. It cascaded down in folds to her ankles and under it she was wearing very stylish granny shoes. Her platinum hair was in a neat braid down her back. She wore a minimum of makeup and there was a tiny line of freckles right over her nose.

"I know I'm not pretty," she said, made uncomfortable by the close scrutiny, "and I'm built like a boy."

He smiled. "Are you still naive enough to think that looks matter?"

"It doesn't take much intelligence to see that pretty girls get all the attention in class."

"At first," he agreed.

She sighed. "There are so few boys who like to spend an evening listening to exciting discoveries like a broken bowl of charred acorns and half a soapstone pipe."

"Mississippian," he recalled, from their discussion about the find last year.

She beamed. "Yes! You remembered!"

He smiled at her enthusiasm. "I did a few courses in cultural anthropology," he confessed. "Not physical anthropology," he emphasized. "And so help me, if you say anthropology should be right up my alley...!"

"You didn't tell me that in Charleston," she said.

"I didn't expect to see you again," he replied. He hadn't even planned to come to her graduation. He wasn't sure if he regretted being here or not. His dark eyes searched her pale ones. "Life is full of surprises."

She looked into his eyes and felt a stirring deep in her heart. She looked at him and felt closer than she'd ever been to anyone.

The waitress brought salads, followed by steak and vegetables, and they ate in silence until apple pie and coffee were consumed.

"You're completely unafraid, aren't you?" he asked as he finished his second cup of coffee. "You've never really been hurt."

"I had a crush on a really cute boy in my introductory anthropology class," she said. "He ended up with a really cute boy in Western Civ."

He chuckled. "Poor Phoebe."

"It's the sort of thing that usually happens to me," she confessed. "I'm not terribly good at being womanly. I like to kick around in blue jeans and sweatshirts and dig up old things."

"A woman can be anything she wants to be. It doesn't require lace and a helpless attitude. Not anymore."

"Do you think it ever did, really?" she asked curiously. "I mean, you read about women like Elizabeth the First and Isabella of Spain, who lived as they liked and ruled entire nations in the sixteenth century."

"They were the exceptions," he reminded her. "On the other hand, in Native American cultures, women owned the property and often sat in council when the various tribes made decisions affecting war and peace. Ours was always a matriarchal society."

"I know. I have a B.A. in anthropology."

"I noticed."

She laughed softly. Her fingers traced a pattern around the rim of her coffee cup. "Will I see you in D.C. if I get the job at the Smithsonian?"

"I suppose so," he told her. "You put me at ease. I'm not sure it's a good thing."

"Why? Are you being tailed by foreign spies or something and you have to stay on edge because they might attack you?"

He smiled. "I don't think so." He leaned back. "But I've had some experience with intelligence work."

"I don't doubt that." She searched his eyes. "Is it expensive to live in D.C.?"

"Not if you're frugal. I can show you where to shop for an apartment, or you might want to double up with someone."

She kept her eyes on the coffee cup. "Is that an invitation?"

He hesitated. "No."

She grinned. "Just kidding."

His fingers curled around hers, creating little electrical sparks all along the paths of her nerves. "One day at a time," he said firmly. "You'll learn that I don't do much on impulse. I like to think things through before I act."

"I can see where that would have been a valuable trait in the FBI, with people shooting at you," she said, nodding.

He let go of her hand with an involuntary laugh. "God, Phoebe…! You say the most outrageous things sometimes."

"I'm sorry, it slipped out. I'll behave."

He just shook his head. "I'll never forget the first thing you ever said to me," he added. "'Do you have shovel-shaped incisors?' you asked."

"Stop!" she wailed.

He caught her long braid and tugged on it. His dark eyes probed hers. "I hate your hair bound up like this. I'd like to get a handful of it."

"I know how you feel," she murmured, glancing pointedly at his own ponytail.

He smiled. "We'll have to let our hair down together again sometime," he mused, "and compare length."

"Yours is much thicker than mine," she observed. She pictured it loose, as she'd seen it, when they were tracking people around the toxic-waste site last year. She remembered standing on the riverbank with him while they kissed in a fever that never seemed to cool. If they hadn't been interrupted, anything could have happened. She flushed as she remembered how his hair had felt in her hands that last few minutes they were together as he crushed her down the length of that long, powerful body…

"Cut it out," he said, glancing at the thin gold watch on his wrist. "I have to catch a plane."

She cleared her throat and tried not to look as hot and bothered as she felt. And he tried not to see that she was.

They finished their meal and he drove her back to the hotel where Clayton and Derrie were staying. He parked the car in a parking space a healthy walk from the hotel door, under a maple tree, and turned to her. The difference in their heights was even more apparent when they were seated. Her head barely came up to his chin. It excited him. He didn't understand why.

"I have my own room," she said without looking up. "And Derrie and Clayton won't be back yet."

"I won't come in," he said deliberately. "I don't have much time."

"I wish you could stay and have supper with us," she remarked.

"I left a case hanging fire to come here. It was all I could do to manage one day."

"I don't know anything about you, really," she told him honestly. "You said you were FBI when you were in Charleston, and then you told Derrie you were CIA, then you turned out to be a government prosecutor. You keep secrets."

"Yes, but I don't lie as a rule," he said. "I would have told you more if I'd been around long enough. It wasn't necessary, because I wasn't going to be around, and we both knew it. I came here against my better judgment, Phoebe. I'm too old and too jaded for a woman your age. You haven't even reached the stage of French kissing, while I've long passed the stage of Victorian courtship."

She felt her cheeks burn, but she met his eyes levelly. "In other words, if you stayed around long enough, you'd want to sleep with me."

His dark eyes ran slowly over her face. "I already want to sleep with you," he said. "There's nothing I want more. That's why I'm going to get on a plane and go straight back to D.C."

She wasn't sure how she felt. Her eyes searched his. "You might ask," she said.

"Ask what?"

"If I'd like to sleep with you," she said.

"I might not like the answer."

She studied his hard, lean face. "Would any woman do?"

He touched her cheek. "I'm old-fashioned," he said quietly. "I don't play games. I've only had a handful of women in my life. They all meant something to me at the time, and most of them still speak to me pleasantly enough."

She sighed gently and her eyes were sad as she smiled up at him. "I wish you'd stay," she said honestly. "But I wouldn't try to make you feel guilty about it. Thank you for coming to my graduation," she added. "It was kind of you."

He was watching her hungrily and hoping it didn't show. "It's just as well that you're bristling with principles," he said. "Our cultures won't mix at close range, Phoebe. They're too different. You've studied anthropology for years. You know the reasons as well as I do."

"Good Lord, I'm not proposing marriage!" she burst out.

"Good thing," he mused. "I'm married to my job. But if you're ever in the market for a lover, I'll be around."

She gave him a pointed look. "Thanks bunches."

"Just a thought," he returned thoughtfully. "All the same, you might consider me a friend, if you ever need one. D.C. is a big, exciting place. I'll be close by if you ever get in trouble."

She studied his hard face, seeing the maturity in it. He was devastating at close range like this, and she'd never wanted anything so much as she wanted a chance to have him in her life. But they were already at an impasse, just as they'd been last year. There was a conflict of principles as well as cultures between them, and complicating it all was that formidable age difference. But, oh, he was sexy. She smiled faintly as her eyes roamed over his lean face possessively.

He cocked a heavy eyebrow. "Looking at me that way will bring you to grief," he chided softly.

She shrugged. "Promises, promises."

He touched the tip of her nose with his forefinger. "If I ever make one to you, I'll keep it. Congratulations. I'm proud of you."

She sighed. "Thanks again for coming all this way to watch me graduate. It meant a lot to me." Her eyes searched his and she smiled wistfully. "I hate public places."

He caught her long, thick braid and tugged her closer, so that her head went back against the seat and her face was under his. "This isn't public," he whispered against her mouth.

She barely got over the shock of his warm, hard lips on hers before he drew back and released her. He was already cursing himself for that lapse. He hadn't meant to do it. This whole trip had been against his better judgment, but he couldn't help himself.

She was watching him like a blue-eyed cat.

"Something on your mind?" he prompted.

"Yes. Is that *it?*" she asked pertly. "That's the best you can do?"

"Excuse me?" he asked.

She sighed and touched his chin lightly with her fingers. "I can't help but compare that very anemic peck with the unbridled, passionate kiss you gave me last year on a riverbank," she said outrageously.

He looked down his long, straight nose at her. "That was last year. Things were less complicated."

Her eyebrows went up. "Yes?" she prompted.

He traced her small ear with his forefinger and seemed to be brooding at the same time. "I have a brother, Isaac," he replied. "He's fourteen years younger than I am. About your age, in fact. My parents and I managed to get him through high school, but ever since, he's had one brush with the law after another. Now it's woman trouble. My mother has a bad heart and my father and I are afraid that all this is going to kill her."

She was sorry for his situation, but flattered that he'd be so honest about a personal matter with her. "I'd have liked a brother or sister," she remarked. "Even one who had problems."

He smiled gently. "I know your father is dead. What about your mother?"

"She died of cancer when I was eight," she said simply. "My father remarried and six years later, he died in Lebanon in the Marine barracks attack. My stepmother remarried. I haven't seen her in years. My grandparents and Aunt Derrie are all I have left."

He scowled. She wasn't asking for sympathy, and he didn't offer it. But he felt sad for her. His family was dear to him. He'd do anything for them.

"Heavens, I didn't mean to run on like that!" she exclaimed, laughing self-consciously. She looked up at him with raised eyebrows. "Wouldn't you like to come inside with me and have wild, unprotected sex on the carpet?"

His eyes twinkled with suppressed humor. She was outrageous.

"Listen, I heard a girl say one time that if you used plastic wrap…!" she persisted.

He held up a big hand. "Stop right there," he said firmly, still fighting laughter. "I am not using plastic wrap for birth control."

She sighed theatrically. "What's going to become of me?" she asked the dashboard. "You're condemning me to ridicule when I have to fill in employment forms."

He leaned forward. "What?"

"There's this place where it says sex, and because I'm an honest person, I'll have to fill in that I can't have any because the only man I want refuses to cooperate."

He did laugh, then, shaking his head. "Get out of here!" He leaned over her to catch the door handle.

She was right up against him, with her mouth a scant inch from his, because she didn't move, as he expected her to. At the proximity, she could see dark rims around his black irises, she could feel the minty taste of his breath against her parted lips.

Her fingers touched his warm throat gently. They were like ice. "I dated three boys this past semester alone," she said in a husky tone. "I had to grit my teeth to even let them kiss me good-night."

"Are you making a point?"

Her eyes were eloquent. "I don't feel anything with other men."

"Baby, you're very young," he said in a soft, tender tone, his fingers lightly brushing her full lips. He wasn't even aware of the endearment. His face was solemn. "Somebody will come along."

"He already did, but he keeps leaving," she muttered.

"I have a job," he reminded her. He bent to her mouth and brushed it with his, very lightly. It was like electricity between them. "And a backlog of cases. I wasn't lying."

"I'll bet you never take vacations," she whispered against his lips, tracing them with her own in a desperate ploy to keep him with her.

"They're rare." He nipped her upper lip with his perfect white teeth, and then ran his tongue along the underside of it. His heartbeat increased abruptly and he felt his body responding to her with an urgency that he wasn't used to.

Involuntarily his fingers speared into the bound hair at her nape and tilted her face up to his. "This is not a good idea," he ground out, but his mouth was already on her parted lips, and he was kissing her in a way that made her whole body leap.

She slid her arms around his neck, blind to the possibility of passersby. They were in a secluded area of the parking lot and it was deserted. It wouldn't have mattered if it hadn't been. She was on fire for him.

He groaned into her open mouth and his tongue darted in past her teeth. His big hands slid up her rib cage to the firm, soft thrust of her breasts and he took their delicate weight into his palms, his thumbs rubbing tenderly at the nipples until they went hard.

She shivered.

He lifted his head and looked straight into her dazed, misty eyes. His own were blazing with hunger. His hands contracted and he saw her pupils dilate even as she shivered again with pleasure.

"If you were older," he bit off.

"It wouldn't matter, because you're too attracted to me," she whispered, tightening her arms around his neck. "You'd run like a scalded dog before you'd take me to bed, Jeremiah," she murmured shakily. "Because you'd be addicted overnight."

"So would you," he replied curtly, angered by her perception. The sound of his given name on her lips was strangely intimate, like the way he was holding her.

"I know," she said huskily. She tugged his head back down and kissed him with all the pent-up longing of a whole year, enjoying the way he kissed her back, roughly and hungrily, with no restraint.

But all too soon, he caught her upper arms and pulled them down. His head lifted and the look in his eyes was suddenly remote.

"I have more personal problems than I can handle right now," he said, his tone deep and slow. "I can't manage you as well."

"You want to," she said daringly.

His eyes flashed. "Yes," he said after a minute. "I want to."

The admission changed her. She smiled, dazed.

"But I have to deal with the issues at hand, first," he replied. He drew in a steadying breath and looked down at her soft mouth with real longing. He traced it with a long forefinger. "By Christmas, perhaps, things will resolve themselves. Do you spend it with Derrie, in Charleston?"

"Yes," she replied, beaming, because he wasn't saying goodbye forever.

"Think about the job opportunity I mentioned, will you? I'll get some more details and mail them to you. What's your address?"

Diverted, she fished for her purse and extracted a notepad and pen. She scribbled down Aunt Derrie's address in Washington, D.C., where she lived working for Senator Seymour—except on holidays—and her Charleston address. "I guess I'll stay at Aunt Derrie's place in Charleston for a while, until I know what I'm going to be doing."

"The job I'm recommending you for pays really well," he said, smiling. "And I'd see you often, because I spend a lot of time doing pro bono work in the area of their offices."

Her eyes were bright with hope. "What an incentive."

He laughed softly. "I was thinking the same thing." He hesitated, watching her. "I'm not good with people," he said then. "Relationships are hard for me. Even surface ones. You're demanding."

"So are you," she said simply.

He grimaced. "I suppose I am."

"I'm not pushing you. I'm not even asking for anything," she said quietly.

He touched her cheek with his fingertips. "I know that."

She searched his dark eyes. "I knew you, the first time I saw you. I don't understand how."

"Sometimes, it's better not to try," he replied. "And I really do have to go." He bent and kissed her with breathless tenderness, teasing her mouth with his until she lifted up to him. She moaned softly and tugged at his strong neck. He bent, crushing her against his chest with a harsh groan. She felt her whole body throbbing as the kiss went on and on until her mouth was swollen and her heart raced like a wild thing. He lifted his head reluctantly. But then he let her go abruptly and drew back.

He looked as unsettled as she felt. "We've got things in common already. We'll probably find more. At least you aren't totally ignorant of indigenous customs and rituals."

She smiled gently. "I studied hard."

He sighed. "Okay. We'll see what happens. I'll write you when I get back to D.C. Don't expect long letters. I don't have the time."

"I won't," she promised.

He touched her chin with his thumb. "You were right about one thing," he said unexpectedly.

"What?"

"You said that if I missed your graduation I'd regret it for the rest of my life," he recalled, smiling. "I would have."

Her fingers slid over his long mouth, tingling at the

touch. "Me, too," she agreed, with her heart in her eyes as they met his.

He bent and kissed her one last time before he reached across her and opened the door. "I'll write."

She got out, nodding at him. "So will I." She closed the door and stared down into the car. "I hope things work out for you at home," she added.

"They will, one way or the other," he replied. He studied her with turbulent eyes and an uncanny sense of catastrophe ahead. His father and uncles and the medicine men who were his ancestors would have found that perception a blessing. To him, it was a nuisance.

"What's wrong?" she asked, because the look on his face was eloquent.

He shifted. "Nothing," he lied, trying to ignore the feeling. "I was just thinking. You take care, Phoebe."

"You do the same. I enjoyed my graduation."

He smiled. "I enjoyed it, too. This isn't goodbye," he added when she looked devastated.

"I know." She felt uneasy, though, and she couldn't understand why.

He gave her one last look. His eyes were dark and shadowed and full of misgiving. Before she could ask why he looked that way, he rolled the window up.

He waved, and pulled out of the parking space. She watched him until he was out of sight. Her mouth still tingled from the press of his lips, and her body was aching with new sensations. With a sense of excitement and wonder, she turned and went slowly back into the hotel. The future looked rosy and bright.

2

Three years later

THE SMALL NATIVE AMERICAN museum in Chenocetah, North Carolina, was crowded for a Saturday. Phoebe smiled at a group of children as they passed her in the hall. Two of them jostled each other and the teacher called them down, with an apologetic smile at Phoebe.

"Don't worry," Phoebe whispered to the teacher. "There's nothing breakable that isn't behind glass or a velvet rope!"

The teacher chuckled and walked on.

Phoebe glanced at the board that translated Cherokee words into English. It wasn't exact, but it was an improvement on the board that had hung there previously. The museum had been so ragged and unappealing that the county was thinking of shutting it down. But Phoebe had taken on the job of curator, and she'd put new life into the project.

At the top of the board was the name of the town, Chenocetah, and its Cherokee translation: "See all around." You really could, she thought, considering the tall, stately mountains that ringed the small town.

Phoebe had completed her master's degree in anthropology by doing distance education and spending the required few weeks on campus during the summer in order to graduate. She was given the curator's job in the Chenocetah Museum on the poviso that she was to obtain her master's in the meantime.

Here, only a few minutes away from Cherokee, North Carolina, land was at a premium. The Yonah Indian Reservation, a small stronghold of native people, reached almost to the city limits sign of Chenocetah. On the outskirts of the small mountain town that boasted more hotels per square inch than Myrtle Beach, South Carolina, three construction companies were racing to put up several hotel complexes. One of the conglomerates was erecting a Las Vegas–type theme hotel complex. The other two were luxurious tourist resorts with wildlife trails included in the design. They had the added attraction of being located with their backs to a mountain honeycombed with caves, a sure draw for spelunkers.

Two members of the city council had protested violently at the ecological impact of the mammoth projects, but the other three and the mayor had voted them down. The water rates alone would fill the city coffers, not to mention the tourists they would draw into the already tourist-oriented area.

Phoebe, like the two protesting councilmen, was thinking of the cost of enlarging the sewage system and water delivery system to accommodate the added demands of the huge hotels. They were going up close enough to the Chenocetah Cherokee Museum that they would probably impact the water pressure in the museum, already less than she liked with so many visitors. Another problem was going to be the headache of traffic snarls that would accompany the increased traffic near the small town's city limits at one of the county's worst intersections. One of the sheriff's deputies who flirted with her regularly had mentioned that consequence. She didn't flirt back. Phoebe had a grudge against anyone with a badge these days.

"You frown too much," her colleague, Marie Locklear murmured dryly as she approached her. Marie was half-Cherokee and a graduate of Duke University. She was the museum's comptroller, and a precious asset.

"I smile when I'm alone," Phoebe confessed. "I wouldn't want to upset the staff."

"My cousin Drake Stewart's coming by at lunch, again," she said, naming the deputy sheriff who patrolled the area. "I asked him to bring us a couple of those spicy chicken salads from the new fast-food joint." Marie added, "He's sweet on you."

Phoebe winced. "I'm off men."

"Drake's thirty and drop-dead gorgeous," Marie reminded her. "He's got just enough Cherokee blood to make him sexy," she added. "If he wasn't my first cousin, I'd marry him myself!"

"He's also a deputy sheriff."

"That's right. I forgot. You're down on lawmen."

Phoebe went into her office, with Marie right behind. "I'm down on men, period," she replied.

"Why?"

Phoebe ignored the question. Dragging up the past was just too painful.

"Can we afford to fix that hole in the parking lot?" Phoebe asked. "We're getting complaints."

"If we forego fixing the roof, we can," Marie said demurely.

"Not another leak!" Phoebe groaned. "Where is it?"

"In the men's bathroom," Marie replied. "There's a puddle in front of the sinks."

Phoebe sat down at her desk and put her head in her hands. "And it's November already. We'll have snow and sleet soon and the roof will just collapse under the weight. Why did I take this job? Why?"

"Because nobody else wanted it?"

Phoebe actually chuckled. Marie was incorrigible. She grinned at the younger woman. "No, actually because nobody else wanted me," she corrected.

"I can't believe that. You graduated in the top one percent of your class, and you did a great job with your master's degree, which you completed in record time," Marie recalled. "I read your curriculum vitae," she added when Phoebe looked surprised.

"Credentials aren't everything," Phoebe replied.

"Yes, but your area of expertise is forensic anthropology," came the reply. "There must be a lot of jobs going in that area, because it's so specialized."

"There were none when I needed one," she said quietly, pulling a file toward her. "I wanted to get away from my family, from everything. This is an area where I didn't know anyone, and where I wasn't likely to run into…" She was going to say Cortez, but she bit her tongue.

Marie perched her ample figure on the edge of the desk,

pushing back her long, thick straight hair. "I know you don't talk about it," she said, "but I think you're better now, aren't you?"

She nodded. "Yes. I think I'm over it."

"You will be when you rush out to Drake's car and kiss him blind and beg him to take you on a date," Marie said with a wicked grin.

Phoebe glared at her. "From what you've already told me, Drake's got a girl on every street corner," she said. "He loves women, all shapes and sizes and ages, and they love him. I don't want an overused man."

Marie's eyes popped.

Phoebe realized what she'd said and burst out laughing. "Well, hypothetically speaking," she murmured, flushing. "And don't you dare tell Drake I said that!"

Marie touched her ample bosom. "Would I do that?"

"In a heartbeat," Phoebe agreed. "Get to work. Find me a way to budget roof repair and pothole repair into our fiscal year."

"We could go over to the Yonah Reservation and talk to Fred Fourkiller," she replied. "He can make medicine. Maybe he can influence the board of directors to give us a bigger budget!"

Medicine reminded her of Cortez, who was descended from a long line of medicine men. Involuntarily her hand rested on her middle desk drawer. She jerked it back.

"We may have to try that if all else fails," Phoebe said, turning on her computer. "I'd better get my paperwork done before the school crowd arrives," she added. "We have another busload at eleven, from the middle school." She glanced at Marie wistfully. "When I first came here, we were lucky to get two tourists a month. Now it's busloads of kids every week."

"A lot of people around here have Cherokee blood, because we're so close to the reservation," Marie reminded her with a smile. "They want to learn about their heritage, so history classes like to come here."

"It's nice revenue, like all those regional books on local history that we sell in the souvenir shop," Phoebe had to admit. "I only wish we had a patron."

"It's early days yet," Marie said with a smile. "I'll get to work."

She went out, closing the door behind her. Phoebe's one assistant on staff, Harriett White, was taking the classes through the exhibits. Harriett was widowed, and in her fifties. She'd once been a professor of history at Duke University, but she didn't want to go back to a full-time job. She'd applied at the museum without any real expectation of acceptance, and Phoebe had phoned her the minute she read the application. At first, she couldn't understand why someone with Harriett's credentials would be applying for an assistant's job, but she learned that Harriett wanted a less demanding position that enabled her to continue in the field she loved. The woman turned out to be a hard worker and much appreciated.

PHOEBE HESITATED FOR A minute before she opened her middle drawer and took out a small prayer wheel dangling a feather—not an eagle feather, or she'd have been in trouble. It was an odd little gift. Cortez had mailed it to her the week after her graduation. It was one of only two letters she ever had from him. It contained this prayer wheel, wrapped in rawhide, with the feather attached and a blade of sweetgrass woven into the center. Cortez had said that his father wanted her to have it, and to keep it close. She wasn't superstitious, but it was something of his family... and precious. She was never far away from it.

Next to it was another letter, very thin, with her name and address scrawled in the same hand that had addressed the letter with the prayer wheel. She touched it as if it were a poisonous snake, even after three years.

Gritting her teeth, she made herself take out the small newspaper clipping it contained—nothing else had been in the envelope—and look at it. It reminded her not to get sentimental about Cortez.

She read nothing except the small headline—Jeremiah Cortez Weds Mary Baker. There was no photo of the happy couple, just their names and the date of the wedding. Phoebe never forgot that. It was three weeks to the day from her graduation from college.

She tucked the clipping back into the envelope, pushing back the anguish of the day she'd received it. She kept it beside the prayer wheel always, to remind her not to get too nostalgic about her brief romance. It kept her single. She never wanted to take a chance like that again. She'd thrown her heart away, for nothing. She would never understand why Cortez had given her hope of a shared future and then sent her nothing more than a cold clipping about his marriage. No note, no apology, no explanation. Nothing.

She would have written to him, if for no other reason than to ask why he hadn't told her he was engaged. But there was no return address on the second letter. Worse, the letter she'd written to him at the first letter's address was returned to her, unopened, as unforwardable. She was shattered. Utterly shattered. Her sunny, optimistic personality had gone into eclipse after that. Nobody who'd known her even three years ago would recognize her. She'd cut her hair, adopted a businesslike personality and dressed like a matron. She looked like the curator of a museum. Which was what she was. Sometimes she could go a whole day without even thinking about Jeremiah Cortez. Today wasn't one of them.

She shoved the envelope to the back of the drawer and closed it firmly. She had a good job and a secure future. She kept a dog at home for protection in the small cabin where she lived. She didn't date anyone. She had no social life, except when she was invited to various political functions to ask for funding for the small museum. Sadly, the politicians who came to the gatherings had little money to offer, despite the state of the economy. Probably it was that her small museum didn't have enough political clout to offer in respect to the funding it needed. They got some through private donations, but most of their patrons weren't wealthy. It was a hand-to-mouth existence.

Phoebe sat back, looking around the office which was as bare of personal effects as her little house. She didn't collect things anymore. There was a mandala on the wall that one of the Bird Clan of the Cherokee people had made for her, and a blowgun that a sixth-grader's father had made. She smiled, looking at it. People were always surprised when they were told that the Cherokee people had used blowguns in the past to hunt with. Usually they were more surprised to find that Cherokee people lived in houses and didn't wear warbonnets and loincloths and paint, unless they were portraying the historical Trail of Tears in the annual pageant, "Unto These Hills," on the not-too-distant Quallah Indian

Reservation near Cherokee, North Carolina. People had some strange ideas about Native Americans.

THE PHONE RANG WHILE Phoebe was trying to force herself to answer her e-mail. She picked it up absently. "Chenocetah Cherokee Museum," she announced pleasantly.

"Is this Miss Keller?" a man's voice asked.

"Yes," she replied, ignoring her computer screen. The man sounded disturbed. "What can I do for you?"

There was a hesitation. "You can arrange to have a site dated by organic material, can't you? Don't you have a small foundation budget to help with that sort of thing?"

"Well, yes, although we can date by tree-ring age..."

"I mean skeletal remains," he added. "I have a skull...I have a whole skeleton, in fact. There's a great deal of patination, and in situ in a cave with Paleo-Indian lithic specimens, Folsom point if I'm not mistaken... There are two effigy figures that would certainly date from the Hopewell period, very fine... The skull has an enlarged brain case and wide nasal cavities, the dentition is indicative of...well, the skull is possibly Neanderthal in origin."

She actually gasped. She clutched the phone so hard that her knuckles went white. "Are you serious? We've never dated anything back further than ten to twelve thousand years, and that's at a site in Tennessee, not North Carolina. There simply are no authenticated Neanderthal remains anywhere in North America...!"

"That's right. But I...found some," he said. "I think I... found some."

She sat up straight. "Is this some sort of hoax?" she asked coldly. "Because if it is..."

"I know you're wary—I don't blame you." He paused.

"I'm a doctor of anthropology visiting the area. I know what I'm talking about. This is no hoax. But...they're covering it up," he added in a rushed whisper. "He said that if this gets out, they'll kill him, they'll kill me! They'll do anything to keep the project going. If we tell, they'll be shut down indefinitely while the site's being excavated. Of course, it would mean national publicity as well, and it will bankrupt him!"

"Him, who?" she demanded. "Where's the site? And who are you?"

"I can't tell you...not yet. I'll call you back when I can. They're watching me...!" On the other end of the line, Phoebe heard a loud knock and the sound of a door opening. There was a woman's strident voice in the background, but it was muffled. She guessed that he must have put his hand on the receiver. "Yes, I was just...speaking to my daughter! Yes, to my daughter. I'm coming!" he called to his visitor. Then he came back on the line. "I'll speak to you later...goodbye," he told Phoebe. There was a sudden noise and the phone slammed down.

She pressed star 69 on her phone to get the number that had called her, but it had been blocked at the source. She ground her teeth together and put down the phone. Maybe it was just a hoax, she thought. There had been several such "discoveries" over the years, including one in California that professed to show a set of human remains, which would predate the Cro-Magnon period—and those so-called Neanderthal findings were dated by one of the most famous anthropologists on earth. But the date was controversial and it was discounted by most authorities. There was a similar story from New Mexico which put forth the theory that a set of remains found in a cave were over thirty-five thousand years old, but they mysteriously vanished before they could be scientifically evaluated.

Whether those cases were hoaxes or not could never be proved. The newest archaeological controversy revolved around Kennewick man, a California find, who was purported to be from the Paleo-Indian period, but who did not have predominantly Native American features. That controversy was still raging.

Perhaps this man who'd called her was just some crackpot with time to kill, Phoebe reasoned. But he'd sounded very sincere. And frightened. She chided her own gullibility. It was nothing at all and she was overreacting. She pulled up her computer screen and got back to her e-mail.

THE DOOR OPENED UNEXPECTEDLY, and a tall, well-built man with a light olive complexion, short black hair and dark twinkling eyes stuck his head in. "Time to eat!" he said.

She looked up from her computer screen, smiling at the deputy sheriff. "Hi, Drake. Marie said you were bringing lunch. Thanks!"

"No sweat. I get hungry, too, Miss Keller, and sometimes I have to eat on the run," he drawled, moving into the office with two box lunches. "Which is why mine is still in the car. I'm on my way to a call now. I brought these for you and Marie."

She punched a button on her phone. "Marie, Drake's here with food!"

"I'll be right there!" she called excitedly.

"At least somebody's happy to see me, even if it's just my cousin," he said with mock disappointment. "You're preoccupied."

"I am," she agreed, closing down the computer program.

She looked up worriedly. "I just had a call a couple of hours ago. Maybe he was a crank, or a crackpot. But he sounded scared."

Drake's easy smile faded. He moved closer. "What was it about?"

"He said something about human skeletal remains that might date to the Neanderthal period being covered up by some contractor," she said, boiling the conversation down to its basics. "He hung up abruptly. I tried to get his number, but he had it blocked."

"Neanderthal remains. Uh-huh," he said mockingly.

She smiled. She'd forgotten that he'd taken an internet course on archaeology that had been offered through the museum.

"I suppose it was just a joke," she added.

"Somebody hoping to graduate from high school. He'll trip himself up, like that kid who wrote a bomb threat to his school on his father's letterhead paper," he added.

She nodded. "Thanks for bringing the salads. It's a long way to food from here," she pointed out as she dug in her purse to pay him back.

"I can't get you to come out with me," he commented on a sigh. "It's the next best thing to have lunch here," he added. "I've got to go."

Marie stuck her head in the door. "I'm starved! Thanks, Drake. You're a sweetie, even if you are my cousin!"

He cocked an eyebrow at her. "At least somebody thinks so," he said morosely, with a speaking glance at Phoebe.

"Oh, she's off men," Marie told him chattily.

He frowned. "Why?"

Phoebe shot Marie a warning glance. She held up both hands, looking sheepish, and changed the subject.

3

THE NEXT MORNING, PHOEBE heard sirens racing past her small cabin just as she woke up. She hoped there hadn't been some terrible accident. The mountain roads were narrow and some were dangerous in this part of the area. They'd had flatland tourists go over guardrails occasionally. The drop was inevitably fatal.

She dressed and grabbed a quick cup of coffee before she drove her old Ford to work. The museum parking lot was usually empty at that hour, except for her car and Marie's. But a sheriff's car was sitting at the entrance with the motor running.

Frowning, she got out of her vehicle, shuffling her purse and briefcase. At the same time, Drake got out of the patrol car. But he wasn't smiling, and he looked uneasy.

"Hi," she greeted him. "What's up?"

He rested his hand on the butt of his service revolver in

its holster as he approached her. "You said you talked to a man yesterday about some skeletal remains, right?"

"Right," she said slowly.

"Did he give his name?"

"No."

"Can you tell me anything about him?" he persisted somberly.

She hesitated, thinking back. "He said he was an anthropologist..."

"Damn!"

Her lips parted. She'd never seen easygoing Drake look so angry. "What's happened?" she asked.

"They found a DB on the Rez," he said quietly.

She blinked, trying to recall the terminology. "A dead body," she translated, "on the reservation."

He nodded curtly. "Just barely on it, about a hundred feet or so from the actual boundary. He appears to be of Cherokee descent, because we also found a tribal registration card, with the name and number missing, and we found part of a membership card from a professional anthropological society, which we assume was his—the part with his name was missing. So was his driver's license."

She gasped. "That man who called me...?"

"Looks like it could be. We can't go on Cherokee land unless we're asked. And this makes it a federal matter. But I have a cousin on the reservation police force, and he told me. It's all real hush-hush. The FBI is sending a special agent out to investigate, someone from that new Indian Country Crime Unit they're forming. I just wanted to warn you that they will want to talk to you."

"What?"

"You were the last person who spoke to the victim," he

said. "They found your telephone number scribbled on a pad next to his phone at his motel and looked it up in the phone book. That's when Cousin Richard called me—he knows I hang around the museum a lot." He studied her worried expression. "Somebody killed the guy, in his motel outside Chenocetah, or on the deserted dirt road where he was lying. The road leads the back way onto some construction sites, near a mountain honeycombed with caves. A jogger found him lying on the side of the road early this morning with a bullet in the back of his head. She's still being treated for shock at the local clinic," he added.

Phoebe leaned against a pillar at the front of the museum, trying to catch her breath. She'd never imagined that she might end up involved in a murder investigation. It took a little getting used to.

"Maybe I should join her," she said, and not completely facetiously.

"You're not in any danger. At least…I don't think you are," he added slowly.

She lifted her face and met his eyes. "Excuse me?"

He frowned. "We don't know who killed him, or why," he said. "Unless that story of his was concocted. And even if it is, there are three new big construction projects underway in the area. If what he told you is true, there's no way of knowing where he was looking when he found that site."

"Who did he work for?" she asked.

"They don't know yet. The investigation is still in its preliminary stages. There's one other thing—you can't tell Marie."

"Why not?"

"She can't keep her mouth shut," he replied quietly. "There's an investigation going on, and I'm telling you about it because I'm worried for your safety. I don't want it told all over the county, though."

She whistled softly. "Oh, boy."

"Just in case, have you got a gun?"

She shook her head. "I shot a friend's pistol once, but I was afraid of the noise and I never tried it again."

He bit his lower lip and drew in a long breath. "You live out in the country. If I can get a target, will you let me come out and teach you how to shoot?"

She felt the world shake under her feet. Drake was happy-go-lucky on ordinary days. But he wasn't kidding about this. He was genuinely worried about her. She swallowed hard.

"Yes," she said after a minute. "I'd be glad to have you teach me, if you think it's necessary." She gave him a searching look. "Drake, you know something you aren't telling me," she murmured.

"A site like that, with an unknown set of possible Neanderthal remains..." he began slowly. "If it existed, it would make it impossible for any developer to build on it. We're talking millions of dollars in time and materials and labor, wasted. Some people would do a lot to avoid that."

"Okay," she said, forcing a smile. "So I'll learn to shoot."

"I'll talk to the FBI agent when he, or she, gets here," he added, "and see what we can come up with by way of protection."

But she knew how that would end. Government agencies, like local law enforcement, had the same budget problems that she did. Funding for around-the-clock protection wouldn't be forthcoming, despite the need, and she certainly couldn't fund it herself. All the same, the thought of taking a human life made her sick.

"You're thinking you couldn't shoot somebody," he guessed, his dark eyes narrowing.

She nodded.

"I felt that way, before I went into the Army," he told her. In fact, he'd just come out of it the year before, after a stint overseas. "I learned how to shoot by reflex. So can you. It might mean your life."

She winced. "Life was so uncomplicated yesterday."

"Tell me about it. I'm not directly involved in the investigation, but jurisdiction is going to depend on where the murder actually took place. Just because he was found on the Rez is no reason to assume he was killed there."

"Would a killer really want the FBI involved?" she asked.

"No. But he might not have known he was involving federal jurisdiction. The local boundaries aren't exactly marked in red paint," he reminded her with a cool smile. "The dirt road where the body was found looked as if it was close to Chenocetah. But it wasn't. The reservation boundary sign was lying facedown about a hundred yards from where the tire tracks stopped."

She pursed her lips, thinking. "The killer didn't see the reservation sign. Maybe it was at night…?"

He nodded, smiling. "Good thinking. Ever considered working on the side of truth and justice, fighting crime?"

She laughed. "Your department couldn't afford me," she pointed out.

"Hell, they can't afford me, but that didn't stop them hiring me, did it?" he asked, and grinned, showing perfect white teeth. "You take care of your museum, and I'll do my best to take care of you," he added.

She frowned.

He held up a hand. "In a nice, professional way," he added. "I know you think I'm an overused man."

She did gasp then. "Marie!" she raged aloud.

He laughed. "I'm not offended, but that's why I said you shouldn't share secrets with her." He lifted both eyebrows. "Actually, it's a little like peacocks."

"It's what?"

"A peacock makes a fantastic display to attract females. His feathers may be a little ragged, and the colors may be faded, but it's the effect he's going for. Sort of like me," he added, smiling faintly. "I'm not Don Juan. But if I pretend I am," he said, leaning toward her, "I might get lucky."

She laughed with pure pleasure.

"Didn't you see that movie with Johnny Depp, when he thought he was Don Juan?" he teased. "It worked for him. I thought, why the hell not? You never know until you try. But I had to lose the cape and the mask. The sheriff wanted to call in a psychiatrist."

"Oh, Drake, you're just hopeless," she said, but in a softer tone than she'd ever used with him.

"That's better," he said, smiling. "You've been wearing winter robes. Time to look for spring blossoms, Miss Keller."

"Sometimes you actually sound poetic," she pointed out.

He shrugged. "I'm part Cherokee. Remember, we're not just 'the people,' we're 'principal people' in our own tongue."

Every tribe was "the people" in its own language, she recalled, except for the Cherokee, who called themselves "principal people." They were an elegant, intelligent people who had their own written language long before other tribes.

"No argument?" he asked.

She held up a hand. "I never argue with the law."

"Good thinking," he stated, straightening so that his close-fitting uniform outlined his powerful body.

Before she could reply, the sound of a loud muffler caught their attention. Marie pulled into the parking lot in her old truck, which was pouring smoke from the tailpipe. She cut off the engine and it made a loud popping sound.

Diverted, Drake went to it at once, motioning for Marie to open the hood. He stood back to let the smoke dissipate, waving it with his hand. He peered in over the engine and fiddled with a valve.

He stood up, shaking his head, while Marie waited with a worried look on her face. "It's carburetor backfire, Marie," he told her. "If you don't get it fixed, it could catch the truck on fire."

"I'm not convinced that would cost less than replacing it," Marie muttered. "Oh, I hate this thing!"

"It's just old," he told her, smiling. "Maybe a little... overused."

Marie went scarlet. "I'll go phone my brother at his garage right now!" She didn't even look at Phoebe as she ran past her, fumbling with her key when she realized the door was still locked. Fortunately she didn't think to ask why.

Drake and Phoebe were laughing softly.

"I won't tell her a thing," Phoebe promised.

"I'll see what else I can find out. Maybe Saturday, for the lessons?" he added.

She nodded. "I get off at one."

"I'll arrange my schedule so I'm off that afternoon," he promised. He glanced toward his squad car, where the radio was crackling. "Just a minute."

He strode to the car and picked up the mike, giving his call sign. He listened, nodded and spoke into it again.

"I've got to go," he said. "The FBI agent is on his way. They want us to assist," he added with a grin. "I suppose my investigative abilities have impressed somebody at the federal level!"

She chuckled. "See you Saturday."

He waved, jumped into the car and sped away.

"WHAT WAS GOING ON OUT there?" Marie asked curiously.

"Drake's going to teach me to shoot a gun," Phoebe said. "I've always wanted to learn."

Marie was oddly subdued. She moved to the desk and looked across it worriedly. "I know you don't want to trust me with any important news, after I blabbed to Cousin Drake about what you said. I'm really sorry," she added.

"I'm not mad."

Marie grimaced. "My brother says they found an anthropologist dead on the Rez this morning, and gossip is that he spoke to you yesterday. You're in danger, aren't you, and now you can't tell me because you think I'll tell everybody."

Phoebe was shocked. "How did your brother know…?"

"Oh, we know everything," she said. "It's a small community. Somebody from one clan finds out and tells somebody from another clan, and it's all over the mountains."

"Worse than a telephone party line," Phoebe said, still gasping.

"Really," Marie agreed. "You could stay with me," she added. "Your place is way out."

"Drake's going to teach me to shoot."

She lifted an eyebrow. "You didn't like him."

"He grows on you."

She smiled. "He's my cousin. I think he's terrific. He may strut a little, but he's smart and brave. You could do a *lot* worse," she added.

Phoebe glared. "He's only giving me shooting lessons," she said firmly. "I'm still not ready to get interested in a man, overused or not."

Marie ignored that. "He'll look out for you. So will my other cousins and my brother, if you need it," she told her. "You've done a lot for us. We don't forget favors, especially with family."

"I don't have a drop of Native American blood, Marie," Phoebe said firmly.

Marie grinned. "You're still family," she mused, and turned away. "I'll get to work."

Phoebe watched her go absently, her mind still on the dead man. It was upsetting that someone she'd spoken to the day before had been murdered. What was also upsetting was the destruction of a potentially precious site. If there were Neanderthal remains at a construction site—although she seriously doubted it—it would rewrite the history not only of North Carolina, but of the continent. Certainly it would shut down the developer, no question. Was that a reason to kill a human being? Phoebe, who had no love of money past being able to pay her bills, couldn't comprehend what some people might do for great wealth.

SHE WENT ABOUT HER BUSINESS for the next two days. Drake stopped by to tell her that the FBI agent had arrived, but he was oddly reticent about anything else. And he gave her a look that kept her awake. On Friday morning, she understood what it meant.

Just as she was getting ready to welcome a group of elderly visitors from a local nursing home, a black car pulled up at the steps. It had a government license plate. The FBI, no doubt, she thought idly, watching for the tour bus.

But the man who got out of the car froze her in her tracks. He had long black hair in a ponytail. He was wearing a gray vested suit and sunglasses. He came up the steps and stopped dead in front of Phoebe. He took off the glasses and hung them by one earpiece from his vest pocket.

"Hello, Phoebe," Cortez said quietly. He didn't smile. His scarred face looked leaner and harder than she remembered it. There were new lines around his eyes and mouth. He looked as if he'd never smiled in his life. His black eyes were penetrating, cold, all business.

She lifted her chin. She didn't scream and throw things, which was how she felt. She forced herself to look composed and professional. "Hello, Cortez," she replied, with equal formality and deliberately not using his first name. "What can I do for you?"

"A deputy sheriff named Drake—" he pulled out a pad and made a production of looking for the man's name, which he knew quite well already "—Stewart said that you spoke to the victim the night before his body was found. I'd like to have a word with you, if you have time."

She swallowed hard. "You're investigating the case?"

He nodded. "I'm back with the FBI. I'm part of a new unit being set up specifically to investigate violent crime on Indian Reservations nationwide."

She wanted to ask why he'd given up law, when he loved it so. She wanted to ask why he'd deserted her with nothing more informative than a newspaper clipping, when he'd looked at her as if he loved her. But she didn't.

"Come into my office. Just a minute, please." She stopped

and called to Harriett, who was taking a break. "Harriett, there's a busload of people coming from the nursing home. Can you take it? I have to speak to this gentleman."

Harriett lifted an eyebrow as she looked at Cortez, who towered over both women. "At least the government's taste has improved," she murmured dryly, and went out front to meet the bus, which was just pulling into the parking lot.

Cortez didn't react to the comment. Neither did Phoebe. She went into her office and offered him the only chair in front of her cluttered desk. He didn't sit down because Marie walked in abruptly with a payroll report, since it was Friday. She paused when she saw their visitor. Her quick eyes took in his long hair and dark complexion, the suit and his businesslike bearing. *"Siyo,"* she said in Cherokee, a word of greeting as well as goodbye.

He lifted his chin and his eyes were hostile. "I don't speak Cherokee. I'm Comanche," he said bluntly.

She colored and cleared her throat. "Sorry."

He didn't say a word. He moved aside to let her put the report on Phoebe's desk.

Marie exchanged a bland glance with Phoebe and beat a hasty retreat, closing the door behind her.

Phoebe sat down behind her desk and looked at Cortez. She folded her hands in front of her on the desk. They were working hands, with short nails and no polish. No rings, either.

"What can I do for you?" she asked professionally.

He looked at her for just a few seconds too long. His eyes darkened. There were shadows in them.

He pulled the notepad out of his pocket, crossed his long legs, flipped the pad open and checked his notes.

"You spoke to the man the day before his body was

found," he repeated. He took out a pen. "Can you tell me what he said?"

"He told me that a construction company was trying to cover up a potentially explosive archaeological site," she replied. "Neanderthal remains."

The pen stilled and he lifted his eyes to hers. He didn't say a word.

"I know, it sounds preposterous," she replied. "But he was quite serious. He said that the company was deeply in debt and afraid for the site to be discovered, for fear of being bankrupted during the excavation that would follow."

"There are no recorded Neanderthal remains anywhere in North America," he replied.

"I have a degree in anthropology," she replied coldly, insulted by the insinuation that she wouldn't know that. "Would you like to see it?"

His eyes narrowed. "You've changed."

"So have you," she bit off. "Back to the subject at hand, please. I know it sounds outlandish, but the man seemed to know what he was talking about. I tried to trace his number. He'd blocked it."

"They found your number on a pad beside his telephone, in a motel room. He registered under a false name and address. His ID is missing, except for a card designating him as a member of a national anthropological society."

"If someone stole his credentials, why didn't they take that, too?" she asked.

"It was under the bed. His wallet was thrown on his bed, empty of everything except a twenty-dollar bill. They must have emptied it there. Maybe they tore up the anthropology society ID card and that piece of it fell and they didn't notice. Pretty good work otherwise, though. No obvious clues, although I had our crime technician check the room with a blue light for latent prints. There were none. I sealed off the room and I've already got our crime unit on the scene," he added, naming a group whose purpose was specifically to gather and process trace evidence.

"How about footprints? Tire tracks?"

He shifted restlessly. He was recalling, as she must be, their cooperation in tracking down a polluter outside Charleston by following tire tracks. It was a time when she was young and full of life and hope and ambition. It was a different world.

He forced himself not to look back. "It's early days. We're checking that out. Had you ever heard his voice before?" he added.

She shook her head.

"He didn't mention the developer's name, anything that would help find him?"

She shook her head again.

He grimaced. "There are a number of possibilities, I'm told. Meanwhile," he added, putting up the pad and pen to pierce Phoebe's eyes with his own, "you're the only link we have to a murder."

"I could be the next victim," she assumed.

"Yes." He bit off the word, as if it left a bad taste in his mouth.

"I've already been told that. I have a dog," she said. "And one of the deputy sheriffs is giving me shooting lessons tomorrow."

Something touched his face, something cold and angry. "Do you have a gun?"

"He's loaning me a pistol."

He thought for a moment. "I'll see what I can do about some protection."

She stood up. "You and I both know that no law enforcement budget is going to provide around-the-clock protection for me. Marie's cousins have offered to keep an eye on me," she added.

His eyes narrowed. "This is not a civilian matter."

"That's good, because they aren't civilians. They belong here. They live on the reservation," she replied sweetly. "And you may have jurisdiction there, but you're not going to be met with open arms, either. They don't like feds."

He glared at her and she glared right back.

"Three years," he bit off.

"Your choice," she returned icily. "Haven't you got a crime to investigate, Special Agent Cortez? Because I'm quite busy myself."

She walked to the door and jerked it open, her face so hostile that Marie, walking toward her, actually turned in midstep and went the other way.

Cortez unhooked the sunglasses from his vest pocket and shot them over his eyes and nose. "I'll be in touch," he said curtly.

She almost made a sarcastic remark, but it wouldn't help. Nothing would help. Dragging up the past would only make things worse. She had other concerns, not the least of which was her own well-being.

He walked out, apparently not expecting a reply. A minute later, she heard the engine start and the car pull out onto the highway. He didn't even spray gravel when he left. He was more controlled now than he had been when Phoebe knew him, and that was saying something.

Marie came into the office a few minutes later, watching her boss warily.

"So that was him."

Phoebe wanted to deny it, but there was no use. "Yes."

"No wonder you came up here in the middle of nowhere to work," she replied. "That's more man than I'd want to try to handle."

"My sentiments exactly."

"Drake isn't going to like him, I think," Marie mused.

Phoebe wasn't listening. "I've forgotten a lot of my training," she murmured to herself. "But I do remember that nothing has ever been found in North Carolina older than the last Ice Age, around 10,000-12,000 Before Present Era. The man did mention something about finding the skull in a cave..." she added slowly.

"This whole area is honeycombed with caves," Marie reminded her. "Don't you remember those stupid stories about our huge stockpile of lost Cherokee gold? As if we had anything left after we were rounded up like cattle and walked all the way to Oklahoma in 1838!"

"Of all the tragic stories I know—and I know some—that hurts the most," Phoebe said quietly. "I can't even walk through the Museum of the Cherokee Indians without being reduced to tears. It was a terrible mistake on the part of Andrew Jackson and local governments."

"Gold fever," Marie said. "We were in the way."

"Yes. But your family escaped," Phoebe reminded her gently. "So did a few others."

"Not enough of us did," Marie said sadly. "But, about that gold—there are lots of caves."

"Any at those construction sites?"

"There's a mountain that adjoins all three of them, near a

river, and it's honeycombed with caves," Marie said. "They were bulldozing near them last week. Chances are that no matter what that man found, if it wasn't inside a cave, it's a pile of rubble by now."

"What if," Phoebe wondered aloud, "we could get an injunction to halt construction everywhere until we had time to look?"

"What if we got sued by starving construction workers?" Marie asked, putting things into perspective. "Plenty of men from the reservation work for those companies. It's going to hit a lot of families hard if we shut those companies down. And how would you get the authority to do it, anyway?"

Phoebe grimaced. "I wish I knew."

They went back to work. Alone in her office, Phoebe tried to come to grips with Cortez's unexpected presence in her life. It had wounded her to have to see him again with the past lying between them like a bloodied knife.

She wondered why he'd come here. He couldn't have known she was working nearby. He'd obviously been back with the FBI for some period of time, to be assigned to this case. But where was he working out of?

She tried to recall every single word the murdered man had said. She pulled up a blank file on her computer and started typing. She was able to reconstruct most of their brief conversation, along with putting color into the man's accent. He had a definite Southern accent, which would help place him. He had a way of talking that sounded like a bad stutter, or a lack of cohesive thought. He'd mentioned two people, a developer and another person who was apparently feeding him information. That might be useful. He'd opened the door and someone had called to him while he talking to her, definitely a woman's voice. It had been at exactly 3:10 p.m. the day before. None of it was worth much alone, but it might give the authorities something more to go on.

She wasn't going to phone Cortez. How could she, when she had no idea where he was? But she could give the information to Drake when he came by her house the next morning. He'd give it to the proper people.

She saved the file and went back to her budget plan. Unfortunately she forgot all about it in the sudden arrival of a late group wanting a tour of the facility.

The next morning, she was just finishing her small breakfast when she heard the sound of a truck coming down her long dirt driveway. Jock, her black chow, was barking loudly from his vigil on the front porch.

Phoebe went onto the porch in sock feet, jeans and a sweatshirt, a cup of coffee in one hand. Drake drove up in a black truck and parked at the steps.

"Got some more coffee?" he asked as he dragged out of the truck in boots, jeans, and a black T-shirt under a black and red flannel shirt. "I need fortifying. I've just been flayed, filleted and grilled by the FBI!"

PHOEBE STARED AT HIM. "The FBI?" she asked warily.

"Your buddy Cortez," he replied, following her inside. He'd been wearing dark glasses, but he folded them and tucked them into his shirt pocket. He sat down heavily at her kitchen table. "That man would intimidate a timber rattler!" he exclaimed.

"What did he want to know?"

Drake gave her a wry glance as he poured cream in the coffee she'd given him. "We could make a list of the things he didn't want to know—it would be shorter. I gather you told him I was giving you shooting lessons?"

She grimaced. "Sorry. I did."

"He doesn't think you'll shoot another person regardless of the incentive," he added.

Her jaw fell. She wanted to argue with that premise, but she couldn't.

He shrugged. "I had to agree. Sorry," he added wryly.

"I'm a wimp. What can I say?" She sighed. "But I think I might be able to shoot to wound somebody."

"That would probably cost you your life. We're talking split seconds here, not deliberating time."

She studied him curiously. He'd looked very young when he was coming by her office to check on things, but in the morning light, she realized that he was older than she'd first thought.

He gave her a grin. "You're thinking I've aged. I have. Cortez put ten years on me. See these gray hairs?" He indicated his temples. "They're from last night."

"He's a little abrasive," she agreed.

"A little abrasive," he muttered. "Right. And the Smoky Mountains are little hills." He traced the rim of his coffee mug. It was faded, like most of her dinnerware, but serviceable. "Obviously you've met him before."

She nodded. "He's a sort-of friend," she said evasively.

"He knew you were here before he ever came to investigate the murder," he said abruptly.

Her eyes widened with surprise. "How?"

"He didn't say. But he's worried about you. He can't seem to hide it."

She didn't know how to take that. She stared at her coffee cup.

"Most people who come to small towns like this—people who aren't born here—are trying to get away from something that hurts them," he said slowly. "Marie and I figured that's why you're here."

She lifted the cup to her mouth and took a sip, ignoring the sting of heat.

"And now I understand the reason," he added with

pursed lips. "It's about six foot one and has the cuddly personality of a starving black bear."

She laughed softly.

"I could think up lots more adjectives, but they wouldn't suit the company," he mused. He shook his head. "Damn, that man goes for the jugular. I'll bet he's good at his job."

"He was a federal prosecutor when I knew him," she revealed. "And he was good at it."

"He went voluntarily from a desk job to beating the bushes for lawbreakers?" he asked, surprised. "What would make a man do that?"

"Beats me. Maybe his wife didn't like living in D.C."

He was still for a few seconds. "He's married?"

She nodded.

"Poor woman!" he exclaimed with heartfelt compassion.

She laughed in spite of the pain.

"That explains the kid, I guess," he mused.

"What kid?" she asked, feeling her heart break all over again.

"He's got a little boy with him. They're staying in a motel in town. I noticed a woman going in and out—the babysitter, I suppose. He didn't treat her like the kid's mother."

"A boy or a girl?" She had to know.

"A boy. About two years old," he replied. "Cute little boy. Laughs a lot. Loves his dad."

Phoebe couldn't picture Cortez with a child. But it explained why he might have married in such a rush. No wonder he hadn't been interested in going to bed with her, when he already had a woman in his life. He could have told her…

"I brought a target with me," he interrupted her thoughts. "I thought we could draw Cortez's face on it."

She laughed.

"That's better," he said, smiling at her. "You don't laugh much."

"I'd given it up until you came along," she replied.

"Time you started back. Come on. The coffee was good, by the way. I'm particular about coffee."

"Me, too," she agreed. "I live on it."

He led her to his truck. He reached in and pulled out a wheel gun, a .38 caliber revolver. "This is easier to use than an automatic," he told her. "It's forgiving. The only downside is that you only get six shots. So you have to learn not to miss."

"I don't know if I can hold a pistol steady anymore," she said dubiously.

He pulled out a target shaped like a man's head and torso. "We'll work on that."

She frowned. "I thought targets had circles inside circles."

"In law enforcement, we use these," he replied solemnly. "If we ever get into a shootout, we need to be able to place shots in a small pattern."

The target brought home the danger she was in, and the unpleasant thought that she might have to put a bullet in another human being.

"In World War I, they noticed that the soldiers were deliberately aiming over or past the enemy soldiers when they shot at them," he told her. "So they stopped using conventional targets and started using these." He stuck it in the ground in front of a high bank, moved back to her, opened the chamber and started dropping bullets in. When he had six in the chamber, he closed it.

"It's a double-action revolver. That means if you squeeze the trigger, it fires. The trigger is tight, so you'll have to use some strength to make it work." He handed it to her and showed her how to hold it, with the butt and trigger in her right hand while she supported the gun with her left hand.

"This is awkward," she murmured.

"It's a lot to get used to. Just point it at the target and pull the trigger. Allow for it to kick up a little. Sight down the barrel. Line it up with the tip on the end of the barrel. Now fire."

She hesitated, afraid of the noise.

"Oops. I forgot. Here."

He took the pistol, opened the chamber, laid it on a fallen log. Then he dug into his pocket for two pairs of foam earplugs.

"You roll these into cones and stick them in your ears," he instructed. "They'll dull the noise so it doesn't bother you. Honest."

She watched him and parroted his actions. He picked up the pistol, closed the chamber, and handed it back to her with a nod.

She still hesitated.

He took it from her, pointed it at the target and pulled the trigger.

To her surprise, the noise wasn't loud at all. She smiled and took the pistol back from him. She squeezed off five shots. Three of them went into the center of the target in a perfect pattern.

"See what you can do when you try? Let's go again," he said with a grin and began to reload it.

TWO HOURS LATER, SHE FELT comfortable with the gun. "Are you sure you won't get in trouble for loaning me this?" she asked.

"I'm sure." He looked around her property. The house was all alone on a dirt road. There were mountains behind them and a small stream flowing beyond the yard. There were no close neighbors.

"I know it's isolated," she said. "But I've got Jock."

He glanced toward the dog, lying asleep on the porch. "You need something bigger."

"He has big teeth," she assured him.

"Would you consider moving to town?"

She shook her head. "I refuse to run scared…and I love the peace and solitude out here."

He grimaced. "Well, I'll see what I can come up with for protection."

"On your budget? They'll suggest a string attached to a lot of bells," she replied with a chuckle.

"Don't I know it. But I'll work on it. Listen, if you need me, you just call. The sheriff's department can find me, anytime."

He was really concerned. It made her feel warm. "Thanks, Drake. I really mean it," she added.

"What are friends for?" he teased. "Oh. Almost forgot." He opened the truck and handed her two boxes of shells. "That should do the trick."

"You have to tell me how much it is. I'm not letting you buy my ammunition," she added firmly. "I get a salary, too, you know."

"It's probably less than mine," he muttered.

"We'll have to compare notes sometime. Go on. Tell me."

"I'll tell you Monday," he promised. "See you at your office. Okay?"

"Okay. Thanks again."

"No problem. You keep your doors locked and that dog inside with you," he added. "He's no good to you if somebody gets to him first."

"Good point." She nodded.

He gave her a last concerned look, climbed into his truck and waved as he sped off down the road, leaving a trail of dust behind him.

Phoebe opened the chamber of the pistol, stuck the ammunition in her pockets, and went back inside with Jock right beside her.

SHE WASN'T REALLY AFRAID until night came. Then every small sound became magnified in her head. She heard footsteps. She heard voices. Once, she fancied she heard singing, in Cherokee of all things!

She gave up trying to sleep about five in the morning, got up and made coffee. She sat at the kitchen table with her head in her hands, and suddenly remembered the file she'd made at her office about things she recalled from her conversation with the murder victim. She'd meant to bring it home and give it to Drake, and she'd forgotten. She'd have to try to remember when he came by her office.

There was an odd sound in the distance again, like soft singing, in Cherokee. Puzzled, she got up and went to the door and looked out, but there was nothing there. She laughed to herself. She must be going nuts.

Phoebe left for work a half hour early. As she pulled out onto the main highway, she had a glimpse of an SUV parked on the side of the road opposite her driveway. A man was sitting in it, looking at a map. In the old days, she'd have stopped and asked if he needed help finding something. Now, she didn't dare.

She drove to the museum with her mind only half on the highway. She wondered if she should call her aunt and tell her what was going on. But Derrie would only worry and try to make her quit the job and move to Washington. She wasn't willing to do that. She was making a life for herself here.

When she got into her office, she pulled up the small file she'd written, detailing her conversation with the dead man, and she printed it out. As an afterthought, she copied it onto a floppy disk and put it in a plastic case for Drake. Perhaps something she recalled would help the investigation and solve the crime.

She was inclined to discount the man's story about Neanderthal remains, however. If there had been such a presence anywhere in North America, surely it would have been discovered in the past century.

DRAKE STOPPED BY LATE that afternoon with news about the investigation.

"The FBI guy may be a scoundrel, but he's sure at the top of his game professionally," he remarked with an impressed smile. "He's already turned up some interesting clues." He held up a hand. "I really can't tell you," he said at once, anticipating questions. "I'm in enough trouble already."

"For what?" she asked, aghast.

"It would take too long to tell you. I've asked the guys to do an extra patrol out your way at night," he added. "Just in case."

"Thanks. I owe you for the bullets," she said. "And I've got something for you."

He followed her into her office with a puzzled smile. "For me?"

"Well, for you and the FBI, really," she had to confess, handing him a folded piece of paper and the CD. "It's every little detail I could recall about what the man said, how he sounded, background noise, and so forth. It's not much, but it may trigger some sort of connection when you know more about him."

He was reading while she was talking. "Hey, this is pretty good," he said, nodding. "You've got a good ear."

"I don't go down the road playing my radio so loud that people's houses shake," she replied, mentioning a pet peeve. "And when someone finally tells those people that they're risking not only hearing loss but actual brain damage at those high sound levels, there will be lawsuits."

"Amen," he seconded, chuckling.

"Anyway, I hope those notes help catch whoever did it. Nobody should be killed for being a little crazy," she said.

"You don't think there's a chance he was telling the truth?" he asked hesitantly.

"Not a chance on earth," she said firmly. "Now what do I owe you for those bullets? And you'd better tell me the truth, because I'm calling the local gun shop to ask."

He grimaced and told her. She wrote him out a check.

"And thank you for the lessons and the loan of the pistol," she added. "I'm really grateful."

"No problem. I'd better get back to work. You watch your back," he added.

She smiled. "Sure."

THAT EVENING, WHEN DRAKE got off work, he knocked on the door of the room in a local motel where Cortez was staying.

"Come in," the older man said, sounding weary.

Drake opened the door. There sat Cortez in a chair in his sock feet, jeans and a black T-shirt with a sleeping toddler sprawled on his broad chest. His hair was loose down his back and he looked as if he'd die for some sleep.

"He's teething," Cortez said. "I finally took him to the clinic and got something for the pain. For both of us," he added without a smile, but with a twinkle in his dark eyes. "What do you want?"

"I brought some information." He handed the slip of paper to Cortez and watched him unfold it. "That's what Miss Keller remembers about her conversation with the anthropologist. It was on disk, but I had it transcribed for you."

"She's very thorough."

"She should be doing ethnology, not overseeing some little museum," Drake said. "She's overqualified for the job."

Cortez glanced at him. "What do you know about ethnology?"

"Are you kidding? I'm Cherokee. Well," he corrected quietly, "part Cherokee. My father was full-blooded. My mother was white and she got tired of her family making remarks about her little half-breed. She walked out the door when I was three. Dad drank himself to death. I went into the army at seventeen and found myself a home, where a lot of people have mixed blood," he added coldly.

Cortez studied him silently. "I had a Spanish ancestor somewhere."

"It doesn't show," Drake said flatly. "I imagine you fit in just fine with your people."

"Your people outnumber us."

"Which half of my people do you mean?" Drake asked ruefully.

"The Indian half. And even among my people, there are only about nine hundred of us who still speak Comanche," Cortez said. "The language is almost dead. At least Cherokee is making a comeback."

"No two people speak it alike," Drake said. "But I get your point—it's still a viable language." He looked at the little boy with soft eyes. "Going to teach him how to speak Comanche?"

Cortez nodded. His eyes narrowed thoughtfully as he studied Drake. "But he'll have your problem. His mother is white."

Drake was looking at the sleeping child intensely. "Does she live with your people?"

Cortez's eyes flashed. He averted them. "She…died a month after Joseph was born," he said reluctantly.

"Sorry," Drake said at once.

"It wasn't that sort of marriage," the older man said coldly. "I appreciate the notes. Did Phoebe tell you to give them to me?"

"She said they might be useful to the FBI," Drake hedged.

Cortez's big hand absently smoothed the sleeping child's back. He stared ahead of him without seeing anything. "She lives in a dangerous place, so far out of town."

"I've got the guys doing extra patrols," Drake said. "She knows how to shoot. I think if her life depended on it, she would use it to protect herself."

"She'd shoot to wound an attacker and she'd be dead in seconds," he said flatly.

"You're full of cheer," Drake said with faint sarcasm.

Those coal-black eyes pierced his face. "Why did he call her?" he asked abruptly. "Why not go to the state authorities or local law enforcement…why Phoebe?"

Drake frowned. "Well…I don't know."

Cortez lifted the sheet of paper again and studied it. His eyes narrowed. "He mentioned a daughter."

"That's about as much as we know about this John Doe," Drake said grimly. "His fingerprints aren't on file in any database. That's the first thing we checked."

"I know. Our investigator ran them last night," Cortez told him. "We drew a blank as well, and I won't tell you how our criminalist convinced the lab to leapfrog over other pending cases to do ours."

"The anthropologist was of Cherokee descent," Drake reminded him. "That means he might have relatives on the Rez…"

"That's an assumption. The larger part of your nation is in Oklahoma," Cortez interrupted.

Drake stopped speaking with his mouth still open. "That's right!"

"I live in Oklahoma," Cortez murmured absently. "So we're left with two questions. What the hell was he doing here, and where did he come from? Maybe he has a car, but in another state."

"That's a lead I'll check out as soon as I get back to work. I'll go see the tribal council, too," Drake told him. "Maybe he's got relatives in one of our clans. If so, the same clan in Oklahoma would know him, if he's from there."

"Good thinking. One other thing we dug out," Cortez

added. "Someone staying at the motel saw a dark SUV parked outside the night of the murder. It hasn't been seen since. You might have your colleagues keep an eye out... why are you laughing?"

"I guess you haven't noticed that every other vehicle in this county is an SUV," Drake murmured. "They're perfect for mountain driving, with four-wheel drive."

"Damn." His broad chest rose and fell with a frustrated deep breath. The child made a murmur at the movement and then shifted his little body and went back to sleep. "There's another possibility," Cortez said after a minute, his heavy brows drawn together in thought. "We were told that a lot of Cherokee people work in construction around here. What if our visiting anthropologist was related to one of them?"

Drake pursed his lips. "That's possible. If I can track down his clan, I may be able to dig up a few relations here. I'll get Marie to help. She is a bit of a talker, but she's very smart, too. She and I together have more cousins on the Rez than our tribal council—and that's saying something."

"Marie?"

"My cousin. She works for Miss Keller at the museum."

Cortez averted his eyes. "I remember her. She spoke Cherokee to me. I was...abrupt with her."

"So I heard."

Cortez glanced toward the other man, who was smiling amusedly. "I hadn't seen Phoebe in three years," he said. "It was a difficult day."

Drake hesitated. "I don't know you. Probably I'm going to tick you off for even asking. But Miss Keller is a unique woman..."

Cortez turned his head and looked at the younger man.

Drake held up a hand. The expression was like a loaded gun. "I'm not involved with her, or likely to be," he added at once. "Let me get the words out before you take offense."

Cortez still glared.

Drake cleared his throat. "I've only known her a short time. But Marie's been with her for three years. She said that Miss Keller was a basket case when she came here. An older woman, her aunt, I believe, came to visit and asked Marie to keep a close eye on her, because she'd had some sort of personal problem that almost caused an emotional breakdown. She'd taken some pills…"

"God!" Cortez exclaimed harshly.

The look on Cortez's face stopped the words in Drake's throat. He swallowed, hard.

The toddler stirred and protested. Cortez fought to calm down. He soothed the little boy's back and took a deep, slow breath. His big hand had a faint tremor.

"Miss Keller doesn't know that Marie told me that," Drake said, his voice quieter, softer now. "But I thought you should know, too."

Cortez didn't look at him. He was staring into space again, his whole body tense. "Coyote lies in wait everywhere for us," he said with bridled fury, mentioning a character from Native American folklore which was common to almost every tribe—Coyote, the trickster, the enemy spirit.

"He does," Drake agreed quietly. "But sometimes we can outwit him."

The dark, turbulent eyes met his. "I'd cut off my hand before I would voluntarily hurt Phoebe. What happened… was a family matter that forced me into a decision I would never have made, if I'd had any freedom of choice at all."

Drake frowned. "Would it have something to do with that little boy?" he wanted to know.

"Everything," Cortez said heavily. He looked at Joseph with loving eyes. "I thought it would be easier for Phoebe if she hated me." His eyes closed. "I never dreamed that she might…" He couldn't even finish the thought. It tormented him that a woman like Phoebe, so bright and loving and full of life, could be driven to such sorrow because of him. It wounded his very soul.

"All of us have done desperate things in a moment of despair," Drake said. "We usually have the good fortune to survive them."

Cortez touched the little boy's hair with his fingertips. "I took a month off and spent it breaking wild horses on a cousin's ranch, just after I got married."

The older man was making a point, and Drake understood. "I imagine you didn't even get kicked," he mused.

Cortez laughed without humor. "I got bitten twice." He glanced at Drake. "You can't die when you want to."

"Yeah, I know. I'm not a suicidal person, but I joined a combat unit after my girl dumped me," he replied. "Her people didn't want her to have a half-breed's kids."

Cortez's dark eyes lost their last trace of hostility. "Somebody once told me that we live in a world that no longer discriminates."

"Bull," Drake said passionately.

"That's what I told her," Cortez agreed. "You can't legislate equality or morality. Pity."

Drake chuckled. "Yeah."

Cortez indicated Phoebe's note. "Thanks for bringing this by. I'll share it with the unit tomorrow and we'll see what we can come up with."

"You're welcome. I'll help keep an eye on Miss Keller."

"Thanks."

Drake shrugged. "I like her, too. She doesn't see color, did you notice?"

Cortez gave him a look that spoke volumes.

Drake held up a hand defensively and grinned. "I'll see you around, then. Oh, one other thing," he added from the door.

"Yes?"

"Under the circumstances, don't you think it's a little careless to be sitting in here with a child, with the door unlocked?"

Just as he said that, the doorknob turned and a woman who looked about Drake's age walked in with a bag of disposable pull-up diapers. She stared at Drake intensely with dark eyes in a pretty round face surrounded by long, thick black hair. She grinned suddenly, her white teeth startling in her dark face.

"Are you going to arrest him?" she asked Drake enthusiastically, nodding toward Cortez. "Can I put the handcuffs on?"

Drake was nonplussed. He couldn't think of a reply.

Cortez chuckled. He looked suddenly years younger. "That's Tina," he said. "She's my cousin. My regular babysitter is back in Lawton, Oklahoma, with a bad case of shingles. My father's too old to be a nanny and I couldn't manage Joseph alone, so I talked Tina into coming up here with me. She lives in Asheville. She works in the local library, but she moonlights as a tour guide at the Biltmore Estate on weekends," he added, naming a famous tourist spot.

"Everybody around here thinks I'm Cherokee," she said,

the grin widening. "Hi. I'm Christina Redhawk." She noticed the look her cousin was giving her and she chuckled. "He uses the name Cortez. I like our own family name better."

"I'm Drake Stewart," he replied.

"You live here?" she asked.

"I'm a deputy sheriff."

She made a face. "Another lawman." She shook her head and went to put the diapers down on one of the beds. "He's always playing matchmaker for me, with every new single agent who works with him," she indicated Cortez. "That's why I moved to North Carolina. I dated a policeman in Asheville." She gave Cortez a speaking look. "Of course, he isn't half as cute as you are, Drake," she added with a sly look.

"Drake was leaving," Cortez said at once, standing up carefully so as not to wake the child. "Here." He handed Joseph to her. "He's going to have to sleep in your room tonight. I've got some work to do on the internet."

"I'll take good care of him." She took Joseph and paused at the door where Drake was standing. "Maybe I'll see you," she said with a grin.

Drake chuckled. "Maybe so, if we can ditch him," he jerked his thumb toward Cortez playfully.

"He likes old coins," she said in a stage whisper.

"I've got a 1976 nickel," he told Cortez hopefully.

The other man laughed, rolled his eyes toward the ceiling, and went to the laptop he'd set up at the table by the window.

"Once he turns that thing on, he doesn't know anybody's in the room," Tina said. "We might as well leave. Good night, cousin."

Cortez nodded, already logging on to the internet with nimble fingers.

Drake closed the motel door behind them and gave Tina a curious smile. "You look like him."

"Our fathers are two of three brothers," she said simply. "It's a pity we're so closely related—he's a real hunk. But even if we weren't, there was this young girl at a college somewhere back East. He went crazy for her. Then his brother got killed and the girl he lived with was pregnant. Her people wanted a termination, but Cousin Jeremiah's mother got hysterical and said she'd die if the baby did. So Jeremiah got married." She shook her head, turning away without realizing Drake knew she was talking about Phoebe Keller. "It was bad, too. The girl really loved Isaac. A month after Joseph was born, she hanged herself on the back porch."

Drake could hardly believe the other man's terrible luck. "But your cousin didn't go back to find the girl?"

"He tried to. Her people wouldn't tell him anything except she hated him," Tina replied softly. "He said he'd sent her just a newspaper clipping of the wedding, nothing else. He came home. Lost his job as a federal prosecutor because his mother died and he couldn't leave Joseph with his dad." She shook her head. "He's had a lot of heartache. Losing that girl did something to him. He was laughing tonight, with you," she added. "That's the first time I've heard Jeremiah laugh in three years!"

5

By dawn, Cortez had grabbed a few hours sleep, after exhausting the bulk of the searchable databases for clues to the murder victim's identity. Sometimes cases solved themselves. This one was going to be like pulling teeth, he just knew it.

He dressed in a suit, tied his hair into a ponytail, and left Joseph with Tina while he played a hunch.

The one thing he was certain of was that the murdered man had been in contact with someone in construction working on a local project. He had the crime-lab photo of the dead man's face. He had FBI credentials. He was going to knock on a few doors and see if he could rattle anybody.

The biggest project going was the theme park hotel being erected just inside the Chenocetah city limits. Two projects almost that size were splayed around the mountain that contained caves, also barely inside the city limits.

There was a trailer serving as the construction boss's headquarters. Cortez knocked on the door.

A tall, good-looking blond man of about thirty-five opened it and gave Cortez a curious look. "We're not hiring," he said pleasantly.

"I'm not looking for work." Cortez flashed his ID.

The man grimaced. "Sorry. We've had to turn away a lot of would-be employees this week. Seems like half the reservation's down here looking for jobs."

Cortez followed the man into the trailer and sat down in the straight chair he was offered. The desk was cluttered with blueprints and documents. Among them was a gold-framed photograph of a pretty young blue-eyed blond woman, and a golf trophy.

"I'd offer you coffee, but I just drank the last cup and there's no more until I send one of the guys out to the store," the blond man said politely. He folded his hands on the makeshift desk. "What can I do for the FBI?"

Cortez took the photo out of his pocket and slid it across the desk. "You can tell me if you've ever seen this man."

The other man studied it quietly, frowning. "He doesn't look familiar. Does he work for us in a subcontracting capacity or something?" he asked with genuine curiosity.

"That's what I need to know," Cortez replied. "He was murdered."

The other man was very still. "On our property?"

"No."

There was a sigh of heartfelt relief. "Thank God," he murmured, wiping his forehead with a handkerchief. "I catch hell if there's any delay at all," he explained ruefully. "We had a load of steel drop-shipped here, and they shorted us. We had to sit on our hands until it showed up. I thought the boss was going to skin me alive!"

Cortez took out his pad and pen. "The contractor?" he asked politely.

"I'm the contractor. Sorry. I'm Jeb Bennett," he introduced himself. "Bennett Construction. My company works out of Atlanta."

"How long have you been working here?"

"Three months," Bennett said. "If I'd known how hard the man was going to push us, I'd have thought twice about accepting. I don't like having my men harassed on the job. I've had to use some bad language—and a few threats—to a couple of the owner's subordinates."

That was interesting. A man in a hurry to complete a job would have problems with an archaeological site being discovered on his land. Cortez lifted his dark eyes to the other man's blue ones. "Who's the boss?"

"Theo Popadopolis," he replied. "They call him the 'Big Greek' in hotel circles. He's got a temper almost as bad as mine, and he pinches pennies. He's a self-made man. His dad came here after World War II as an electrical engineer. Within twenty years, he owned a small contracting business. Theo inherited it, and within twenty years, *he* was a multimillionaire."

"Legally?" Cortez wondered.

"Who knows. He's got power. He uses it."

"Do you have a contact number for him?"

Bennett smiled. "Indeed I do. I wish I could be a fly on the wall when you talk to him." He thumbed through a card file and pulled out a business card. "I've got two. You can have this one. You can tell him I referred you," he added with a flash of blue eyes. "That'll give him something to think about."

Cortez's dark eyes twinkled. "Wicked."

"Isn't it?" Bennett mused. "If we down tools, he'll be in a bind, won't he?" He stood up. "If you need anything else, I'll be around, or my foreman will know where to find me."

"Who's your foreman?" Cortez asked on a whim.

"Dick Walks Far," he said. "He's Cherokee. Hard worker. Honest man," he added, averting his eyes as if he didn't want to say more. "He worked for me in Atlanta."

"North Carolina Cherokee?" Cortez wondered.

He hesitated and then shook his head. "Oklahoma."

"Could I have a word with him?" Cortez asked immediately.

"Sure." Bennett stuck his head out the door and yelled for the foreman. He didn't need a bullhorn.

Cortez held his ear.

Bennett chuckled when he noticed. "Loud voices go with the job," he told him.

A minute later, a tall, dark man in working gear and a white helmet walked up the steps. He stopped dead when Cortez took out his ID and showed it to him.

"What'd I do?" he asked immediately.

Cortez's eyebrows arched. "If you don't know, don't ask me."

The Cherokee's face relaxed and he chuckled. *"Osiyo,"* he greeted in the Oklahoma Cherokee greeting—Eastern Cherokees omitted the *O*.

Cortez narrowed one eye. "I'm Comanche."

"Ah. In that case, *Ma ruawe! Unha hakai nuusuka?*" he said in Comanche, grinning. "Hello. How are you?"

Cortez was impressed. He answered him, in Comanche. *"Tsaatu, untse?"* He smiled. "How is that you speak the tongue of the people?" he asked in his own dialect.

"My mother is Comanche," Walks Far replied pleasantly in English. "What's the FBI doing here? Bennett cheat on his taxes?" he teased the boss.

"No. Homicide investigation," Cortez replied, palming the photo of his victim. He flashed it under Walks Far's nose. "Ever see this guy?"

The reaction was immediate, but quickly hidden. Walks Far blinked twice, frowned, and leaned toward the photo. "Yeah," he said after a minute. "He came by last week, asking about caves."

"Caves?" Cortez asked.

"He said he was an archaeologist," Walks Far continued. "Somebody had told him about a big find, but not where to look. He said all he knew was that it was a building site under construction, in a cave. So he wanted to see ours."

"What did you tell him?" Cortez asked.

"I showed him the caves," Walks Far replied. "He looked around, said thank you, and left."

"Was he driving?" Cortez asked.

"Search me," Walks Far replied and seemed uneasy. "I didn't see where he went."

"What are you going to do about the caves?" Cortez wanted to know, in case he had to bring the investigators over to check for clues.

"Nothing," Walks Far said, surprised at the question. "They're on the back side of our site, near the river, hidden by a grove of fir trees."

"We plan to leave the caves on our property," Bennett said. "As a tourist attraction. The Big Greek knows a local guy who specializes in spelunking. He's going to offer cave tours." Bennett grinned. "More tourist revenue, unless somebody gets stuck in one."

Walks Far chuckled. "I'm not going in no cave," he told the other two men. "Bats in there!"

"We'll ask the bats to leave before the tours open," Bennett promised.

"Good luck," Cortez told him. He slid the photo back into his pocket, covertly watching the two men for reactions, but nothing was forthcoming. "You don't know any of the other crews working in the area, by any chance?"

"Well, I know one," Bennett said, and his face tautened. "Paul Corland and his gang. They're from somewhere in South Carolina. They put up a shopping mall and a wall collapsed. Killed two workers. They were shut down while it was investigated, but it was attributed to substandard materials."

"You don't believe that," Cortez noted, reading the younger man's cold expression.

"No, I don't," Bennett said. "When you've been in this business a while, you learn the good guys from the bad guys. Corland's rotten. Anybody who hired him without knowing him had better carry big liability insurance." He pointed north. "He's building a hotel for some local investors, about a mile past our site over near the river. You might check with the licensing guys at the state capitol and the local planning commission. Just a hunch."

Cortez extended his hand. "Thanks," he said.

Bennett shook it and shrugged. "I run a clean shop. I don't like people who cheat."

"That makes two of us," Cortez replied.

"Three," Walks Far interjected. "Take it easy," he told Cortez solemnly.

"You do the same," Cortez replied. He thanked Bennett for his time and asked for directions to the caves.

"Do you mind if I have a look around them later?" he asked Bennett.

"No problem," the contractor replied. "Help yourself."

"Thanks."

CORTEZ DROVE BY THE CAVE on his way out of the building site. Perhaps there was sign there, something he could read. It hadn't rained since the dead man's body was found, and it wasn't predicted for several days. There might be tire tracks, a gum wrapper, a cigarette butt that he could trace to the victim. He was going tracking.

Tomorrow, he was going to check out Corland's operation.

He stopped by the motel to check on Tina and Joseph, changed into jeans and pulled a checked, long-sleeved flannel shirt over his black T-shirt. As an afterthought, he let his hair down and put on his sunglasses.

On a whim, he whipped the car into the parking lot of Phoebe's museum and took the steps in three long strides.

Marie, just coming out of Phoebe's office, stopped dead at the sight of him.

"Siyo," he said politely in Cherokee as she moved aside. "Excuse me," he added, going right past her into Phoebe's office. He closed the door behind him.

Phoebe, who was on the phone, looked up. It was like a baseball bat hitting her stomach. Her lips parted on a soft explosion of breath. Time stood still. She was back in Charleston, back in time, back in love. He looked exactly as he had the first day she knew him, when he took her to track a polluter's truck.

He took off the sunglasses and stuck the earpiece in his pocket. "I'm going tracking," he said. "Want to come?"

The phone was still in her hand, poised in midair. A voice was repeating, "Hello? Hello?"

She blinked and brought it back to her ear. "I'm sorry, I'll have to…to call you back. Thanks."

She hung up, missing the first time before she fumbled the receiver back into the cradle.

She got to her feet unsteadily, her blue eyes glittering, glaring at him as surprise gave way to fury. He thought he could walk back in and wipe out what he'd done to her by asking her to track with him? He thought it was going to be that easy? Her temper exploded.

"Three years," she said icily. "Three long, empty years. You sent me a damned newspaper clipping…!" She fumbled in the drawer for it and waved it at him. "A newspaper clipping, without a word of explanation, apology, anything! You didn't even have the courtesy to explain why you'd talked about a future with me and then married some other woman overnight! And then you come walking in here in the middle of my workday like nothing ever happened and you want me to go tracking with you?" She threw the newspaper clipping at him. Her eyes were blazing. "You go to hell! You vicious, cold-blooded, insensitive, second cousin to a desert sand viper…!"

He was around the desk before she could get it all out. He reached out, slammed her body into his, bent her back across his hip and kissed her as if he were facing imminent execution.

"You…!" she muttered, fighting him. She tried to kick

him. He simply wrapped his ankle around hers and she fell heavily against him, holding on to keep from falling.

He wrapped her up tight, his mouth forcing hers open, his arm like steel around her back. She hit him with her fist, but he didn't feel it. He was alive, on fire, burning with desire for the first time in three years. It was like an explosion of joy in his whole body. He groaned in anguish against her lips.

She really wanted to keep fighting. But his mouth was so familiar, even after three years. He smelled as she remembered, a cologne scent that still reminded her of fir trees and solitary places. His mouth was hungry, expert and demanding on her lips. His body, against hers, was hard and hot. He wanted her. He couldn't pretend. Neither could she, for that space of seconds.

With a little sob of pleasure, she relaxed in his arms and her lips parted. Her hands went to his lean face and her fingers tangled into the long, thick, clean strands of his black hair. The past and the present merged. She kissed him back with something like anguish.

But after a few insane seconds she managed to get her brain to work again. She heard voices in the distance. They weren't speaking Cherokee. They were giggling.

She drew her lips from under the devouring crush of his mouth. "Jeremiah…do you remember…that the upper part of my office door…is glass?" she got out.

He blinked, his own mind whirling. "Is that relevant?"

She turned her head toward the door. His followed. Outside were a host of little grinning faces and fingers looking back. Over their heads was Marie's pop-eyed expression. Behind her, five total strangers, including a well-dressed blond woman, were also getting an eyeful.

Cortez cleared his throat and quickly moved Phoebe back into an upright position. He steadied her before he removed his hands and stepped back, but with his own back carefully turned toward the glass part of the door. He was reciting multiplication tables in a furious attempt to relax his aching body. His sunglasses had fallen out of his pocket onto the floor. He bent slowly to scoop them up and tuck them back into the pocket.

Phoebe smoothed the jacket of her pantsuit and put a nervous hand to her hair. Her mouth felt swollen. She was glad there wasn't a mirror.

Their audience melted away in a dull buzz of giggles. They were alone again.

"How could you do that?" she demanded. "You're married!" she choked.

"I am not!" he replied shortly. "I was widowed over two years ago."

She was still trying to breathe normally. It wasn't easy. Her knees shook. She dropped down into her desk chair with the last dignity she could summon. "Oh."

He was able to relax, too, finally. He perched himself on the edge of her desk facing her. His face was solemn. "I'll tell you all about it one day, when you're ready to listen."

"Don't hold your breath," she bit off.

"I told you once that I never do anything unless I've considered all the consequences," he replied. "I thought… hating me might spare you any sadness."

"Why should I have been sad?" she asked in what she hoped was a normal voice. "We were friends."

He shook his head. "More than that."

"No."

Her mutinous expression said it all. She wasn't giving in,

no matter how passionately he tried to convince her that he still cared. He had to bide his time.

She'd kept the newspaper clipping. That registered. Then his eyes went past her to the open desk drawer and he saw the charm his father had made for her three years ago. She still had it!

She saw where his eyes were looking and she closed the drawer abruptly.

"Do you remember what I wrote you about it?" he asked. "My father said to keep it with you always. I didn't understand why. He said it would save your life one day."

She shifted in the chair. "You said he was a medicine man."

"Yes. He still practices. He mentioned that charm again when I told him I'd found you."

The wording was odd. She lifted her eyes to his. "Found me?"

He averted his gaze. "Bad choice of words. Met you again," he corrected. "He said that you must put the charm in your pocket, and put these behind it. You must do this every time you go out alone."

He drew two large Mexican peso pieces out of his hip pocket and handed them to her. They were heavy and still warm from his body.

She felt the weight and thickness. "What are these?"

"Very old, Mexican pesos that have been in my family for a long time," he said. "My father was very specific about where you keep them, too—in your right slacks pocket or a fanny pack."

She traced the heads on the heavy coins, touched by his father's concern. "Why does he think these will save my life?"

"He has visions," he told her. "A psychiatrist would call them delusions or the aura from migraine headaches—which he also has. But he knows things. He has two brothers. One is disgustingly normal and lives in California. The other lived with his Apache wife in Arizona until her death, and stayed on there to raise his son. He has the same gift of precognition that my father has. His son is in the CIA. He always knows when something's wrong with him."

"I've known people with that gift," she confessed, meeting his dark gaze. "Your father knew I was in danger before you came here!" she said suddenly, as the thought occurred to her.

He nodded. "He gave me those coins a month ago. He said I was going to see you when I came to North Carolina."

"Did he know…that you were coming to North Carolina?"

He glanced down at the big coins in her hand. "Yes. God knows how. I was working out of Oklahoma until this summer. But because I'm Native American, and they're starting this new organization, I've been attached to the Indian Country Crime Unit. They sent me here when they got the news of the homicide on the Yonah Reservation this week." He hesitated. "I took a week off back in the summer and went to Charleston."

Her lips parted. "I haven't been to Charleston in three years," she blurted out.

His expression was hard to describe. "I know," he said with feeling.

"You…were looking for me."

His face gave away nothing.

"But you never wrote," she bit off.

His eyes closed. "How could I? What could I have said that would undo the pain, Phoebe?"

She refused to think of the past. It was too painful. She took a deep breath. At least he didn't know how far she'd gone over the edge when she got that newspaper clipping. It spared her pride.

"It was all a long time ago," she said primly. "Water under the bridge."

He traced a pattern on one clean, flat fingernail. "Come tracking."

She looked at him, aghast. "I'm the curator," she began.

"Give yourself two hours off."

This was nuts, she told herself. "I'm not dressed for outings."

"I'll drive you by your house to change."

"I can't," she began.

There was a perfunctory knock on the door, and Marie peered in. "Sorry," she said. She moved closer to Phoebe, nodding toward a well-dressed blond woman who was standing with another adult near a group of children. "There's a schoolteacher out here. She was looking in the window a few minutes ago. She says she wants to talk to you about the deportment of the staff." She grinned.

Phoebe cleared her throat. She felt a blush flaming on her cheeks. "I'm sorry, I can't do it right now. I'll be out of the office for two hours," she told Marie at once. "Tell her to speak to Harriett."

"Harriett said you'd say that. And she said to tell you that you'll have to buy a doughnut in the morning. Coffee, too."

Phoebe stood up. "She can have two doughnuts. Tell her that I'm assisting the FBI."

Marie's eyes twinkled. "Is that what it's called?" she asked with raised eyebrows.

Red-faced, Phoebe squeezed by Cortez, grabbed her purse and rushed out the door.

Cortez paused long enough to reach in her desk drawer and retrieve the charm before he followed her. As he passed Marie, he didn't crack a smile. But he winked before he slid the dark glasses back into place.

Marie stood at Phoebe's door, waving her hand in front of her face to cool it. He might have a bad temper, but he was the most dashing man she'd ever seen, and he was bristling with charm and good looks. Poor Phoebe wouldn't stand a chance.

IT WAS LIKE OLD TIMES. Cortez pulled up in front of her house and sat in the car while she rushed in past a barking Jock to change into jeans and boots. When she came back out, with sunglasses perched over her nose, it was like a glimpse into time past. She wore reading glasses, but she didn't need vision correction for distances.

Cortez got out to open the door for her. She climbed in and fastened her seat belt before he slid in under the wheel and did the same.

"Nice manners," she murmured.

"My mother was a stickler for them. Isaac never listened. I did."

Isaac. His brother. She heard an odd note in his voice and stared at him curiously. "How is he?"

"He's dead," he said shortly. He started the car and put it in Reverse.

She folded her hands in her lap and looked out the window, uncertain about whether or not to press the issue. "Recently?" she asked.

"Three years ago."

Three years ago he'd married another woman. There was a child. She was feeling sick. What if…?

She turned toward Cortez with wide, curious eyes.

"She was three months pregnant with Joseph," he choked out as he headed down the driveway toward the highway. "Her parents wanted a termination. My mother had a heart attack over it. Isaac was dead."

"So they sacrificed you to save the child."

His eyes closed for an instant on a wave of pain. She was as perceptive as he remembered.

"Joseph," she persisted. "Not your son. Your nephew!"

There was a long pause. He drew in a harsh breath. "My nephew."

She turned her attention out the window again, feeling numb all over. "You couldn't have managed to put that in a letter? Even four lines would have done it."

"I was married."

"You said you were widowed…"

He stopped the car at the road, threw it out of gear and turned off the engine. He turned to her, ripping off the sunglasses. "A month after Joseph was born, she left him with me so she could take a walk. She needed to be alone, she told me. I was on the internet on a case, and I didn't realize how long she'd been out. Three hours later, I thought she'd been gone long enough. Joseph was hungry and I was still new to formula and bottles. I left him in his crib and went outside to find her." His face tautened. "She'd gotten the extra rope from the barn and tied it to the rafter on the back porch. I found her hanging there. Dead."

She put a hand to her mouth.

"I didn't love her. She was Isaac's girl. She loved him. She grieved for him. It would never have been a real marriage, if we'd been together ten years. She couldn't live without him."

She almost told him she knew how that felt.

"I know how she felt."

The words echoed in the car, but in his voice—not hers.

She looked back at him with wide, anguished eyes in a white face.

"Three years," he said heavily. "I could only imagine how badly I'd hurt you. I would have tried, even then, to explain. But my mother had a second heart attack. She'd been taking care of Joseph, while I worked out of Oklahoma City, and my father couldn't cope. I'd already had to give up my job as a federal prosecutor, because I was needed at home so badly. I'd phoned my old boss at the FBI. He's high up these days. He gave me a job and pulled strings to get me assigned as close to Lawton as he could."

"Lawton?"

"It's in Comanche County, Oklahoma," he explained. "I was within easy driving distance of home, so that I could commute to the field office to work. After my mother died, I tried again to find you. I thought if I could get assigned to the southeast, I might eventually catch you at Derrie's apartment in Charleston. But you weren't there. I gave up the idea and went home after my vacation."

"I came here," she explained. "I couldn't stay in Charleston. Too many bad memories." She hesitated to ask the question, but it was killing her not to.

"You want to know why I didn't ask Derrie for your address," he guessed.

She nodded.

He drew in a long breath. "I did. She said that you told her never to give it to me. She said that you'd go to your grave hating me." He shrugged. "I wasn't giving up, even so. It's taken a hell of a long time to find you…but I finally succeeded."

"How did you end up here in the FBI?" she wanted to know.

"Because of the new Indian Country Crime Unit I'm in, I've had assignments all over the southeast—even down into Seminole country." He smiled slowly. "When my old boss knew about this homicide, and remembered that I'd told him you moved here, he got me assigned to the case. It's a good job, and I'm happy doing it. But it's been a long three years, Phoebe."

"You knew I was here?" she asked.

He nodded.

"How?" she exclaimed.

6

"YOU WON'T BELIEVE ME if I tell you," he said.

"Try me."

"My father told me. I don't know how he knew," he added. "But in addition to amazing psychic skills, he does have a number of friends in high places. Even in law enforcement. But he knew." He stared at her hungrily.

She stared back at him with uncertainty plain on her face. He was here. She'd grieved long and hard for him. But she didn't—couldn't—trust him. He'd walked out on her without a word three years ago.

He sighed. "I can see the wheels going around in your mind. I almost know what you're thinking. It's going to take time for you to ever trust me again." He gnawed on the tip of the earpiece of his sunglasses in deep thought. "Suppose we pretend we've just met. I'm a widower with a child. You're an attractive museum curator. We're working together on a case. No complications. No recriminations. We're just friends."

She gave him a suspicious look. "Just friends? You bent me back over my desk in my own office!" she pointed out, trying to hide the heat that memory generated. "And now I'm going to be in deep trouble with the board of trustees if that schoolteacher files a complaint!"

"If she does, I'll talk to the trustees. I'll tell them you stopped breathing and I was giving you CPR," he promised dryly. "You can faint while they're in your office and I'll demonstrate how."

She didn't want to laugh, but he had the most wicked look on his face. She smothered the laugh and cleared her throat. "You said we were going tracking. What are we looking for?"

"I'm not sure," he said, his expression lighter as he started the car. "But if we find it, I'll know."

As they pulled out onto the highway, she glanced where the SUV had been parked the morning she took the information about the murder victim to Drake. She almost mentioned it to Cortez, but there was no reason to. After all, it probably had only been a lost motorist. She put it out of her mind.

THEY DROVE ALONG IN A companionable silence to the caves at the Bennett construction site. Cortez parked the car, pausing to take his .45 caliber automatic in its leather holster out of the pocket of the car and stick it in his belt.

Phoebe gave it a worried look.

"I have credentials," he reminded her. "I work for the government, and I know how to shoot a gun if I have to."

She grimaced. "So do I, but I don't want to have to."

"That's why Drake had you out practicing. If it's instinctive..."

"I can't kill someone, Jeremiah," she said miserably. "Not even to save my own life."

He studied her in a tense silence. "It may come to that. Whoever killed the professor isn't going to stop if there's a real threat to his income. I've seen people murdered for less than fifty dollars by people who were very surprised to find how little money their victims had on them. We aren't talking about rocket scientists."

She looked at him with what she hoped was veiled hunger. He was still the sexiest man she'd ever known. He was beautiful, in a masculine sort of way.

"No time for that now," he said, deadpan.

"You have no idea what I was thinking!" she retorted.

He made a sound deep in his throat that set her hair on end before he got out. She extricated herself before he had time to come around the car.

"I thought you liked my nice manners," he accused.

She flushed. "I can open my own doors."

He didn't comment. "Go that way," he indicated the worn ruts in the road. "Look for a car track that comes to a stop and then backs up in its own space."

"There are a lot of tracks here," she pointed out.

He was remembering an odd sort of track that he'd seen in the dirt parking lot at the reservation motel where the professor had stayed. It was in front of the dead man's apartment.

"Look for tracks with a missing tread mark in the middle, vertically. It will be on the left."

She pursed her lips. "Scientific stuff, huh? Okay." She bent down and started looking. It was impossible not to remember the last time she'd gone tracking with him. "You said you might come to my graduation, and when I hesitated, you made some snide remark."

"You threw a tree limb at me," he recalled, bending over a suspicious track.

"You were obnoxious," she replied, glancing at him. "You still are. I hope I'll still have a job to go back to when that teacher gets through with me."

"You can come to work for me," he murmured. "You'd be worth your weight in gold in a forensics lab. One of your professors in college said you had a natural feel for forensic dentition."

"I didn't tell you that," she said, hesitating. "How did you hear that?"

"I thought your forensics professor might know where you were," he said simply.

She felt empty. Hollow. Sick at heart. Everyone had tried to protect her from this man. She'd asked them to. She had no idea of the real situation. Now that she knew it, she hated realizing she'd cut her own throat three years ago. He hadn't turned away out of disinterest. Circumstances had unfolded to keep him away.

He stood up abruptly, frowning. Then he strode back to the car, to Phoebe's surprise, and drew out what he'd taken from her desk drawer. He walked back and handed her the charm. "Put this, and the pesos, in your right slacks pocket."

She knew it would do no good to argue. He trusted his father's mystic powers too much. "Okay, okay." She slid the two pieces together and inserted them in her pocket. Then she turned back to follow the track when she felt a sudden thrust that knocked her completely off her feet. A fraction of a second later, there was a sharp crack like thunder.

"Phoebe!"

Cortez had his gun out and was firing from a kneeling position toward the direction the shot had come from. There was another crack and dust flew up near Cortez, but seconds later, there was a loud thud and the sound of an engine firing. It was followed by a vehicle spraying gravel in the near distance.

Cortez didn't wait for it to fade. He was already kneeling beside Phoebe, his hands quick and deft on her body. "Are you hit? Tell me!"

She groaned, rolled up into a ball. "Oh, it hurts!" she ground out.

"Phoebe, are you hit?!" he demanded, each word deliberate.

She managed to uncurl her legs with an effort. Her hand went to the right side of her stomach. "I don't…feel blood," she whispered.

He unzipped her jeans and stripped them down over her hips before she had time to protest. There was no wound, but there was the beginning of a terrible bruise near where her appendix should be. He felt just above it and his knuckles brushed the heavy pesos he'd just made her put in her pocket. He felt sick.

They exchanged a stunned look. He slid his hand into the pocket and pulled out the charm and the coins. There was a hole through the center of one peso and a bullet was embedded in the second one behind it. His father's foresight had spared her life.

"It would have hit the femoral artery," he said in a

ghostly tone. "You'd have bled to death before I could have gotten you to a hospital."

She shivered. "He knew...your father knew!"

He gathered her close and sat down in the dirt, holding her tight. He rocked her, mindless at the thought of what could have happened.

"The shooter got away," she whispered into his throat.

His arms tightened. "First things first." He kissed her temple and took a long, heavy breath. He jerked up the cell phone he wore on his belt and pressed in numbers with one hand.

"I need an ambulance and Yonah County deputy sheriff Drake Stewart to come immediately to the back of the Benning construction site. It's located at the end of Deal Street at a cave in a stand of fir trees. It's just outside the city limits of Chenocetah," he said. "We're about a hundred yards from the boundary of the Yonah Indian Reservation on a dirt road."

"Who is this?" a bored voice replied.

"Special Agent Jeremiah Cortez, FBI," he replied tersely. "There's been a shooting. Tell Stewart to come to the dead end and look in the woods on the right."

"Just a sec!" the 911 operator said. "I'll dispatch him. Stay on the line."

"No time," Cortez said. "The perp's getting away."

He hung up and pressed in more numbers while Phoebe lay against him, still in pain. "I need an evidence team out here in Jones's van," he said. "I'll give you directions."

"That was my unit," he told Phoebe when he completed the call. He ground his teeth together. "Listen, I'm going to have to put you in the ambulance. I can't go with you." It seemed to be killing him that he couldn't. "I have to wait for my unit to get here to gather evidence. With any luck, there may be a shell casing."

"It's all right," she said huskily. "I'm a big girl. I can ride in an ambulance all alone."

He didn't smile, as he might have once. "You could have been killed," he growled.

She met his tormented eyes evenly and forced herself to smile through the pain. "His mistake. He slipped up. We'll get him."

"I never expected danger out here," he said, as if he couldn't believe it. "I'd never have asked you to come with me if I'd had any idea this could happen!"

She reached up a hand and touched it to his mouth. "This is much better than explaining myself to an angry grammar-school teacher. Trust me."

He caught the hand and kissed the palm hungrily.

His concern unsettled her. She hadn't expected that strong a reaction. "I'm going to be fine. Then we're going to catch this fool and put him away. Right?"

"Right," he said in a strangled voice.

"You just keep that in mind and stop flogging yourself. Who would have expected somebody to start shooting the minute we got out of the car?"

"I spooked somebody," he said coldly.

"How?"

He started to answer her, but the sirens drowned him out. Drake slid to a stop just behind the ambulance. The paramedics were beside Phoebe in less than three minutes with a gurney.

Cortez explained what had happened while they worked on Phoebe. Drake was furious.

"One of us needs to go with her," Drake said flatly.

"My unit's on the way," Cortez said through his teeth, having reluctantly released Phoebe to the paramedics. "I can't leave."

Drake turned to him. The other man's face was rigid with frustrated concern. "Don't worry. I'll go with her. She'll be all right…I promise."

That seemed to calm Cortez, but only on the surface. He couldn't get the image of seeing Phoebe dead out of his mind.

"She's all right," Drake said firmly, looking stern. "You just catch the perp, okay? I'll take care of her."

Cortez took a steadying breath. "When I find him," he said through his teeth, "he's going to wish he lived on another continent."

"Good man. I'll get you some more bullets for your gun," Drake promised, clapping him on the shoulder and smiling forcefully. "Now go to work. Phoebe's going to be fine."

Cortez paused by the gurney when the paramedics had loaded Phoebe up and voiced the opinion that it wasn't going to be serious.

He caught her hand in his and held on tight. "I'll be along when I get through here. Drake's going with you."

"Ah," she surmised. "The indigenous people closing ranks."

He smiled gently. "Something like that." He kissed her fingers and laid them back at her waist. "Do what the doctor says."

"Where's my charm?" she asked at once.

Cortez grimaced. "Material evidence."

"The coins are. The charm isn't. Give it here," she added.

With a sigh, he produced it and laid it in her hand.

"Your father," she says, "really knows his business."

"I told you so. Be safe."

"You, too. You're not bulletproof and you don't have one of these." She held up the charm.

He pursed his lips, reached into his pocket and produced a charm identical to hers. "He said I wouldn't need the coins."

She made a face, and then she smiled to reassure him. He did look so worried.

Drake climbed into the back of the ambulance with her after radioing for another deputy to pick him up at the hospital emergency room later and take him back to his car. The paramedics closed their back door on a somber-faced Cortez, still holding his charm.

"What's with the charm?" Drake asked.

"Cortez's father made it for me three years ago," she said, wincing. The bruising was really starting to hurt. "He added two Mexican pesos to it today. Jeremiah had just told me to put them in my pocket, exactly where his father said to keep it, when someone shot me. If I hadn't had them there, I'd be dead. It hit just beside my femoral artery."

Drake whistled. "That's heavy medicine."

"Tell me about it. Jeremiah's father is a shaman. He also has some sort of precognition. I'm not sure I believed in all that before—I do now."

"No wonder. What were you and Cortez doing out there?"

"Investigating some caves the murdered anthropologist had visited. The caves were behind the Bennett construction site. We got shot at almost as soon as we arrived." Phoebe closed her eyes, then opened them wide.

"I just want to get patched up and help you find the

person who fired that shot. Then I want five minutes alone with them!"

"I'll give you some lessons in martial arts first," Drake teased.

She let out a tautly held breath. "This really hurts. It didn't break the skin, but it bruised me really bad." Her hand pressed gingerly against the point of impact.

Drake changed the subject, trying not to think how much damage a traumatic blow could do to flesh, even without penetration. He'd seen a blow to the ribs produce bruising in the lung which led to internal bleeding, even to death.

Later, at the hospital, they did all sorts of tests before the doctor, a young, dark-haired woman, holding a chart, walked into the room they'd given Phoebe.

She glanced over the clipboard and raised her eyebrows at the slight young blond woman in the bed.

"If somebody had shot me," the doctor pondered aloud, "I'd be screaming my head off. You're calm for a woman in your condition."

Phoebe sighed. "I'm an anthropologist. Indiana Jones?" she prompted. "Fedora hat, long black whip, attitude problem…?"

The doctor chuckled. "Okay, I get the point."

Drake stuck his head in the door. "I have to leave," he told Phoebe. "Another deputy's picking me up out front. They need me to help interview people near the construction site—even the part-timers have been called in. Is she going to be okay, Doc?" he asked the physician.

"Yes," the doctor said.

Drake gave her a thumbs-up. "I'll call you later," he told Phoebe, and then he was gone.

"Now," the doctor said, leaning against the wall near Phoebe's headboard to thumb through the lab work. "You've got some bad bruising in your groin, in an area substantially larger than where a bullet would have hit you. Which brings to mind another question, why didn't it penetrate?"

"I was carrying two thick Mexican pesos in the pocket where the bullet hit," Phoebe said matter-of-factly. "It went through one and was imbedded in the second."

The doctor's thin eyebrows arched. "You expected to be shot and prepared ahead?"

Phoebe grimaced. "Sometimes truth is stranger than fiction."

"I'm a doctor. I've seen a man shot at point-blank range with both barrels of a shotgun walk a mile to get help and survive," the doctor said, holding out her hand palm-up. "Let's have it."

Phoebe told her.

The doctor didn't say anything for a minute. Her eyes went back to the lab reports. "I'd send that shaman a birthday present for the rest of his life."

"I intend to. He saved me."

"Why were you shot, do you know?"

"I was helping an FBI agent track a suspicious vehicle in a homicide investigation," Phoebe replied calmly.

The doctor blinked. "The FBI?"

She nodded. "He's part of the new Indian Country FBI Crime Unit. He came here to investigate a homicide on the Yonah Reservation."

"And you can track."

"Assist," she clarified.

"Was there some particular reason you went with him?"

"Yes. He'd just kissed me half to death in the museum where I work. A grammar-school class stopped by to watch. It was either go tracking or explain myself to a very angry teacher." She grimaced. "I picked the lesser of the two evils. I like to think of it as exercising the better part of valor."

The doctor burst out laughing. "Well, you're lucky. Or blessed. Or you have a guardian among the little people."

"Leprechauns?" Phoebe asked.

"Nunnehi," the doctor corrected. "The Cherokee say the little people protect travelers in the woods. They can hear them singing sometimes in the distance. Lovely legend, isn't it?"

Singing. In the distance. In Cherokee. Phoebe didn't say a word, but her mind was busy recalling the melody she'd heard in the wee hours of the morning a few days ago.

SIX HOURS LATER, A WEARY Drake, who had returned to the hospital, drove her home. The staff had wanted to keep her overnight, but they couldn't find anything severe enough to warrant it. Phoebe had good insurance, but she didn't want to have to use it on something non-life-threatening.

When they got back to her house, Cortez was pacing on the front porch.

"He phoned me every hour on the hour," Drake confessed. "I had to tell him we were on the way, or he was going to storm the hospital."

She smiled wearily. "No problem." In fact, it touched her that Cortez was that concerned, but she wasn't admitting it.

Drake pulled up in front of her house and cut off the engine. He got out to open her door, but Cortez was there first. He slid an arm around her waist and helped her into the house.

"I was expecting you to pick her up and carry her in," Drake teased.

"He can't lift," Phoebe said simply. "He caught some shrapnel in the shoulder when he was in Vietnam during the last days our troops were stationed there."

Drake pursed his lips.

Cortez's eyes softened. "I'd forgotten that I told you that," he said.

Phoebe cleared her throat, embarrassed.

"Sometimes we get second chances," Drake said to nobody in particular.

"Like Phoebe just did," Cortez replied. He was wearing jeans and a flannel shirt. His long hair was loose, but untidy, as if restless hands had mussed it. "And that's why I'm not leaving her out here alone in the wilderness all night."

Phoebe hesitated. Then she realized that something was missing. "Jock!" she exclaimed, immediately fearful that her would-be assassin had gotten to her dog.

"He's being boarded at the local animal hospital," Cortez replied at once. "They're going to spoil him rotten."

"But, you can't do that!" she exclaimed.

"I just did. Pack a bag, Phoebe," Cortez said quietly. "You're moving in with Tina and me at the motel for the duration."

"Duration?"

"Until we catch the guy who's doing this," Cortez said. "And you'd better remember that he was aiming to kill. If it hadn't been for my dad's foresight, you'd be in the morgue."

Phoebe felt the blood leave her face. She sat down heavily on the arm of her sofa.

"Sorry," Cortez bit off. "I didn't mean to put it like that."

"He's right, though," Drake jumped in. "You can't stay out here alone. He won't stop. Next time, he won't rest on one good shot, either."

"Exactly," Cortez replied.

Phoebe ground her teeth together. "It will look like I'm running!"

The two men exchanged a complicated look. "Think of it as advancing to the rear," Cortez said after a minute. "Even Quanah Parker, one of our greatest Comanche warriors, did that from time to time. Nobody would ever call him a coward. Right?" he asked Drake.

Drake nodded. "Right."

She gnawed her lower lip worriedly. "It won't look right..."

"You'll be in Tina's room, with Joseph," Cortez said patiently. "I'll be right next door. You'll be safe."

In the room with the baby. The baby was the reason Cortez had deserted Phoebe and married a woman he didn't even love. It wasn't the child's fault, but it would revive a painful memory. She hated the whole idea of it. But staying here alone was terrifying, especially now that he'd removed her only protection—Jock.

"You'll like Tina," Drake coaxed. "She's really nice."

"Yes, she is," Cortez assured her.

"Is she kin to your late wife?" she asked Cortez.

"She's my cousin," he said slowly.

Sometimes people married their cousins, she was thinking...although she didn't say it aloud. It didn't exactly put the mysterious Tina out of the running as a romantic rival. She glanced from Drake to Cortez. That was when she noticed that they both looked as exhausted as she felt. It had been a very long day.

"I'm sorry," she said at once, struggling to her feet. Her belly was terribly sore. "I'm making waves, when you're both dead on your feet, too. I'll pack what I have to have. Did you find anything out there?" she asked Cortez.

He relaxed a little, shoving his hands into his pockets as he moved to the window to look out. "Not much. A shell casing. Garden variety .45 caliber. Could have been fired from a handgun or a rifle." He turned. "But judging from the velocity," he added, staring at her, "it was a handgun. A rifle shot would have most likely penetrated the silver and gone right into your body."

"Then the shooter was close by," she guessed.

He nodded. "We found the shell casing about two hundred feet from where you and I were standing. But the shooter had to be a marksman, just the same. It isn't that easy to bring someone down at that distance without a scope."

"You've got ballistics on it?" Drake asked.

Cortez nodded. "I overnighted the bullet to our FBI lab in D.C.," he added. "If we get lucky, they may be able to tell us where it was purchased, even the sort of handgun that fired it."

"Were there any latent prints?" Drake persisted.

"One," Cortez said with a smile. "A partial, but it might be enough. We found one other thing—a cigarette butt."

"So the shooter smokes," Phoebe guessed.

He nodded. "If it was his," he added. "There's no way of knowing when it was left there."

"It rained night before last," Drake pointed out.

"The butt hadn't been touched by water," Cortez replied. "So far, so good."

"Can I at least go back to work?" Phoebe asked when she'd packed her toiletries and three changes of clothing. She had them in a suitcase, which Cortez picked up with his left hand.

"She'd be around people," Drake pointed out.

"Good point," Cortez said after a minute. "All right, but you don't leave the office unless one of us is with you."

It wasn't her choice, but then, she didn't seem to have one. She glanced from one of them to the other. Talk about being stonewalled…

"All right," she agreed.

Cortez checked his watch. "We'd better go. I've got an early appointment."

"With another developer?" Drake asked. "Should we tail you, in case there's another shooting, too?"

Cortez chuckled. "That was below the belt."

Drake shrugged. "Just checking."

"I'll lock up," Phoebe said. She went from room to room, checking windows and doors until assured that they were all secure.

"It doesn't look like anybody lives here," Drake murmured. "No photos, no souvenirs, no keepsakes…"

"Most of my stuff is at my aunt Derrie's place," Phoebe remarked. "It seemed sort of useless to bring along a lot of stuff that I'd just have to move again, eventually."

"You're planning to leave?" Drake asked.

"Not today," she said wryly. "I meant someday. It was a figure of speech."

Cortez didn't say anything at all. He opened the front door and walked out onto the porch.

TINA MET THEM AT THE DOOR of her room, giving Phoebe a curious look. "So you're the famous Phoebe," she murmured dryly. "I'm really happy to meet you. *He* doesn't tell me anything," she indicated Cortez.

"You are not to pump her for information," he cautioned his cousin. "You aren't to let her out of your sight, either," he added firmly.

"Yeah, I know why," Tina said, quickly sobering. "I'm glad you're still in one piece. Good thing Jeremiah's father is a shaman, huh?"

"A very good thing," Phoebe replied. "I'm only bruised. It could have been so much worse."

"You'll be safe here," Tina assured her. "I'm Christina Redhawk. That's his last name, too, but he won't use it," she told Phoebe, indicating Cortez. "He has a really vicious sense of humor."

"He does?" Drake asked, grinning at Tina, who actually blushed.

"Well, the great-grandfather who kidnapped Jeremiah's great-grandmother was named Cortes, with an *s*," Tina mused.

"Kidnapped her?" Phoebe asked, glancing curiously at Cortez.

"Held her in a log cabin for two weeks until she was disgraced and had to marry him," she continued. "They had ten kids. He lived with her Comanche people, learned the language, even went on raids with his in-laws. Jeremiah's grandfather was the youngest of those kids."

"Were they together a long time?" Phoebe asked.

"Fifty years," Tina said, sighing. "Isn't it romantic? They were enemies. Her people had just attacked his and killed several of his extended family, too. I guess love does conquer all."

"Stop jabbering and let her go to bed," Cortez told his cousin, tweaking a lock of her long black hair. "She's had a rough day."

"I'll keep an eye on her," Tina promised.

"I can keep an eye on myself, thanks," Phoebe told Cortez firmly.

The other three adults exchanged knowing glances.

"Nobody can see a bullet coming," Phoebe defended herself.

"Jeremiah's dad did," Tina piped up.

"Bed. Now. How's my boy?" he added, stepping into the room behind Phoebe and Drake.

Joseph was sitting in the middle of one of two queen-sized beds, playing with some cloth blocks. He looked up at Cortez and grinned, opening his chubby arms wide.

"Daddy!" he exclaimed.

Cortez swept him up, hugging him close, and kissed his little cheek. "How's my boy?" he asked in a tone so soft that it made Phoebe's heart ache.

"Daddy, I can count to five!" He held out four fingers. "Where was you? I was lonely! She wouldn't let me have the cake!"

"Chocolate cake," Tina defended herself. "He'd have been up all night."

"I wanted cake," Joseph muttered. He looked past his father's shoulder. "Who are you?" he asked Phoebe.

"This is Phoebe," Cortez told the child, turning him toward Phoebe. "She's been hurt. She's going to spend the night with you and Tina. You have to help take care of her."

"Okay," Joseph said at once. He studied Phoebe carefully. "You got blond hair."

"Yes. I have blond hair," Phoebe said. She didn't want to like the child. But he had beautiful dark eyes and a smile like an angel.

"You like to read?" he asked.

"Yes." She realized that she was beginning to sound like a parrot. "Do you?"

Joseph grinned. "I like Bob!"

Phoebe glanced at Tina. "Bob the Builder," she was informed. "It's a cartoon show on TV."

"Oh."

"Can you tell stories?" Joseph persisted.

"She can, but we're going to bed soon," Tina said, rescuing her. She took Joseph from Cortez. "That means everybody who isn't a little boy or a woman has to leave." She gave the two men a pointed look.

"We're being evicted," Drake puzzled it out. "Okay. If you need us..."

"I'll be right next door," Cortez told the women.

"And I'll be right next to my phone," Drake added. "He's got the number." He jerked a thumb toward Cortez. "One last thing, stay away from windows."

Phoebe saluted him.

He chuckled and went out the door. Cortez gave her a wink and followed suit.

"Men are a lot of trouble," Tina told Phoebe as she carried Joseph back to the bed. "And it looks like you've got two of them on your case."

"I'm off men for life," Phoebe said firmly.

Tina's eyes twinkled. "That's what they all say!"

"I'm really sleepy!" Phoebe broke in.

Tina chuckled. "Okay. I get the message. I'm a little sleepy myself. Joseph's teething again. Jeremiah and I didn't get much sleep last night."

"Teething?"

"It's an ongoing process, I'm afraid," Tina said. "You'll see."

Phoebe didn't understand the statement until two in the morning, when Joseph let out a wail and started bawling.

JOSEPH WAS CRYING IN great sobs. His little face was hot and he was drooling.

"Hurts, Tina," he muttered against Tina's shoulder.

"I know, baby, I'm sorry," Tina said. "I'll get the medicine. Phoebe, can you hold him? Here, sit down so you don't strain your stomach. I guess it's really sore now."

"It is," Phoebe replied, reluctantly letting Tina put Joseph into her arms.

"Hurts," Joseph sobbed, clinging to Phoebe.

His little head was pressed hard against her breasts. He smelled of soap and baby powder. His hair was very clean, kind of medium brown in color. His face was wet against the soft cotton of the T-shirt she slept in.

Phoebe hadn't had much to do with little children. There were none in her family. She'd seen them at the museum, of course, but she hadn't interacted with them. This was

Cortez's child, even if only by adoption. He was the child of Cortez's brother. He shared the same blood, the same family, the same history.

Her body had been stiff at first, but now she relaxed and took the child's weight quite naturally. Her hand went automatically to his back. She smoothed over it gently.

Tina came back with a teaspoon full of medicine. "It's cherry," she coaxed, ladeling it into Joseph's mouth. "You swallow that, my baby, and I've got something to make your poor tooth feel better, too."

He made a face. "Don't want it," he moaned.

"A lot of things we don't want are good for us," Tina said comfortingly. She ran her finger into Joseph's mouth and rubbed the clear liquid on it into his gumline.

"Yuuck," Joseph muttered.

"It will help," Tina assured him. She looked over her head at Phoebe as she wiped her finger on a tissue. "Just a minute and I'll take him in with me..."

"No!" Joseph wailed when she tried to separate him from Phoebe. "Don't want to go with you."

The women exchanged puzzled glances.

"Bee-bee's nice," he said drowsily. "Bee-bee smells good." He burrowed his face closer against her chest.

Phoebe had never felt such a warm sensation in her life. The child clung to her. He didn't want to be taken away. He even had a name for her—Bee-bee. It felt odd to be needed. She wasn't sure she ever had been before. Her father had always been independent and the picture of health. Even her mother hadn't had much illness before her death. Her stepmother, long since remarried, ignored her. Derrie, her aunt, had her own interests and never needed caring for. But here was this tiny human being whom Phoebe had resented from the day she knew of his existence. What an irony that he needed her.

"Want Bee-bee," Joseph muttered again, burrowing into Phoebe's chest and holding on with all his small might.

Phoebe drew him closer instinctively. A pulse of pure joy overwhelmed her. "It's okay," Phoebe said when Tina looked ready to make a second try for Joseph. "Really. He can sleep with me. I don't mind."

"Nice Bee-bee," Joseph whispered, his little eyes closing as he slumped securely in Phoebe's embrace.

"It will hurt your stomach," Tina said reluctantly.

"No, it won't," Phoebe said tenderly, brushing the child's hair. "Come on, little man," she whispered. "Let's try to go to sleep, okay?"

"Okay," he murmured.

Phoebe climbed back into bed, settling Joseph against her shoulder. She smiled at Tina and closed her eyes. Scant minutes later, she was dead to the world and so was the child.

THE NEXT MORNING, CORTEZ stood in the doorway gaping at the sight in the bed next to Tina's. Joseph was draped over Phoebe's slight breasts, sound asleep. So was Phoebe. They looked like a work of art.

"He wouldn't let go of her," Tina explained softly, laughing. "At least he's sleeping."

Cortez studied her in a stunned silence. His heart ached to gather them both close and hold them, never let them go. It was a revelation. He hadn't expected Phoebe to take to the child. She'd been reluctant even to stay in the same room with him, although she'd pretended it didn't bother her. Joseph had found a way to reach her, it seemed.

Tina noted the expression on her cousin's face with hidden amusement. In recent years, he'd lived like a hermit. He hadn't even dated anyone. But when she saw him with Phoebe, all her questions were answered. Tina could see what he felt for the blond woman. It was written all over him. No wonder Drake had looked so odd when she told him about the blond woman Cortez had loved and lost. It was Phoebe and he knew her! He liked her a lot, too, or Tina was no judge of character. She wondered how Phoebe felt about Drake.

"I have to wake her soon," Tina said regretfully, "or she'll be late for work."

"I'm going to drop her by the museum on my own way to work."

Tina gave him an amused glance. He ignored it. He moved to the second bed and touched Phoebe gently on the shoulder.

She opened her eyes. They were the pale blue of an autumn day. She blinked. "Jeremiah?" she murmured drowsily.

He brushed back her tangled hair. "How do you feel?"

She moved, felt Joseph's weight, and grimaced as her leg shifted and aggravated the bruising. "Ouch," she muttered.

Joseph felt the movement and opened his eyes. "Daddy," he murmured, smiling. "Bee-bee smells nice."

"Bee-bee?"

Phoebe managed a smile. "That's me. Feel better, baby?" she asked Joseph, brushing back his damp hair.

"Better," he nodded. He yawned. "Sleepy."

Tina came forward and took him, cradling him against her shoulder. "Bee-bee has to go to work."

"No," Joseph protested. "Bee-bee stay!"

Phoebe dragged herself to her feet, hurting. She touched Joseph's face with her fingertips. "I'll be back later. I'll bring you a surprise."

"Surprise? Tiger?"

She laughed. "We'll see." She glanced at Cortez with quiet curiosity. He looked...odd.

He turned. "I'll wait in the car," he said. "I'll drop you off at the museum on my way."

"Where are you going?" she wanted to know.

"To talk to some more construction people."

"Wear body armor," she retorted.

He just closed the door, without comment.

"He'll get himself killed," Phoebe muttered as she gathered up her clothes and got into slacks and a neat embroidered top with a jacket to put over it. Dressing was difficult, because of the bruising.

"He's no cream puff," Tina assured her. "Didn't that doctor say you were to rest for a couple of days?" she added.

"I just sit at a desk all day—it can't do much damage," Phoebe reassured her. She ran a brush through her hair and put on light lipstick and powder. "Have you known him a long time?" she asked.

"Jeremiah, you mean?" Tina laughed. "All my life. He used to take me to school in the mornings when he was still at home. The bus was sort of hit or miss because we lived so far out in the sticks. His dad still does. His father really hates modern society. He says it's the cause of all our problems, that people were never meant to live in cities."

"He's got a point," Phoebe had to admit. She pressed her fingers against the big bruised place under her slacks. "But he's got amazing foresight. I'd be dead if not for him."

"He's spooky sometimes," Tina commented. "He knows stuff."

Phoebe searched for her purse. "We had a woman like that near where my aunt grew up, in South Carolina. She could read the future—not like those people you see advertising their services on television—she could really read the future. She said it was a curse. Most of the things she knew beforehand were bad things. She wasn't Native American, or a shaman. She was just sensitive."

Tina cocked her head. "I guess you know a lot about indigenous people, with your background."

Phoebe nodded. "I think the wisdom of the earth resides in ancient, indigenous cultures," she replied. "Maybe someday, the knowledge of indigenous people will allow a portion of mankind to survive."

"Survive?"

Phoebe picked up her purse. "Mankind has evolved into a very small niche, dependent on exhaustible fuel. One of my anthropology professors said that any culture so specialized is doomed."

"You'll like Jeremiah's dad…he talks just like you," Tina chuckled. "He's always telling us the story of the Rainbow Warrior."

Phoebe smiled. That was the basis of her opinion about the wisdom of ancient cultures, that one day they would be called on to save the human race. Native people called it the legend of the Rainbow Warrior.

"He really wanted Jeremiah to go to college—just like he did," Tina added.

That was surprising. Phoebe, despite her exclusive education and her intimate knowledge of native peoples, had pictured Cortez's shaman father living at less than standard levels. She was ashamed of herself for stereotyping him. "He really went to college?"

Tina pursed her lips. "Yes, he did. Education is the only escape from poverty, he always says. He loves history."

Phoebe's eyes brightened. "Imagine that."

"He knows all about you, of course," Tina persisted. "You were all Jeremiah talked about when he came back from Charleston that time." She winced. "It was terrible, Isaac getting killed like that."

"Like what?"

But before Tina could answer, the door opened and an impatient Cortez peered in. "I'm on the clock."

Phoebe started for the door. "God forbid that I should keep you! Lead on."

Tina laughed. Cortez didn't. He'd had more than enough to make him irritable the past two days.

HE STOPPED IN FRONT OF the museum and cut off the engine. It was raining all at once, with lightning flashing crazily in the distance.

He looked at Phoebe with narrowed eyes. "I don't like letting you out of my sight," he said bluntly.

"I'm not going to get shot in my office," she promised him. "But speaking of being shot, aren't you pushing the edge of the envelope going to yet another construction site? You're asking questions that somebody doesn't like."

"Do you think there's a Neanderthal skeleton hidden somewhere around here?" he asked seriously.

"No," she said at once. "I won't deny the possibility that indigenous people were here long before the last ice age ended, but it's improbable that we wouldn't have found evidence of it by now."

"Then why do you think that professor made such a flat statement about it?"

She pondered that. The rain was falling harder. It was loud where it hit the metal of the car body. "I think he wanted someone to investigate a crime, but he didn't think he'd get help unless he made it sound sensational. I do think human remains have been covered up. But not Neanderthal ones. Someone's breaking the law trying to keep construction on schedule. That much I'd bet on, and they're willing to kill people to prevent any holdups."

Cortez looked pensive. "That's what I thought."

"You must have spooked somebody at that site we went to yesterday," she said, choosing her words carefully. "Any idea who?"

He traced a pattern on the steering wheel while he thought. "The construction boss is from Oklahoma and he has Cherokee blood. Our visiting professor appears to have had Cherokee kin as well. I think there's some sort of a connection."

"Me, too. Can you get Drake and Marie to help?" she added. "Between them, they know most everybody on the reservation."

"I already have," he replied. He searched her blue eyes quietly. "Getting you shot wasn't part of the plan."

"Your father saved me," she said with a smile. "I'm tough as old boots. You just go get the killer."

He laughed shortly. "You make it sound simple."

"It probably is," she replied. "Find the money and you find the motive. Somebody's in hock up to his eyebrows and desperate to stay afloat financially. Right?"

He pursed his lips. "Right."

"So can't you subpoena financial records from the companies you suspect?"

He chuckled. "Listen, I work for the FBI…I can do just about anything I want." He gave her a stern look. "But I don't want you to go around asking questions. You're in enough danger as it is."

"Think of me as your assistant," she said innocently.

He touched her short hair lightly. "I loved it long," he remarked.

She averted her eyes. "I went a little crazy when I got that clipping," she confessed. "I got drunk and went to a wild party, ended up in bed with a man I didn't even know…"

He closed his eyes briefly and turned his face away. His fault. His fault!

She wanted to tell him all of it, but the wounds were still raw from his desertion. She turned her face toward the window. "I'm older and wiser now," she bit off. "I guess there's no way to run away from pain. You just have to get through it."

He drew in a sharp breath. He didn't dare say what he was thinking. It was enough that they were speaking again. He had no right to recriminations. "You aren't the only one who acted irresponsibly," he said gruffly. "I wasn't thinking. So much happened, in such a short time. I couldn't cope, for the first time in my life. I thought hating me might spare you some of the pain."

She laughed coldly. "Fat chance."

"Yes. Hindsight is a wonderful thing." He reached out and tugged on a short lock of her hair, his dark eyes smoldering with feeling as he looked at her. "I had dreams."

Her lower lip trembled. "So did I," she choked.

The emotion he saw in her face wounded him. Their eyes locked and the pain mingled with sudden, terrible desire. She thought her heart would jump right out of her chest.

"I'm starving to death. Come here," he demanded, tugging her face under his with an insistent hand at the back of her neck.

His mouth ground into hers with no warning, no preliminary tenderness. He kissed her as if he'd never see her again in his life.

She moaned helplessly at the first touch of his hard mouth. It was just as it had been in her office yesterday, as if the three years since they'd been apart fell away the minute he touched her.

She linked her arms around his neck, oblivious to the tug of the seat belt, the pain of her bruise. She fed on his kiss, drowning, aching to be part of him.

He found the release on her belt and then on his, and pulled her over the console and into his lap. His arms contracted, grinding her breasts against his hard chest. The kiss grew slower, harder, deeper with every passing second. The only sounds were the harsh metallic ping of the rain hitting the car and the muffled sighs of their breathing as they kissed feverishly.

He groaned out loud as his hand smoothed possessively over her small breast and contracted, feeling the hard nub in his palm.

"Jeremiah," she whimpered into his mouth. She was on fire for him. She trembled helplessly as her nails bit into the back of his neck.

"Easy," he whispered, easing the embrace. His mouth lifted, brushing hers tenderly as his hand gentled on her breast. "Easy. It's all right. I ache just as much for you, Phoebe..."

She arched her body against his, feeling his warm strength, the hardness of his chest muscles against her. She loved the slow tracing of his fingertips over her breast. The pleasure made her shiver helplessly.

He nibbled her upper lip, then her lower one. All the while, he was searching for a way under the embroidered top she was wearing. He was successful. His hand found the catch of her brassiere behind her back. He flipped it open. His hand circled back, taking the weight of her soft, warm breast.

"Beautiful," he whispered into her parted lips.

"Beautiful," she managed shakily, lifting closer to the tender caress.

Somewhere there was the sound of an engine cutting off and a door slamming. Neither of them realized what it was.

There was a sudden rap on the window. Cortez lifted his head and looked around. The windows were all completely covered with fog. It was impossible to see anything outside. There was a long shadow near the driver's side.

"Someone's out there," Phoebe said unsteadily, lifting herself away from him and back into her own seat. Her hand shook as she pushed back her hair.

"Someone," Cortez agreed. He straightened his tie and jacket and slowly powered the window down.

"Carbon monoxide can be deadly," Drake said with a straight face.

Cortez blinked. "Thank you for that health bulletin, Deputy Stewart," he replied, in what he hoped was a composed tone.

"I had a speck," Phoebe said primly. "Jeremiah was helping me get it out."

"Out of what?" Drake mused, noting the disarray of Phoebe's blouse.

She folded her arm over her sore breasts indignantly. "Never mind what! What do you want?"

He grinned. "Remember that teacher who was here yesterday for an explanation?" Drake asked. "Marie phoned me, looking for you, and said she was on her way over here to talk to you. I guess that was her who drove up a couple of minutes ago in the only cab we have in town."

"Oh, no," Phoebe groaned, her face in her hands, imagining what the woman would have seen before the windows got so fogged.

"Marie headed her off," Drake said after a minute, chuckling. "She's inside waiting for you, though. You might want to announce your engagement while there's still time to save your job."

"I will not..." Phoebe began, embarrassed.

"Yes, you will," Cortez said with an amused glance. "Tell her I proposed yesterday and you accepted. That will get her off your back."

"It's dishonest," Phoebe fluttered.

Cortez gave her a long, slow look. "Tell her. We'll work out the details later." He checked his watch and grimaced. "I'm late. I'm going to talk to the contractor Bennett told me about."

"You watch your back," Phoebe said immediately.

"Good advice," Drake seconded.

"I'm going inside before I get into any more trouble," she murmured, getting out of the car. She was painfully aware that her bra was still unfastened. She'd make a run for the ladies' restroom once she got through the front door. No need to give that teacher more ammunition than she already had.

"I'll pick you up at five," Cortez told her firmly.

She started to argue and couldn't find a reason to. She nodded, smiled at Drake, and rushed into the building.

When she was out of earshot, Drake bent down to the driver's window, his good humor gone.

"Bennett of Bennett Construction has a record," he told Cortez at once. "He was arrested and charged with violation of the clean-water act for dumping paint thinner into a stream in north Georgia, along with containers of paint and glue."

"Was he convicted?" Cortez asked.

"No. He pleaded no contest, though, and got probation. It was a first offense. But it's well-known locally that he's invested his last dime in this new project, in partnership with the 'Big Greek.' Apparently he was involved in some sort of reparation in another case and it almost bankrupted him. I couldn't find out the circumstances. But suffice it to say that he can't afford work stoppages, not even for a week. Now his site foreman Walks Far, on the other hand, actually did do time for theft by taking. He stole some items from a museum in New York City, among several other items. He spent three years in prison."

"So Bennett's not exactly squeaky clean," Cortez mused, thinking out loud. "Why would he hire an ex-con?"

"Because Walks Far is married to Bennett's only sister," Drake replied.

He and the deputy exchanged curious looks.

"Bennett's wealthy. Or he was," Drake added.

"And Walks Far apparently isn't," Cortez said. "If he's working for wages, and Bennett's sister has champagne tastes, maybe he's trying to protect his boss from losing it all."

"Not bad," Drake said with a faint grin. "Ever thought of working in law enforcement?"

Cortez gave him a speaking glance.

"But why shoot at Phoebe?" Drake wondered.

Cortez's black eyes flashed angrily. "Maybe because of her phone call with the dead professor." He paused. "But that's just speculation at this point. She might have just been caught in the crossfire."

"You mean, maybe he was aiming at you?"

"It's a possibility." Cortez sighed with irritation. "If he's killed once, another death won't matter much, considering the penalties. But none of this makes sense! There has to be more to murder than avoiding a work stoppage. I'm still going to speak to Paul Corland, and the builder working on the other project. I can't go any further without knowing all the facts. Bennett may be involved, but all the evidence so far is circumstantial."

"It does look that way. I'll be on duty today if you need backup," Drake offered.

"Thanks," Cortez said quietly, and he meant it.

"I'll keep an eye on Phoebe, too." He smiled. "No worries," he added when Cortez's face tautened. "I know the lay of the land." He glanced toward the still-fogged windows. "Making out in a museum parking lot, for God's sake. Don't they have dirt roads in Oklahoma? We have lots of them in North Carolina."

"You know what you can do with your dirt roads," Cortez said pleasantly, starting the car. "I'm going to work."

"Me, too. Take care."

"You do the same."

PHOEBE INCHED OUT OF THE restroom and into her office, hoping for a reprieve. It didn't come. Seconds later, a worried Marie led a trim older woman into Phoebe's office and ran for her life. The woman seemed nervous. Her eyes shifted constantly. She had blond hair, blue eyes and a nice figure. She was wearing a designer suit that seemed more expensive than a schoolteacher could afford.

"I'm Marsha Mason," the woman began. "I was here yesterday." She hesitated. "I teach grade school. I told your assistant I wanted to discuss a moral issue with you…"

"I'm Phoebe Keller," came the quick reply. "I'm sorry about what you saw in my office yesterday. My…fiancé had just proposed," she began.

"Proposed?" The woman seemed confused.

"Uh, yes," Phoebe replied, forcing a smile. "We've known each other for three years, but we'd been apart for a time…he's an FBI agent."

The woman seemed to flinch, but her face was calm. "He is? I see."

"I am keenly aware of my responsibilities here," Phoebe said softly. "But the circumstances were…quite overwhelming."

"Apparently." The woman frowned. "You don't have a ring," she added, noting Phoebe's bare ring finger.

"Not yet," Phoebe agreed with a shy smile. "He's very impulsive."

The teacher cleared her throat. "Well, under the circumstances, I expect it was understandable. But in future…"

"It won't happen again," Phoebe said firmly. "Was there anything else?"

The woman hesitated. "No. Yes," she corrected at once. "I notice that you have quite a nice collection of Paleo-Indian artifacts. The effigy figure in the front display case is...especially impressive. Could I ask where you purchased it?"

Phoebe frowned. That was a strange question. "Why?"

The woman hesitated again, as if she were thinking hard. She ground her teeth together. "There was a robbery at a museum in New York City, a year or so ago," the woman said solemnly. "I don't mean to make accusations or anything, but I was, uh, I taught near the museum and often took my classes through it. I saw photographs of the pieces that were lost. One of them resembles that effigy figure in your central case."

Phoebe felt faint, but she hid it quickly. She'd forgotten about that particular piece. It was less than a month old. She'd been approached by an art dealer and she'd taken him before the museum's board of governors to suggest the purchase. The governors had approved it, at a substantial price. But she didn't want to admit that to the teacher before she spoke to Cortez. It was odd that the woman had brought it up. The woman didn't really look like a typical schoolteacher, either. She was carrying what was definitely a designer purse and so were her shoes, like her suit. Not exactly items that can be bought on a modest schoolteacher's salary.

"How interesting," Phoebe said with feigned surprise. "I've seen a couple of effigy figures like it over the years. One, of course, was an admitted forgery."

The woman's eyes were shrewd. "Yours doesn't look like a forgery."

Phoebe's eyebrows lifted. "You studied archaeology?" she asked curiously.

"I have some knowledge of artifacts," the woman said quickly. "You know, there are people who rob archaeological sites for valuable artifacts," she said.

"Indeed," Phoebe agreed, her face darkening. "Pot hunters are the lowest form of life to any true archaeologist."

The woman lifted her eyebrows. "Where would museums like this get their treasures without them?"

"Reputably," Phoebe replied curtly. "From archaeologists who find them on site and arrange their donation to museums through the legitimate channels. I can assure you that our effigy figure came from a reputable source, an art dealer from New York City. He was very knowledgeable about it. Apparently it was a piece from Cahokia that had been in the hands of a private collector who died."

"How interesting." She hesitated. "My school would like to add a few inexpensive pieces to our collection, in our display case. Do you have the man's name?"

Stranger and stranger, Phoebe was thinking. She blinked. "He gave me a business card, but I lost it, apparently." She let out a short laugh. "But I'd know the man anywhere. I could pick him out of a crowd. Perhaps I could call his gallery and inquire for you. I do have that number written on the purchase file itself…"

The woman had gone pale. "On second thought, I don't think we could afford him. Perhaps if you hear of a dig nearby you could contact me and I could beg some potsherds from the archaeologist."

"That's a possibility," Phoebe said.

"Forgive what I said about the effigy figure," Miss Mason said primly. "I'm sure that your exhibits don't come from suspect sources."

"I never thought you were making accusations," Phoebe said, smiling.

Miss Mason smiled back, but it didn't reach her dark blue eyes. "I'll go, then. Congratulations on your engagement, by the way."

"Thank you," Phoebe replied.

"You're…very sure that your art dealer was legitimate?" the blonde asked suddenly, flushing as she met Phoebe's suspicious gaze.

"Of course I am," Phoebe lied.

"Well, then." The blond woman smiled wanly and walked out of the museum, climbing quickly into the cab that had been waiting for her out front. Phoebe watched her go, but didn't feel the relief she'd expected to have the episode put behind her before it threatened her job. Miss Mason had made a disturbing comment about that effigy figure. Phoebe was going to tell Cortez. But first, she was going to check her records and trace its history. She gave the effigy figure in the case another quiet scrutiny.

8

PHOEBE MADE A CAREFUL search of her files to look for the man who'd brought them the effigy figure. The business card he'd given her wasn't actually lost. She'd told the woman it was because there was something suspicious about her.

But the business card wasn't what she expected. It had the man's name—Fred Norton—and his business address along with the name of his gallery in New York City. It didn't have a telephone number.

Impulsively Phoebe dialed information and gave the name of the gallery. The operator told her there was no such listing. There was one that was close, so Phoebe called it and asked for Norton. She was told that no one by that name worked for them.

She hung up and stared at the telephone curiously. What

if the man who sold her the effigy figure was the same man who'd stolen it in the first place?

Impulsively she phoned the school the teacher had said she worked for. She asked for Miss Mason and waited while the woman was called to the phone.

"Miss Mason?" Phoebe asked carefully.

"Yes, what can I do for you?" someone replied in an unfamiliar voice.

"I'm Phoebe Keller at the Chenocetah Museum," she introduced herself. "I wanted to ask you a question in regard to our conversation in my office this morning."

There was a long pause. "Excuse me, but you must have the wrong number. I have never been to your museum."

"But your class was here yesterday," Phoebe argued.

"Another teacher's class did come there," came the soft reply. "But it wasn't mine. I've had the stomach virus. This is my first day back."

Phoebe stared at her desk blindly. "But the woman said her name was Marsha Mason," she protested.

"But that's impossible," the voice said worriedly.

Apparently it was. Phoebe was ready to grasp at straws. "Then can you tell me the name of the teacher who was here yesterday?"

"Just a moment, please." There was muffled conversation. Miss Mason came back on the line. "Are you still there, Miss Keller?"

"Yes," Phoebe said.

"Constance Riley brought her first-graders to your museum, and I was certainly not with her," came the reply. "I believe I should report this matter to the police. I don't like the idea of someone using my identity," Miss Mason said urgently. "It's rather upsetting."

"I'm sure I'd feel the same way. I think it's a good idea to report it to the authorities. They can contact me if they need verification. Thank you, Miss Mason."

"No, thank you, my dear," came the quiet reply. "I'd never have known if you hadn't phoned."

"You're very welcome."

Phoebe hung up, feeling unsettled. She'd told her mysterious visitor that she'd know the man who sold her the effigy figure if she saw him again. What if the woman was in league with him, and had only come to the museum to check out what Phoebe knew? She sat down, hard, feeling threatened.

CORTEZ TRACKED PAUL CORLAND out to his building site, where he was overseeing the placement of rebar. The site wasn't too far from Bennett's.

He was a tall, rough-looking man with dark eyes and blond hair. Cortez flashed his FBI badge. "My name is Cortez," he said. "If you can spare a few minutes, I'd be grateful."

"I've already explained to the authorities that someone sabotaged my shipment of steel," Corland said angrily. He took off his hard hat for a moment to wipe the sweat from his forehead. He slammed it back in place, looking furious. "I don't cheat on support beams!" he growled. "My record probably does look bad, but I can assure you that what happened in Charleston was not my fault!"

"I'm not here about the construction," Cortez replied calmly. "I want to know if you've had anything suspicious going on around here in the past week or so."

"May I know what you're looking for?" the man asked bluntly.

"I'm investigating a homicide," Cortez replied with equal bluntness.

The other man cocked his head. "The archaeologist, right?" he asked.

Cortez's eyebrows jerked. "Yes."

"He came to see me," he told Cortez. "Spouting some sort of nonsense about finding ancient remains that were moved. He thought we'd done it. He wanted to look through some cave on the site here. I wouldn't let him."

"Why not?"

"Because I can't afford a work stoppage, especially on such a flimsy damned excuse," he replied coldly. "We're in hock up to our noses after the lawsuits we faced down in South Carolina. I've got my men on overtime as it is, trying to catch up. We were shorted our last shipment of steel. I'm still waiting for it to get here and calling every day to find out where it is in transit."

"Where is the cave?" Cortez wanted to know.

"I'm not saying," the man said belligerently.

Cortez gave him a measuring look. "I don't make threats," he said coldly. "But if you want a work stoppage, you're going the right way to get one. I'm looking for a murderer. I'll go through you if I have to. All it's going to take is a search warrant and a couple of reporters."

The man cursed roundly.

"That won't help matters," Cortez replied. There was cold determination in his face. "You don't want me for an enemy."

"One FBI agent isn't much of one."

"I spent several years as a government prosecutor," Cortez told him.

It was a veiled threat, and it worked. The other man set his thin lips in a line. "What do you think you'll find?"

"I don't know. I may not find anything. If I don't, you won't see me again."

"Nice incentive," Corland said sarcastically. "I'll take you to it."

CORTEZ FOLLOWED HIM INTO the woods beside the building complex and up a ledge to two caves.

"Wait here," Cortez told the other man, waving him back. He bent down, looking for a sign.

"You tracking?" Corland asked abruptly.

"Yes."

Corland moved to one side, toward the other cave. "I'm a hunter," he said, bending. "I can track a deer over rock."

Cortez glanced at him. "If you see anything, sing out."

He nodded.

They spent half an hour getting to the entrance of the caves. But there were no footprints, not even in the sandy soil under the overhanging rock ledges.

"Nothing," Cortez said finally. "I'd stake my life on it."

"Same here."

Cortez turned. "Thanks for the help."

Corland nodded curtly and Cortez turned to go back to his car.

"Hold up a sec," Corland said suddenly. "There's one other site with caves, just south of town," he told the taller man. "Ben Yardley's putting up a hotel there. I only know about it because the site boss approached me at lunch a few days ago about a mutual employee. He said he'd seen activity on his building site late at night and ran off an SUV on the property. He wanted to know if it was one of my guys up to some bad business. It seems a reputation follows people for life," he added bitterly.

Cortez moved back toward him, scowling. "One of your guys?"

"I fired a man for laying out of work a few days ago," he said. "He went to Yardley for a job. Yardley's site boss asked me why I fired him, and I told him."

"He drives an SUV?" Cortez murmured, pulling out a pad and pen. "I need the man's name."

"Fred Norton," he said. "He drives a late-model black Ford SUV."

Cortez wrote it down. "Did Yardley hire him, do you know?"

"Nobody's desperate enough to hire a layabout in these hard times," Corland said indifferently. "I'm not convinced that Norton wanted a job. He wasn't much of a hand, according to my foreman. He lazed about and went home."

"Thanks," Cortez told him. "You're off the hook. I won't be back. But if you think of anything else, call the sheriff's department and ask for Deputy Stewart. He can get in touch with me."

"I will," Corland replied.

Cortez nodded and left him there. He liked Corland, despite what he'd heard about him from Bennett. Now he was going to see the man Yardley, and do some more checking about those caves.

BOB YARDLEY WAS SIXTYISH, short and balding and a live wire. He shook Cortez's hand firmly and grinned.

"I'll bet you're here about that murder investigation," he told Cortez. "Right?"

The corner of Cortez's disciplined mouth curved up. "Nice deduction."

"I started life as a cop," he replied. "Construction pays better. Sit down."

Cortez dropped into a comfortable chair across the desk from the other man. "I understand that there's a cave on your building site," he began.

"The mountain's got plenty of them, but there's only one here. It's seen some midnight visitors just lately," Yardley told him. "I was going to call the police, but I never got a look at the person who was roaming around out there. After all, they weren't touching anything on my site."

"You told Corland the intruder was driving an SUV?" Cortez pursued.

"That's right. It was dark-colored but I couldn't see it all that well."

"How many times have you seen it out there?"

"Only once, myself, when I came to the office to get some paperwork. But one of my men saw activity out there a few days ago." He grimaced. "From what I gather now, it might have been the night that man was killed."

"If you figured out the possible connection, why didn't you alert the authorities?" Cortez asked.

"I didn't want to send them on a wild-goose chase in case I was wrong," he explained with a shrug.

Cortez's pulse leaped. "I'd like to look around the cave."

"Sure. I'll drive you up there."

"Thanks."

THE ENTRANCE TO THE CAVE was through another section of woods. There weren't many flat building sites in this part of North Carolina, which was mountainous and rocky. The track went over a small wooden bridge and then down a rutted path.

"Stop here, if you don't mind," Cortez told the man.

Yardley stopped his pickup truck and cut off the engine.

Cortez got out, bent, and started looking for signs. There were plenty, including a track with a vertical tread missing. His heart jumped up into his throat. Pay dirt!

He flipped open his cell phone and called his unit. "Make it fast," he told the lead technician. "I'll wait right here."

"We're on the way," she replied and hung up.

"Found something, did you?" Yardley asked.

Cortez smiled. "Yes, I think I did."

The technicians bagged evidence, made plaster casts of the tire tracks, and even attempted to lift prints from the smooth granite outcroppings outside the cave. Inside, there was evidence of traffic, but otherwise the search was a disappointment. They found nothing like human remains.

On the other hand, there was a blood splatter on rocks inside the cave. The technicians were very careful to get as much of the sample as they could by employing a diamond saw to lift the section of rock on which the splatter rested.

"That's a lot of work for a little piece of evidence," Yardley murmured, having been far too interested in modern forensics to leave the site.

"That's Alice Jones," Cortez mused, indicating the lead technician who was supervising the saw. "I've seen her have walls cut out, not to mention floors, to obtain evidence. She's something of a legend back in Texas."

Yardley shook his head. "Well, she's thorough. I had some good people in my department, years ago." He looked up. "Looks to me like the perp killed him here. What do you think?"

Cortez smiled at him. "You know I can't respond to that. We'll see what the evidence shows us." But inwardly, Cortez agreed with the former cop.

IT WAS DARK BEFORE CORTEZ got back to town. The museum was dark, and he had a momentary fear that Phoebe might have gone out to her cabin alone. But when he got to the motel, she was sitting on his bed with Joseph, reading him a book.

Cortez moved into the room, sliding the motel key back into his pocket. "What are you two doing in my room, and where's Tina?"

"Drake had a night off and he wanted to see that hot new sci-fi flick that's out, so he took Tina with him. I'm babysitting," she added with a smile. "How'd it go?"

"We found a cave and we think it's where the victim was murdered. We got trace evidence," he added wearily. He fell onto the bed beside them and laid back. "God, I'm tired!"

"Have you eaten?"

"No time," he murmured.

"We have pizza," she said. "Drake brought it. He said you'd be hungry and you wouldn't feel like going out."

He turned his head and looked at her. "Did you encourage him to think that?" he mused.

She smiled. "I knew you'd be tired," she said. "Joseph, sit with Daddy while I fix his supper, okay?"

"Okay, Bee-bee," Joseph murmured. He crawled up next to Cortez and patted his chest. "Hello, Daddy!"

"Hello, son." He pulled the child into his arms and kissed him lazily. "Have you been a good boy?"

"Been good boy," Joseph agreed, smiling widely.

Watching them together, Phoebe was amazed. She'd never been able to picture Cortez with a child, but he was a natural at parenting. He loved the little boy, and it showed. The feeling was obviously mutual; anyone could see how much Joseph loved his father.

Cortez felt her scrutiny and glanced at her with a grin. "Didn't know I had it in me, did you?" he murmured dryly.

"I haven't said a word," she protested.

She opened the pizza box and took out two hot slices of pizza, lobbing them onto a paper plate. "What do you want to drink?"

"Do we have a beer?" he murmured.

"You drink beer?"

"Once in a while, when I'm really wired," he confessed, throwing his legs off the bed. "It's been a long day."

"Yes, it has," Phoebe agreed as she handed him the plate and the beer from the minibar.

She climbed back onto the bed with Joseph while Cortez sat at the desk and ate his pizza. "The so-called schoolteacher who came to see me this morning was an impostor," she said.

The beer stopped at his lips. "What?"

"I backtracked her to the elementary school, but the woman I asked for was a stranger. She's never been to our school. They don't know who the woman was." She grimaced. "She asked where we got our effigy figure and mentioned a recent robbery at a big museum in New York. She actually told me that the figure looked like one that was stolen."

He scowled. "Did she say anything else?"

"No, but I traced the art dealer who sold us the effigy figure a month ago, too. He had a bogus business card.

There's no such gallery and no such person." She hesitated. "I told her I'd know the dealer anywhere if I saw him again."

He put the beer bottle down hard.

"I know, it was a stupid thing to do," she confessed. "But at the time I thought she was a schoolteacher. She even said she wanted to talk to him about buying some pieces to exhibit in the school." She brushed back her hair nervously, feeling like a prize idiot. She was scared, and it showed.

"You couldn't have known," he said softly. "Come here."

She went to him and he pulled her down onto his lap and bent to kiss her gently. "We all make mistakes. Even big-shot FBI agents like me," he added with a warm smile.

She smiled back and bent to kiss him back, enjoying the sudden intimacy of their relationship. She already felt as if she were part of him.

"Bee-bee kissing Daddy!" Joseph laughed.

Phoebe lifted her head and grimaced. "Little pitchers…" she mused, glancing at the laughing child.

"…have big ears," Cortez murmured. "And even bigger eyes."

She got up and went back to Joseph. He hugged her and kissed her cheek. "I kiss Bee-bee, too!" He laughed.

She kissed him as well, hugging him close. "You heartbreaker," she accused.

Cortez chuckled at the byplay as he finished his food. "I'm going to have a quick shower, if you can handle Joseph," he told Phoebe, loosening his long hair from its neat ponytail.

"I certainly can," she assured him. "I'm reading stories about the Cherokee to him."

He gave her a hard look. "Comanche stories would be more appropriate."

"Don't have any," she replied with a sigh. "This isn't exactly Comanche territory," she added ruefully.

He smiled. "Point taken. I won't be long."

He took off everything but his slacks on his way into the bathroom, and Phoebe did her best not to stare when the shirt came off. He had an amazing physique, muscular and tanned and sexy. His broad chest was lightly covered with hair.

He noticed her rapt look and turned toward her with an eyebrow lifted.

She needed an excuse to be gaping at him. She cleared her throat. "We were taught that Native Americans didn't have hair on their faces or chests."

"My great-grandfather was Spanish," he reminded her with a wry smile.

"I forgot."

He studied her almost hungrily, with black eyes that coveted her trim figure under the neat jeans and long-sleeved, yellow V-neck sweater. It matched her blond fairness. "You look pretty good yourself, Phoebe," he said quietly.

She flushed and laughed self-consciously. "Pull the other one."

He moved toward her, reaching down to pull her up off the bed and into his arms. "You don't have an ego at all, do you?" he asked huskily. "You're devastating, Phoebe," he added, his eyes dropping to her mouth. "Irresistible, in fact."

She opened her mouth to speak and his lips came down to cover it, teasing her lips apart even as he caught her hands and smoothed them into the hair over his chest.

"Daddy kissing Bee-bee!" Joseph piped up.

Cortez let Phoebe go at once, laughing uproariously. "So much for privacy," he mused, moving away. "Wrong time, wrong place."

Phoebe watched him go with a frantically beating heart. It was the first time she'd touched him like that, and her body throbbed with unexpected needs and longings.

"Story, Bee-bee!" Joseph said insistently, sitting in the middle of the bed with the storybook Phoebe had been reading from. The print was extra-large, a good thing because her reading glasses were back on her desk at work.

She plopped back down on the bed. "Right," she said, smiling as she gathered him up onto her lap. "Come here and we'll finish this up!"

THERE WAS A CARTOON MOVIE on, which Phoebe watched with Joseph while Cortez worked at his laptop computer on the internet. He didn't speak, but his hands were busy. Phoebe found herself watching him covertly while he worked. His long, thick black hair was loose and clean. He was wearing a black T-shirt with black sweatpants and bare feet. He looked very sexy.

Joseph dozed off and Phoebe tucked him gently into bed, lying down beside him while Cortez continued with his work.

There was a light tap on the door much later. Cortez opened it and Tina stuck her head in.

"Sorry I'm late, there was a crowd!" she whispered, glancing past him to Phoebe and Joseph. "I can take Joseph back with me…"

"Joseph and Phoebe will be staying in here," Cortez

said quietly. "I've got some things to discuss with Phoebe. Joseph can bunk down with her in the second bed."

Tina gave him a curious look. "Something's happened, hasn't it?" she asked worriedly.

"Yes," he replied. "You lock your door and if you hear anything out of the ordinary, you bang on that wall as hard as you can. Got that?"

She grimaced. "Drake said something was going on, but he wouldn't tell me what. You're not going to, either, are you?"

"I can't, honey." He smiled. "Did you have a good time?"

Her eyes were dreamy. "Yes. He's really nice."

He cocked an eyebrow. "What about the policeman in Asheville?" he teased.

She grimaced. "Ouch!"

"Sorry," he replied. "Don't sweat it. You're single."

"Yes, I am," she said uneasily, and with a covert glance at Phoebe, who didn't see it. "But Drake and I are just friends," she added quickly.

"Of course," he agreed.

She peered past him and waved at Phoebe, who waved back. "Does she know she's staying with you tonight?" she whispered to Cortez, because Phoebe was watching the movie and not paying much attention to the conversation.

"Not yet," he confessed with a chuckle. "But she'll be fine. I'll loan her a T-shirt."

Grinning, Tina said good-night and went back into her own room.

WHEN THE MOVIE WAS OVER, Phoebe got up and turned off the television. She glanced over at Joseph, who was sleeping soundly in Cortez's double bed. "I suppose I should go to bed," she began, oddly reluctant to leave.

Cortez left the computer and got up to tower over her. "I told Tina I'm keeping you in here tonight. You can have the other bed. I've got an extra T-shirt." He smiled gently. "Considering the difference in our sizes, it should reach down to your knees."

She searched his black eyes quietly. "What do you know that I don't?"

"Drake remembered seeing a black SUV parked at the end of your driveway the day he taught you to shoot," he said.

"Yes," she replied at once. "I meant to mention it, but the man inside was looking at a map. I assumed he was a lost tourist."

"The murder suspect drives a dark SUV, Phoebe," he replied. "And you're the last person who spoke with the murder victim."

She whistled softly. "Oh, boy."

"It could be worse," he said. "But you've got plenty of protection, as it happens."

"I shouldn't have mentioned the art dealer to that bogus teacher," she said miserably. "Or told her that I could pick him out of a crowd."

"Curious that she'd mention a robbery to you," he replied, eyes narrowing in thought. "Maybe she was in league with the pothunter and now they're having differences of opinion. She might have meant for you to give his name to the authorities and implicate him."

"No honor among thieves?" she wondered.

"It depends on how much money's at stake, from my experience," he told her. "If he's a thief, he might also be a murderer. Maybe she's involved and she doesn't want to be charged an accessory to murder. Life in prison wouldn't appeal to many women."

"Truly."

He went to the dresser, opened a drawer and pulled out a clean black T-shirt. He handed it to Phoebe. "I've got a little more work to do. Why don't you climb in with Joseph and try to get some sleep?"

"Is the alarm clock set?" she wondered.

He nodded. "I'll make sure you get to work on time," he promised

"Thanks."

She went into the bathroom and had a quick shower before she dried her hair with the motel hair dryer and pulled the tee shirt over her clean body. It was so big that it swallowed her, looking more like a casual oversized dress than a shirt. She laughed as she gathered up her clothes and went back into the other room.

Cortez was still concentrating on the computer screen. She gave him a hungry glance before she climbed in beside Joseph and pulled the covers over them both. The child curled naturally into her arms, his soft breath calming as she closed her own eyes.

Something woke her in the early hours of the morning. Joseph was sleeping on his belly on the far side of the bed. Cortez was sitting on the edge next to Phoebe, brooding as he looked down at her in the semidarkness of the room.

She rolled onto her back and looked up at him drowsily. "Is something wrong?" she asked.

"There's been another attack," he said quietly. "I have to leave. I'm going to go next door and get Tina to come in here with you while I'm away."

"Who's been injured this time?" she asked.

"We don't know yet. It's over at the Bennett construction site." He leaned over her and brushed back her hair gently. "Call Drake and get him to drive you to work. I don't want you going there alone."

"All right," she promised. She reached up to his cheek and stroked it, loving the smell of his clean body in the black T-shirt that matched the one she was wearing. "You be careful," she added huskily.

He drew in a long breath and leaned down to put his mouth ravenously against hers. She melted into him at once, her arms linking around his neck as she opened her lips, inviting a deeper intimacy.

He had vague regrets for the innocence she'd lost because he'd betrayed her, but perhaps it wasn't so bad that she was experienced. Their first time wouldn't cause her any discomfort.

With that in mind, his hands slid under the T-shirt and pushed it out of his way as he brought her closer. He paused to strip off his T-shirt before he kissed her again and drew her bare breasts against his naked chest in an agony of pleasure.

"Jeremiah," she exclaimed, shaken at the contact.

His big, lean hands slid up and down her bare back, smoothing her closer as he built the kiss hungrily. "I love the way your breasts feel against me," he bit off against her mouth.

She knew she was blushing, but she was too involved to care. He couldn't see anyway…

His hands slid up to cup her breasts and rub softly at the nipples, so that she gasped. He lifted his head and suddenly pushed her down on the bed, onto her back, holding her hands beside her head as he stared at her bare breasts.

She shivered. The moment was explosive. She moved restlessly on the bed, aching for more.

His eyes went down to her pale pink briefs, to the length of her elegant, pretty legs. He drew in a rough breath. "You can't imagine how tempted I am to strip you out of those briefs and have you where you lay."

Her lips parted on a rough breath. "Joseph…!" she cried.

He glanced toward the sleeping child and his lips made a thin line. He breathed harshly as he turned his eyes back to her prone body. His hands left her wrists and caressed her breasts with arrogant possession. She arched into them helplessly and moaned.

"You're experienced. So am I. There's no reason we can't have each other. Not tonight," he managed with visible regret. "But soon, Phoebe. I'm going to have you to the roots of your pretty hair. I'm going to make you scream with pleasure. I'm going to make you claw my back raw while I'm having you. When I finish, you'll never get the memory out of your mind!"

She shivered helplessly. What had he said about her being experienced? She wasn't, but he didn't know that. She didn't want to tell him, either. What he said was inflaming her senses. She wanted to take off her clothes and pull him down on her, feel his body harden with desire, taste his mouth grinding into hers.

He bent and kissed her breasts with exquisite tenderness, enjoying the involuntary motion of her young body, the soft moans that tore out of her throat.

"You're beautiful, Phoebe," he whispered as he lifted his head. "And one way or another, before I finish this investigation, you're going to sleep in my arms."

CORTEZ MET HIS EVIDENCE team at the Bennett property, where they found a man badly beaten and unconscious in Bennett's office. It was the site boss, Walks Far, and he had been covered with light dust. They'd bagged his clothing and boots as evidence before he was rushed to the hospital in an ambulance. According to the most recent update from the doctors, Walks Far was in critical condition.

"A passing off-duty police officer noticed the lights on and got suspicious," Alice Jones, the evidence technician, indicated a city policeman in jeans. "Forensics indicates that the man wasn't assaulted in here," she told Cortez decisively.

"Make a guess of what you think happened," he invited.

Alice drew in a long breath, squinting one eye. "Something like a rock was used to inflict this kind of blunt-force trauma to the head."

Cortez narrowed his own eyes. "How about the dust on his clothing?"

She bent to the victim's discarded clothing and sniffed. "Nothing surface," she said, almost to herself. "There's a dank odor. He'd been digging or he's been underground. His shoes are wet," she added, noting the traces of mud and dried water on the leather boots. "And there were spider webs in his hair." She recalled the dried blood and cobwebs. "At a wild guess, he's been near a water source and in a cave."

Cortez's heart leaped and he stood up. "I'm going hiking," he told her, borrowing a flashlight from one of the Chenocetah patrol officers. "I need backup," he added, glancing at the men, all three of whom were almost half his age.

"I'll go with you," the tall blond man in jeans, the off-duty police officer who'd loaned him the flashlight said. "Dawes," he called to his colleague in uniform, "loan me your flashlight, would you?"

"Here," Dawes said. "I've got a spare one in my squad car."

"We won't be long. Dawes, give me your cell phone number," Cortez added, knowing that the local officers had been given cell phones just recently because their communications equipment was so outdated.

Dawes wrote it down for him on a slip of paper torn from his ticket book.

"If I don't call you every fifteen minutes, you come looking for us," Cortez told him somberly. He gave the man directions to the cave on the back of Bennett's lot.

"Watch for bears," Dawes told the men.

"Any bear that can catch me is welcome to eat me," Cortez murmured absently. "Jones, as soon as the tests are completed on the dirt on his shoes and that stuff on his shirt, I want to know."

Jones looked at the shirt closely and frowned. "That material looks uncomfortably familiar," she murmured, returning it to the evidence bag.

"I'll check with you later," Cortez murmured as he and the officer went out the door.

There were tire tracks at the cave entrance. Cortez bent down with the flashlight, studying them. One of the treads had a missing vertical bar. He smiled to himself as he cautioned the officer to avoid the track and walked into the cave. He was going to tell Jones about that, the minute they got back to the crime scene, so that she could get a plaster cast of it. Good thing her equipment van was fully equipped, he mused. She carried trowels, picks, brushes, and a broad-mouthed shovel, in addition to her store of paper bags for evidence. Jones rarely used plastic ones—they encouraged moisture and, therefore, mold.

The sight that met his eyes surprised him. There was a skeleton, laid out on the dirt floor. There were also pots and flaked tools, in addition to what looked like stone pipes and small sculptures.

"What the hell is that?" one of the policeman asked.

"At a guess, a stash of stolen artifacts, but I need to verify that. I have to get an anthropologist out here."

"Lots of luck finding one at this hour," the policeman chuckled.

Cortez lifted an eyebrow. "Oddly enough, I know exactly where to find one."

PHOEBE WAS SLEEPING SOUNDLY when she was shaken gently awake. She opened her eyes and looked up into Cortez's face.

"What time is it?" she murmured.

"Two in the morning," he said softly, smiling as he pushed the hair out of her eyes. "I need you to get up and get dressed. I think I've just found the missing artifacts from the New York museum robbery."

She was awake at once. "You're kidding!"

"I'm not." He tugged her gently to her feet. "Get dressed. I'll wait for you outside," he added, whispering so that he didn't wake Joseph and Tina.

It was exciting for Phoebe to be involved in an actual investigation. She threw on jeans and a T-shirt with a denim jacket, socks and sneakers. She didn't even take time to comb her hair or put on makeup. Exactly five minutes later, she was in the car.

Cortez smiled approvingly. "You're quick."

"I had a friend who took half an hour just to put on her makeup," she commented with a chuckle as she fastened her seat belt. "Of course, she was gorgeous. I never had looks to begin with, so I don't usually bother about making up."

He frowned. "But you're lovely," he said unexpectedly. "Didn't you know?"

She just stared at him, surprised. Although this wasn't the first time he'd complimented her appearance, she still had a hard time believing it.

"You have the least ego of any woman I've ever known," he murmured as he started the car and backed out of the parking spot in front of the motel. "You're intelligent, you're pretty, you're openhearted. I could go on," he added with an amused glance, "but I wouldn't want to make you conceited."

She smiled. "Thanks."

He shrugged. "I mean it," he replied. "I don't suppose

you even know that I had plans to come back for you three years ago."

She was very quiet.

He glanced at her set features. "I even had the plane ticket to Charleston. Then Isaac…died." His expression hardened as he paused for a traffic light. "You can't imagine the turmoil in my family. Isaac's girlfriend was pregnant. Her parents wanted her to have a termination. My mother had a bad heart, and she ended up in the hospital. She begged me to save the child. The only way I could manage to do that was to wed Mary. She agreed reluctantly, and told me she wanted a divorce when Joseph was a month old."

She didn't want to ask, but she had to know. "Did you… could you…love her?"

"No," he replied flatly. "And she couldn't love me. She never stopped mourning my brother. Joseph was just barely a month old, and I'd started divorce proceedings, as she'd requested, when she killed herself. She left a note, just three words—Gone to Isaac."

She bit her lower lip, hard. She could imagine how the young woman had felt. It was how she'd felt when Cortez never came back.

He turned his head toward her, his eyes narrow and watchful. "That's how you felt. Wasn't it?"

Her expression was one of surprise. "Well…yes," she confessed.

"It's how I felt, too," he bit off, averting his face. "I couldn't have cared less about my work or even my life. I switched jobs because it involved a lot of travel and I liked it. I didn't have to look at her grieving for Isaac. I didn't have time to grieve over you."

"You grieved for me?" she asked, fury overcoming her

for the second time in a week. "You grieved? And you had the gall to send me three column inches of type about your marriage!" she said harshly. "You didn't write me even one single, damned word...!"

Although they'd hashed this out already, she still hadn't forgiven him for the heartless way he'd broken the news of his marriage.

He pulled the car into a deserted parking lot, cut off the engine and reached for her. His mouth ground into hers as if he wanted to become part of it. He unfastened her seat belt and dragged her across his lap, the kiss building, heating up, devouring. He groaned as if he were in pain.

She had no thought of resisting him. Her body throbbed all over. She wound her arms around his neck and held on for dear life while she returned the hot kiss with everything in her. It was as if the past three years hadn't even happened. She wanted him so much. She loved him more than her own life. He groaned again and the pressure of his mouth increased. She opened her own mouth and felt the world spin away in a haze of pure, aching desire.

It seemed a very long time before he lifted his head. They were both breathing as if they'd been running. His eyes found hers in the dim light from the streetlights. She looked devastated. There was a faint tremor in her slender body that matched the unsteadiness of his arms. His hands went under her jacket and blouse, and she never protested once. Her own hands were busy under his jacket and shirt, delighting in the feel of thick hair and warm muscle. Her mouth pushed up hard against his and she moaned huskily.

Totally involved, with no other thought in his mind except relief, his hand went to the button and zip of her jeans. But her hand pressed against his hard mouth and she drew away.

"Aren't they waiting for us?" she whispered unsteadily.

"Who? Waiting for us where?" he asked, dazed.

"Evidence technicians. At the crime scene?" she prompted.

He took a deep breath and slowly, the crush of his arms relaxed. He stared down at her as if he'd only just realized he was holding her. He helped her up and let her move back into her own seat.

"So much for restraint," he murmured with black humor as he refastened his seat belt and started the car. The windshield and the windows were completely fogged. He laughed softly. It was a repeat of their heated interlude in front of her museum. He turned on the defroster and leaned back to let it work.

He turned to her, his eyes quiet and somber. "That was too rough. Did I hurt you?"

"I wouldn't have felt it if you had," she confessed, her gaze trapped in his. She was still fighting to breathe normally. Her hands trembled as she fastened her own seat belt.

He noticed her hands shaking. He caught one of them and held it close, tight in his own as he stared at her. "Whatever happens, I'm not losing you again," he said curtly.

She knew that her eyes were eating him. She couldn't help it. He was the most important thing in her life. She returned the firm pressure of his hand, her eyes brimming with tears.

"Don't cry, sweetheart," he whispered, bending to brush his mouth tenderly over her wet eyes. "Don't cry. It's all right." His mouth moved to her nose, her cheeks. His heart was raging in his chest. This woman meant more to him than life itself. "Phoebe," he murmured as he found her mouth again. But this time, the kiss was tender, soft, searching. His lean hand found her cheek and traced it while he kissed her.

Somewhere in the back of his mind, he heard a sound like purring. He was so involved in the taste of Phoebe that he didn't realize a car had stopped beside them. Before he could draw back from her, there was a perfunctory tap on the window and the door opened abruptly.

Deputy Sheriff Drake Stewart shook his head, grinning. "I knew it was you when I saw the fogged-up windows," he began.

Phoebe was flushed and breathless. Cortez let her go and sat up straight, his chest rising and falling on a bemused breath.

"Don't you work?" he asked Drake.

Drake grinned. "Now, here I was just about to ask you that same question," he remarked. "We had a call from your crime unit. They were worried about you because you said you'd be right back."

Phoebe straightened her denim jacket, glanced at Drake's amused expression, and cleared her throat. "I fainted and he was reviving me," she said deadpan, using the explanation he'd suggested to her the other time they got caught in the car in a compromising situation.

Cortez burst out laughing. "Phoebe, you can't faint when you're sitting down," he explained.

"Turncoat!" she exclaimed. She pointed at Drake. "He was buying it!"

"No, he wasn't," Drake said, chuckling. "Listen, you guys had better get going. It's blowing snow," he added, holding out a gloved hand palm-up to demonstrate the precipitation. It wasn't really surprising to have snow in the last week of November in the North Carolina mountains.

"We're already gone," Cortez replied. He hesitated. "We've got an assault victim in the hospital—Walks Far from Bennett Construction," he added. "If this stash we're investigating is what I think it is, Phoebe's life is going to be at risk even more than before. How about doubling the patrols near the motel where we're staying and the museum?"

"I already have," Drake assured him, sobering. "I heard about the assault on my police radio. You watch your back," he added.

"You do the same," Cortez replied.

He pulled out of the parking lot, glancing at Phoebe with indulgent amusement. "No need to look so embarrassed," he told her. "Drake's human."

She cleared her throat. "Of course."

"Unless you were embarrassed for another reason than the one that came to my mind," he added slowly, frowning. "Did you have anything going with him before I showed up?"

"Yes," she agreed at once. "Salads, three days a week. He came by the museum and brought lunch."

He held her eyes. "Nothing else?"

She could have lied. She was even tempted. But she wasn't very good at it. She grimaced and folded her hands in her lap. She looked out the window. "I think he was attracted to me," she confessed with a sigh. "But it wasn't mutual." She glanced at him bitterly. "As if I wanted to get involved with a man, ever again."

He felt bad about that, but elated just the same. He turned

the car onto the road that led to Bennett's building site. "He's a good man."

She smiled. "Tina thinks so."

"She was dating a policeman in Asheville," he said. "I don't know that he'll ever forgive me for dragging her here to babysit."

"She's old enough to make up her own mind about men," she told him.

"I know that." He smiled. "She's special."

"She said that your father went to college."

"That surprised you?" he asked amusedly. "Did you expect him to live in a teepee and walk around in full battle regalia?"

She laughed at her own notions. "Even if I did, I'd be ashamed to admit it."

He shook his head. "You'd be amazed how many people see us like that," he told her. "Movies and fictional stories haven't helped."

"We're all guilty of stereotyping, to a degree," she replied. "But I should know better."

He reached out and curled her hand into his big one. "You're doing okay."

She held on tight. "I'll remind you that you said that."

The crime unit, led by Alice Jones, was marking time when Cortez and Phoebe walked carefully around the small wooden stakes and string that marked the limits of evidence-gathering, and into the cave where Jones indicated.

"Good Lord!" Phoebe exclaimed as she looked at the skeleton. Blind to the people around her, she moved toward it, careful to step on hard ground where there was no disturbed dirt. She knelt by the skull. "May I pick it up?" she asked.

Alice waved a hand. "We've already gone over it for prints and trace evidence," she said. "We've had a lot of time for that," she added pointedly, noting Phoebe's swollen mouth and disheveled hair...and Cortez's guilty expression. "I've already got plaster casts of the tire tracks, we've bagged all the trace evidence, and the photographer's come and gone, both at the trailer and here." She held up a gloved hand to catch snow. "Isn't it lucky that we didn't get covered up like living snowmen and women or eaten by black bears while we were stuck here in the cold?"

Cortez apologized, but Phoebe wasn't listening. She was examining the ridge above the brow. "Male," she murmured to herself. She turned the skull, noting the high cheekbones and large sinus cavities. She checked the dentition of the upper jaw—the only one with the remains since the lower jaw was missing—and checked the pattern of tooth wear. She went on to assess the double-arched brow ridge, the backward slope of the cheekbones, and the high, rounded orbit of the eye sockets. The low forehead, added to the other points, was more than enough for a decision even before she painstakingly examined the rest of the skeleton with its large shoulder, hip, elbow and ankle joints and its short, thick-walled tibia.

"These remains are Neanderthal," she said finally, looking at Cortez as she examined the skull one more time. "I'd stake my professional reputation on it."

"Neanderthal?" Alice Jones muttered, scowling. "That would make them..."

"I know," Phoebe replied. "Between forty thousand and two hundred thousand years old, depending on their location. They come from Europe, Africa and the Middle East primarily. There's never been a Neanderthal skeleton identified in the Americas. And this one isn't indigenous, either," she added firmly. "You'll need to do tests to prove that, however."

"You can tell that from a skeleton?" one of the police officers asked, fascinated.

"You can," Alice Jones answered before Phoebe could, smiling at Phoebe's surprise. "I did courses in physical anthropology long before I decided on a career in forensics. I've been on digs. In fact, I remember you from one forensic course I took at the University of Tennessee. You're Phoebe Keller. You were in my class!"

Phoebe laughed as she recognized the other woman. "Yes! You were! Nice to see you again, Alice!"

"What about the other artifacts?" Cortez prompted.

Phoebe grimaced, hating to put the skull down. It was speaking to her. From the bones alone she could tell the age, sex, physical health, and perhaps even the manner of death. From the dentition she could garner race and eating habits and age. She didn't want to stop. But he was right, it was a crime scene, not a lab.

She picked up a piece of pottery and turned it in her hands, noting the media and the pattern. "Late Southeast Woodland Period, two thousand years old," she said to herself. She put it down and went over the projectile points. "Folsom spear points," she murmured. "They could be Paleo-Indian, dating back around twelve thousand years, or they could even be Mousterian." She smiled at their blank stares. "That's Neanderthal lithic technology. Handmade stone tools." She frowned as she studied the other artifacts. There were pipes made of red pipestone, very old, but difficult to date without her lithic textbooks. There were two effigy figurines, funerary ones, very old and very expensive.

She lifted the first with great care, turning it around in her hands to note the workmanship and the media. "Hopewell period," she mused. The other figure was the same period. The two pipes, very rare and valuable, also dated from the Hopewell period. She put it down gently and stood up, still frowning.

"What is it?" Cortez asked.

"These artifacts are a mixed bag," she said. "The skeletal remains are Neanderthal. As for the pottery, it's Swift Creek pattern. It dates from the Woodland period—that means it's from one thousand to just under two thousand years old. But the projectile points are Folsom—that dates them to before 12,000 BCE. They could be much older, even possibly Neanderthal, although I won't believe that without corroboration. On the other hand, the platform pipes and the effigy figures are from the Middle Woodland Period, the Ohio Valley Hopewell Culture of the first and second centuries CE that was prevalent in the Southeastern United States and denotes the mound builders," she added. "I've seen museum exhibits of funerary effigy figures almost identical to these in New York City. In fact, our effigy figure that we purchased just over a month ago looks similar to these." She turned to the technicians. "It's impossible all these artifacts came from one single site. Just impossible."

"I agree," Alice Jones added.

"What did you say about that effigy figure your museum bought last month?" Cortez asked her.

"It looks like a match for these two," she said flatly. "I think this is the loot that was stolen from the museum in New York City. That would explain finding it all in one place. With no regard for its age, either. This is a sloppy job of stashing for artifacts so precious."

"There's something else here that doesn't add up," Alice broke in. "Remember that sample of matter I took from the victim's shirt? I won't know until I can get it to a lab, but I'm pretty sure that it's brain matter. And it's not the victim's."

Cortez whistled through his teeth. That could very easily mean there was another victim, a dead one, somewhere in the area. "This is not adding up."

"Tell me about it," Alice said.

"Let's get those tests underway," Cortez told Alice. "I need answers fast."

"You can count on me, boss," she replied, grinning.

"I'll check out that museum robbery with our computer, and feed that description and the information Phoebe gave me about the art dealer who sold her the effigy figure into the computer as well and see if it rings any bells in our databank," Cortez said, referring to a national databank of known criminals. "Let's put a twenty-four-hour guard on this site."

"Great, who do we really dislike?" one of the local policemen mused, staring pointedly at his blond colleague who'd gone to the site with Cortez.

"You can draw straws," Cortez said, "but I don't want anyone wandering around here after we leave. Furthermore, I want you in hiding. If anybody does show up, you cuff him and bring him in. Got that?"

"I got it," the blond policeman said smugly.

"I'll take you back, Phoebe," he told her, taking her arm. "See you guys later."

DAWN WAS BREAKING AGAINST the mountains. Phoebe wasn't even sleepy. "Do you think you could stop by my house on the way to the motel?" she asked him. "I really need a change of clothes, and I'd love a shower."

"You could do that at the motel," he pointed out.

"Yes, but I don't have my soap or my shampoo or my bath powder," she reminded him.

He glanced at his watch. "I suppose we've got time. It's a little late to go to bed now."

"I'll be quick," she promised. "I have to be in my office at eight-thirty."

Leaving Cortez in the kitchen making coffee, she made a dash for the bathroom. She undressed quickly and wrapped a bath towel around her while she adjusted the showerhead. She was just undoing the towel when the door behind her swung open.

She gasped audibly, staring straight into Cortez's dark eyes.

He couldn't look away. "I was going to ask if you wanted a biscuit to go with your coffee," he murmured, only half-aware of what he was saying.

His dark eyes slid down her body, over the wealth of bare skin unhidden by the towel, which barely covered her breasts and hips. She looked beautiful like that, with her hair wavy and mussed.

He felt his whole body clench. He ached to rip that towel off her and throw her down on the floor. His teeth ground together as he struggled with temptation.

She looked back at him with wide, soft eyes. He was so handsome. The stuff of dreams. He'd never been out of her thoughts for longer than ten minutes in the past three years. She'd dreamed of loving him in the darkness, of growing big with his child. The desire was much worse since she'd shared a room with him and Joseph. She'd gone hungry for him. But he had a child and a career, and he was only here temporarily, looking for a murderer. He'd solve the case, and he'd go away again. If only she could go with him, and they could have children of their own…

The light went out of her eyes as she met his.

"What were you thinking about just then?" he asked suddenly.

"Ba…babies," she faltered.

His face contorted. Then his gaze fell to her waistline and began to glitter with feeling. Three years ago, if he hadn't been so inflexible about taking her virginity, he could have taken her to bed and had memories to live on. But he'd gone away, rejected her, hurt her so badly that she'd ended up in another man's bed out of anguish. Her first time had been with a stranger, in a drunken encounter. Because of him. Because of him!

Yet, if she'd become sexually active, there was no reason on earth he couldn't have her now. He'd ached for her ever since she let him take off the T-shirt and look at her. The need had grown by the minute until it was unmanageable and stark.

With cold deliberation, his hands went to his jacket. He stripped it off and tossed it onto the clothes hamper by the door. His shirt followed it while Phoebe gaped at him with parted lips and pulsing heart.

He took his hair down before he reached for the fastening of his slacks. Everything came off except the black satin boxers he was wearing under his clothing, then he walked toward Phoebe with intent.

She opened her mouth to protest, but it was already too

late. He ripped her out of the towel and riveted her to his powerful body even as his mouth pushed down against hers and knocked any thought of resistance right out of her mind.

"I left you at your hotel three years ago and never looked back," he groaned against her parting lips. "A bigger fool was never born. I'm not walking away this time, Phoebe. And neither are you."

His mouth bit into hers again as he stripped off his boxers and let them fall to the floor. He stepped out of them, and Phoebe felt him against her with awe and faint fear, absorbing the strength of his warm body and the urgent threat of his masculinity pressing against her bare flesh.

She should tell him, she thought dizzily. It might hurt. Could he tell? They said men couldn't...

He groaned against her mouth and suddenly took her right under the shower with him. She felt the water at her back as his hands smoothed up and down her body, exploring her nudity with slow, tender motions that shocked as much as they aroused.

He soaped her body and then his, drawing her hands to him, coaxing her to explore him as he learned the exquisite contours of her own body. He shampooed her hair while his chest moved enticingly against the hard tips of her breasts, arousing her even more. While she rinsed her hair, he shampooed his own and then held his face under the spray to wash out the soap.

When they were through, he cut off the shower and helped her out of the tub, following to retrieve the bath towel she'd dropped and use it to mop away the moisture. He pulled another towel from the cupboard to dry himself before he retrieved a third to wipe away most of the water from their hair.

He plugged in the blow dryer and used it first on her short, blond hair and then on his own long black strands.

When he finished, he put the dryer aside and held her at arm's length, looking blatantly at her nudity.

She was holding her breath, fascinated, shocked, delighted by the intensity of his scrutiny.

He caught her hand and led her out of the bathroom and into her bedroom, where a quilt lay covering a double bed. He stripped back the covers, exposing a neat floral fitted sheet. He eased her down on it, noticing that she accepted the action without a single protest. He could see the whip of her pulse at the hollow of her throat, the hardness of her nipples, the tense shiver of her limbs as she waited for him to ease down alongside her in the bed.

He smoothed back her soft hair and bent to kiss her, softly, his lips barely touching hers. He nibbled her upper lip and then the lower one, easing his tongue under the moist softness in a silence that only magnified the roughness of their breathing.

One long leg inserted itself slowly between both of hers, spreading them apart. He looked into her eyes deliberately as his hand slid down, tracing maddening patterns on the inside of her thigh, just at the top.

She gasped and her body shivered.

"Let me," he whispered, ignoring the sudden urgent protest of her fingers.

She was nervous and trying not to show it. Involuntarily, her eyes moved down his body to his masculinity.

He saw her blatant curiosity and lifted away from her, to

give her a better view. The look on her face aroused him even more and his breath became unsteady.

His hand moved again, boldly, against her, feeling the soft dampness under his fingers. She jerked helplessly and a soft cry escaped her tight throat.

It must have been a long time for her, he thought hungrily. Her reactions were those of a novice.

He touched her deliberately, with a gentle rhythm that made her hips arch off the bed to push closer to his touch. She couldn't help it. She ached for the pleasure he was teaching her to feel. Her eyes closed and she shivered.

"I didn't know it would…feel like that," she whispered brokenly.

The words didn't quite register. He was throbbing with pleasure as she moved against him. Her body was almost liquid, melting into him, pleading for more.

She shivered again and again as his touch began to intrude, to penetrate. She opened her legs on a shudder.

But seconds later, his hand stilled and he looked down at her with shock.

She realized that he'd stopped touching her. She opened her eyes and could barely talk. She almost vibrated with delight.

"Don't stop," she whispered brazenly.

He moved closer, his black eyes biting into her light ones. His hand moved, hard.

She gasped and ground her teeth together.

"Yes," he bit off. "Apparently your one-night encounter wasn't quite as reckless as you told me it was, Phoebe," he said accusingly.

He drew away from her with a harsh breath and sat up, resting his head in his hands. His body ached with frustration.

10

She drew in a long breath, watching him. He was hurting. She could see it in the stiff lines of his body.

Her hips moved involuntarily on the sheets, restless for more of the delightful sensations he'd been arousing in her.

"I'm twenty-five," she whispered.

He drew in a rough breath of his own. "And still a virgin. I can't, Phoebe."

She sat up, shivering with desire, and looked down his body. "Yes, you can," she breathed. "Oh, yes, you can!" She moved, pressing her breasts against his back, her arms linking around his broad, hair-covered chest. She had no pride left at all. "I can't do this with anyone else! I just can't! Please," she whispered in anguish.

His back arched closer to her breasts. "Phoebe, I don't have anything to use," he ground out.

She stilled. Neither did she. But she ached so terribly. Worse than she'd ever ached in her life.

He turned and pulled her down across his body, so that her head rested in the crook of his elbow. His fingers traced over her belly, over the bruise where the bullet had hit her, up across her hard-tipped breasts. He groaned.

She arched backward, her eyes closing to slits. Her hips moved helplessly. "I'm dying," she cried.

"So am I," he replied roughly. He traced around a hard nipple, watching her heart race at her throat. "When was your last period?" he asked almost in desperation.

"Two weeks ago," she moaned.

"This is the worst possible time," he muttered.

Her pale eyes met his dark ones. She thought about a baby. It softened her body, made it shiver with the possibility of a child of her own.

His face tautened as he saw the hunger in her eyes. "I've never thought of deliberately making a baby."

She swallowed. "Neither have I."

His hand cupped her soft breast, moving so that he could feel the nipple hard in his moist palm.

She tried to breathe normally, but she couldn't. Her hand went to his broad chest and moved involuntarily over the hair-roughened muscles. Her head tilted back, inviting his mouth.

He shifted her back onto the bed, sweeping the pillow out of the way. Slowly, deliberately, he knelt between her soft thighs and pushed them wide apart. His black eyes stabbed down into hers. His breath was audible as he looked down at her with possession.

She shivered as he caressed her with slow, tender movements and watched her reactions.

"Your maidenhead is almost intact," he bit off. "You're going to feel it when I go into you."

"I don't care," she whispered feverishly.

"I do." He moved down over her, catching his weight on one elbow while his hand continued its maddening sweep against the moistness of her body. "I'm going to make you climax. When you do, I'm going inside you."

The blunt statement made her flush, even through the desire that was overwhelming her. Her lips parted on a shocked breath.

"It would have been hard, in any case," he whispered, bending to her breasts. "You're going to be tight, and I'm unusually aroused."

She wondered if she could faint lying down. What he was doing to her body was like slow torture. She opened her legs even more, coaxing him, as the pleasure began to build into something frightening.

Her helpless little cries of pleasure were arousing him intensely. His mouth opened on her breast and his tongue worked at the hard nipple while his hand became insistent on her body.

She was shivering rhythmically now, lifting her hips to encourage him, incite him, to give her pleasure. Her head thrashed on the pillow. Her hands gripped it on either side of her head. She moaned harshly, her teeth clenching, as she started up a spiral of incredible tension.

He lifted his head and looked straight into her eyes, feeling the tension build. "Open your eyes and look at me," he bit off.

She could barely focus. Her body was lifting and falling with every throb of pleasure. She ached for something just out of reach. Her mind was focused on the distant goal that was so very close. She gasped with every touch, her dazed eyes staring into his almost fearfully.

"Tell me when," he whispered roughly, unblinking. His own heart was shaking him. He felt his body throbbing with insistence.

The words didn't make sense, and then they did. She was reaching, reaching, almost there, almost…there…!

"Oh!" she cried hoarsely as her whole body suddenly convulsed on a wave of pleasure so intense she thought she might die of it.

"Yes," he moaned. He moved suddenly, pushing down, impaling her.

She felt the sharp intrusion, but it was only part of the pleasure, part of the throbbing heat that shook her body.

His lean hands gripped her wrists and his weight crushed her into the mattress as his hips moved roughly, his body penetrating in a fever of anguished need.

She stared into his eyes as she convulsed, seeing his face harden, tighten, his eyes like glittering black diamonds. He was groaning, his body shivering as the rhythm became insistent, urgent, fiercely demanding.

He bent to kiss her bruisingly, his breath mingling with hers in the anguished rush for fulfillment. His body was throbbing in time with hers, his powerful legs trembling as he drove into her.

He lifted his head and looked into her eyes at point-blank range as the rhythm built to utter madness and the sound of the springs was as loud as their rough, frantic breathing.

Suddenly he arched down into her and stilled, his eyes wide and black as his lean body began to convulse.

"Phoebe," he ground out hoarsely. "We're making a

baby," he whispered unsteadily, holding her eyes while the world went blazing into oblivion.

The words made the fever burn even higher. She watched him as satisfaction shook him above her, his face clenched hard, his eyes closing finally in the maelstrom of passion that rocked his own body.

It was beyond imagining. She felt him burst inside her, felt the heat of their passion explode. He cried out and she watched until he blurred in her wide, shocked eyes. She relaxed suddenly, feeling him impale her even farther as he drained the climax of its final weak throbs.

He collapsed into her arms, damp with sweat, shivering in the aftermath, as she was. She held him weakly, tears rolling down her cheeks as she moved involuntarily against his still-aroused body to hold on to the echoes of fulfillment that stabbed into her with exquisite little thrills of pleasure.

He lay over her, feeling her body move. He was awed. No sexual experience of his entire life compared with it. He pushed against her gently, groaning as the pleasure shot through him again.

Her long legs slid over the backs of his, increasing both his potency and his possession.

He lifted his head and looked into her wide eyes. He moved again, watching her face. He realized that he still had her wrists in a death grip. He released them, letting his hands take his weight as they rested on either side of her head. He lifted up deliberately and looked down at their bodies, to where they were still completely joined.

He caught her eyes with his and lifted again, not quite enough to separate them. "Look," he coaxed.

She did…and her breath caught. She'd never dreamed it

would even happen, much less that pain would be the least of her concerns.

"Would you like to tell me again about the wild encounter you had the night you got my clipping?" he asked roughly.

"I did try," she muttered. "He wasn't you. I couldn't."

"Neither could I," he bit off.

She stared up at him in the soft afterglow of satiation. "You were married," she said slowly.

"She loved my brother. She didn't want anyone else. Neither did I. I wanted you, Phoebe. I still do."

"It's been three years!" she cried, astonished.

"Yes, I noticed." He looked down their damp bodies again. "I've had you, and I'm still aroused, can you feel it?"

Her face flamed. "You're…very blunt."

He met her eyes. "Very hard, too," he murmured, moving his hips. He caught his breath as the movement increased what was already an alarming capability.

Phoebe's lips parted.

She was intimidated by him; that would never do. He smiled tenderly. "It won't hurt at all this time," he whispered softly, lifting so that he slid against her in the most arousing sort of way, watching her expression change from apprehension to anticipation.

She looked at him while he moved on her, feeling her body quicken, feeling the pleasure build all over again.

"We didn't use anything," she managed weakly.

"You love children," he said quietly. "So do I." He pushed down against her in a long, slow thrust that made her shiver with pleasure. "I want to make a baby. I didn't say it to bring your blood up. Although it did, didn't it, honey?" he whispered, bending to kiss her with lingering pleasure.

"It brought my blood up, too." He nibbled her lower lip. His breath was coming roughly now, echoing the sharp, hungry rhythm of his body on hers. "I've never made love like this, Phoebe," he whispered unsteadily. "I've never felt anything like this!"

"Neither…have I," she whispered, arching suddenly. "Good…heavens!" she exclaimed as the movement suddenly convulsed her.

"Your body is sensitized, like mine," he breathed into her mouth. "If I'm slow enough, I may be able to give you an orgasm."

She didn't answer. She couldn't. The pleasure had her on the rack. He looked into her eyes as his movements became slower and deeper and more powerful. Her face was flushed, her eyes wild, her body answering his in a silence thick with delight.

All at once, her mouth opened wide and she gasped. She'd thought the pleasure had reached a peak, but it was only a plateau. She hung there, helpless, terrified that he might stop moving. Her small hands gripped his wrists as she arched, pleading wordlessly.

"I'm not going to stop, baby," he whispered, reassuring her. "You're not quite there, even yet, are you? Lift up. That's it. Lift up. Do it again. Do it again. Yes!" One lean hand went under her, to catch her thigh and jerk her hips up into his. She was gasping helplessly, her eyes blind, as she grasped for fulfillment.

"Jeremiah!" she cried out, her voice throbbing with mingled fear and delight.

"Yes, baby," he whispered urgently, pushing against her intently. "Yes!"

She stiffened suddenly, her eyes stabbing into his as she stopped breathing, her teeth clenched, her face fiery.

"Beautiful," he whispered while he could, fascinated with the joy he saw almost tangibly in her face. And then the pleasure took him, just as fervently as it was taking her. He groaned harshly, his body going rigid as he convulsed.

It was almost pain. He felt her body so close that they seemed to share the same breath, the same soul. He wanted to watch her, but he couldn't. His eyes were closed tight as he savored every silvery throb of the delight that sent him as rigid as steel above her.

Blinding light flashed behind his eyes. Finally he collapsed on her, spent, wrung-out. He could barely breathe. Under him, he felt her own ragged breathing, her frantic heartbeat. He rolled off her and pulled her to him, lying on his side with one powerful leg thrown over hers while they fought to get a whole breath of air.

"I can't believe you let me do that," he whispered shakily.

"I can't believe I felt that," she whispered back, shivering. "I thought I was going to die."

His hands smoothed over her soft skin. "Me, too," he murmured. "I've never experienced this kind of passion before."

Her face flushed and became radiant, but just as soon, her expression fell. "You aren't saying that because we just made love?" she asked suspiciously. "I read this article about how men say a lot of things they don't mean in bed."

His eyebrows lifted and he smiled, amused. "Probably some men do. I never have." His hand smoothed over her cheek. "But we do have a new complication now."

She grimaced, searching his dark eyes. "Neither of us

was thinking about how complicated the lack of protection could be."

"That's exactly what I mean." He groaned silently as he recalled what he'd said to her in the heat of passion. At the time, creating a child had been irresistible. Now, it felt as if he'd railroaded her into an intimacy she might not have wanted, subconsciously. She wasn't the sort of woman to have a termination. She'd have the child and resent it, and him, for the rest of his life. He felt guilty.

She traced his wide, firm mouth with her forefinger. He was beautiful to her. She loved looking at him, touching him. She was keenly aware of the powerful lines of his body so closely pressed to hers, of the lazy strength of it. She felt safe with him.

She thought of his child growing inside her, and her breath caught. She wanted to tell him that, but all of a sudden, he seemed remote. He'd withdrawn from her without moving away an inch.

She moved her hand into the hair at his shoulder, to bring him back to her.

He smiled and tested the soft texture of her hair even while her own hands slid into the thick, cool strands of his long, black hair.

"I love your hair," she said softly. "I always have."

"I loved yours long," he replied.

She smiled sadly. "I cut it the day I got the newspaper clipping."

His eyes closed briefly. "I couldn't think at all, the day I mailed it." He drew in a long breath as he studied her oval face. "Phoebe, there was more to it than just Isaac dying. He died running from the police. He'd been in trouble with the law for years. He drank to excess and didn't know what he was doing until he was arrested. The day he died, he'd just robbed a liquor store and seriously injured the owner of the store. He'd have done time, if he'd lived."

"Your poor mother!" she groaned. "And with a weak heart, too."

"A violent death is the worst kind for any family to cope with," he replied. "I went a little crazy. That's why I didn't write to you." His eyes mirrored his sadness. "What happened broke my heart. I loved my brother."

"I would have understood, if I'd just known what was going on," she replied heavily.

He smiled faintly. "I realize that now…years too late."

"I really tried to date other men," she added. "But when it came right down to it, I didn't trust men anymore. I'd given up on a happy, shared future when I came to Chenocetah. I planned to be a career woman and live for my work."

"So I gathered, when I finally located you," he replied with a rueful smile. "But knowing where you were didn't help much. I couldn't find a good excuse for coming to see you. Then fate arranged it for me."

"Yes. Everything fell into place like links in a chain. You know, I really resented Joseph at first," she confessed.

"I knew that," he replied quietly.

"It didn't last long," she murmured, remembering little arms clinging around her neck. "He snuggled close to me and refused to let go. I was hooked."

He laughed. "He has a way with women—Tina can tell you that."

"He looks a lot like you," she noted. "Only someone who knew for sure wouldn't think he was your own son.

Are you going to tell him about his father, when he's old enough?"

"Yes," he said. "Isaac wasn't a bad person," he added. "He was just weak when it came to alcohol. He was one of those people who become violent when they've had too much. He started drinking when he was barely in his teens. We tried hard to get him away from it, but we couldn't. We all felt guilty when he died the way he did."

"You can't fight fate," she said absently. "I lost my grandparents two years ago in a train wreck in Europe, of all things. They'd gone on vacation. It was really hard for Derrie and me."

"I didn't know that."

She searched his dark eyes. "I didn't know about Isaac or your mother."

He returned the curious, intent stare. She looked like a woman who'd just discovered the meaning of pleasure. He was glad that he'd given her that. But now he wondered if her surrender had been desire…or just curiosity. She was overwhelmed with the newness of intimacy. That didn't mean she loved him, or that she wanted a traditional marriage. Hadn't she just said that her goal was to become an independent career woman?

He stared past her, feeling uneasy all over again. He grimaced and let go of her, getting to his feet. "Not much sense in going to bed. It's eight in the morning. We'd better have a quick shower and get out of here. You can have the bathroom first."

She'd almost suggested that they shower together, but he was standing with his back to her and he didn't turn when she got out of bed. With a worried sigh, she went toward the bathroom.

IT WAS A SILENT DRIVE to the museum. The intimacy of the past hour might never have happened. It had spoiled something between them. She'd thought it would bring them closer, but it had split them apart instead.

He pulled up at the door of the museum. "I need everything you can get me on the man who sold you the effigy figure," he said. "The notes helped, but I need as much information as you can get from the other museum personnel if they saw him."

"I'll talk to the directors for you, too," she told him. "One more thing. That woman who came here was tall and elegant and blond. She was wearing designer shoes and a designer purse—Aigner," she added, naming a famous French designer. "She had a mole on her right cheek, just above her upper lip. She had a Southern accent, not thick but noticeable, and dark blue eyes."

"You're a wonder," he said gently.

She managed a smile. "Not really. I just have a fairly decent memory." She searched his eyes intently. "You be careful. This is getting dangerous."

"You're the one I'm worried about," he countered. "Wait here until I pick you up. If I can't make it, I'll ask Drake to take you to the motel. The local police are going to step up patrols through the area as well. We've got a would-be murderer on the loose. I don't believe he'll quit."

"Neither do I," she replied. She wanted to say more; she wanted to ask how he really felt about what they'd done. But in the end, she was too shy. She smiled and got out of the car. "See you around, FBI," she teased.

"You, too, 'Indiannetta Jones,'" he murmured with a forced smile.

She laughed all the way into the museum.

BUT WHEN SHE WAS BY HERSELF, it felt like the end of the world. Cortez acted as if nothing had happened. Were all men like that? Were they truly unconcerned once they'd fed a physical hunger? Or did Cortez just have a guilty conscience, because he knew now that she'd been innocent?

Worrying about it, she decided, was only going to increase her gray hairs, without solving anything. She turned on her computer and printed out the telephone numbers of the museum's board of directors. She was going to get everything she could about the mysterious man who'd sold them the effigy figure. If there was anything that she hadn't already given Cortez. Perhaps he was only asking to keep her busy, so she wouldn't worry. It did the job.

Cortez, meanwhile, was in Jeb Bennett's office.

"I can't believe Walks Far is in the hospital," Bennett said wearily, when he was informed about the events of the night before. "He's a good worker, honest and loyal. Who would want to hurt him? And why?"

"That's what I was hoping you could tell me," Cortez said quietly. He was wearing a suit and his hair was in a neat ponytail. He looked the part of an FBI agent.

Bennett leaned back in his chair. "I'm afraid I don't know a lot about him," he said tersely, and didn't meet the other man's eyes. "He's worked for me for several years. I've never had a complaint."

Cortez was noticing something he vaguely remembered from his last visit to Bennett's office. There was a picture in a frame, a pretty blue-eyed, blond woman in an expensive dress. She had a mole on her cheek. What was it Phoebe had said about the mystery woman's appearance?

"Is that your wife?" Cortez asked, nodding toward the frame.

"What? Oh. No. I'm not married," Bennett said with a grimace. "At least, not now. That's my sister, Claudia."

He had to fight not to let show how interested he was in this new possible connection. "Is she in construction, too?" he asked.

Bennett laughed. "Claudia doesn't like getting her hands dirty. She's an art dealer."

An interesting answer, and Bennett looked as if he'd said too much and was regretting it. Cortez noted that Bennett hadn't owned up to the fact that Walks Far had spent time in prison or that he was married to Claudia. "How is Walks Far?" he asked quickly, as if to divert his guest.

"He's still unconscious," Cortez told him. "Head injuries are tricky. If he dies, we'll be looking for a murder suspect."

Bennett sat up straight, looking uneasy.

Cortez's dark eyes narrowed. This man was involved in the case. He leaned forward. "If you know anything, and you don't tell me, you could end up charged as an accessory. It carries a stiff penalty."

Bennett's dark eyes met his and he hesitated.

Before he could speak, Cortez's cell phone began to vibrate insistently in his pocket. He pulled it up and flipped it open. "Cortez."

It was Alice Jones. "I've got a preliminary report on that stuff I got from the victim's shirt. It's definitely brain matter. There was some dirt as well. It's from another cave, not the one we were in last night. I got a biologist out of bed and in front of a microscope to analyze it for me. The dirt is from a living cave, a wet one—and a cave with bats."

Cortez's heart jumped. Yardley's cave. He was certain of it. "Jones, you're worth your weight in pizzas! Get your team together and meet me in the parking lot at the corner of Harper and Lennox streets. Got that?" he added, directing them to a neutral point so that he didn't have to speak in front of Bennett. He didn't trust the man.

"Got it, boss," Alice said, and hung up.

"I've got to go," Cortez said, rising and shaking hands. "It looks as if we've got a break in the case."

Bennett seemed to hesitate. "What is it?" he asked suddenly.

"I'll be in touch," Cortez said without answering the question. He left the office deep in thought.

Once he was out of sight, Bennett picked up the phone.

AT THE MUSEUM, PHOEBE was dodging curious looks from Marie. She was certain that nobody knew she'd been alone with Cortez that morning, but it seemed as if Marie had some idea of it. Finally she decided that the best way to deal with the problem was to meet it head-on.

She called Marie into her office and closed the door. "You've been giving me strange looks all morning," she told the woman. "What's wrong?"

"I wasn't sure how to mention this," Marie confessed, sinking onto a chair with something like relief.

Phoebe felt uncomfortable. She was old-fashioned, in her way, even though she'd given in to a three-year starvation diet of unfulfilled desire for Cortez. But she didn't want to share that with the community at large.

Marie grimaced and averted her eyes. "You know that Drake's my cousin."

"Yes, of course I do," Phoebe replied, sidetracked by the statement.

"Well, it's just..." She grimaced again. "He was kissing

Cortez's cousin Tina last night. Really kissing her, you know?" She looked at Phoebe with compassion and regret.

Phoebe's eyebrows arched and she almost slumped in relief. "Was that what you didn't want to tell me?"

"Yes. I'm very sorry. I know that Drake paid you a lot of attention, and I know that he was really attracted to you…!"

Phoebe held up a slender hand and smiled with pure relief. "I like Drake a lot," she said. "He's a wonderful man. But I'm not in love with him, Marie."

"Thank goodness!" Marie said, pressing a hand to her ample bosom. She laughed breathlessly. "I hated having to tell you, but I didn't want you to find it out by accident. I think he's got a case on Cortez's cousin."

"I think he has, too," Phoebe replied. "She's nice. You should see her with Cortez's nephew," she added softly. "She loves kids."

"Is she involved with anybody, do you know?" Marie persisted.

"She was dating a policeman in Asheville," she replied, "but just between you and me, I think he's out of the running. Drake is special."

Marie beamed. "I think so, too, even if he is my cousin." She cocked her head. "I heard something about a man getting hurt and sent to the hospital last night."

Phoebe wasn't certain how much Cortez would want her to say to an outsider. She only smiled. "Did you?" she asked.

Marie cocked an eyebrow. "You're not talking, right? I tried to pump Drake for information, and he said just about the same thing. But another one of my cousins said you and Cortez drove out of town in the early morning hours, and that there was a whole group of police and sheriffs' cars at a cave on a building site close to here."

"You have too many cousins, Marie," Phoebe said firmly. "And I need to get to work, or we'll both be out of jobs."

Marie chuckled. "Fair enough." She got up, waved, and went to work.

Phoebe let out a sigh of relief. At least nobody was speculating about her and Cortez. Not yet, at least. It was a secret she didn't want to share just yet.

THE NEXT DAY CORTEZ DROVE to the Yardley building site ahead of his crime-scene unit's big van, Drake's squad car, and a local police officer in his own vehicle. It was going to attract attention, but that couldn't be helped. He had a cold feeling in his gut that this was going to be a second crime scene.

They crossed the small bridge and drove down the rutted path into the woods that led to the small rock ledge overhang. The stream could be heard gurgling in the distance.

Cortez waved the team back as he bent to look at a fresh tire track. It was missing a vertical stripe, just like the suspect vehicle he'd tracked before. He indicated it to Alice Jones and her team before they walked carefully around it and toward the entrance of the cave.

The sun was high and it was warm for a late November day in the mountainous region. He didn't see anything suspicious, but as they moved closer to the cave, his stomach clenched. He ground his teeth together as a faint, unmistakable odor hit his nostrils. He knew what it was.

So did Alice Jones. She exchanged a grim look with him. He stood aside to let her go first, indicating for the other officers to follow in his footsteps.

Only a few feet inside the overhang, in the damp cold of the wide cave, a pair of shoes came into view. They were attached to a man who was lying in the dirt.

The man was dead.

11

THE VICTIM WAS LYING facedown; half of his face was disfigured, the rest was bloody. His own mother wouldn't have known him. There was blood around his head in a pool on the dusty ground. Splatters of blood and specks of gray tissue were visible on rocks to one side of the victim, far above the dead man. There was one visible shoe print, and brush marks where several others had been erased. The tall, thin man was dressed in an expensive suit and leather shoes that looked equally expensive. His arms were bent on either side of his head. He was stiff. Alice Jones was working deftly to arrive at an approximate time of death. Nobody paid a lot of attention to what she was doing. Death was disturbing, even to experienced investigators.

The medical examiner hadn't yet arrived. Tanner, one of Cortez's FBI crime unit guys, was walking around taking photographs of the body and the immediate surroundings.

He had a camcorder in a case sitting on his car hood, which would be used as a backup to document the crime scene. Alice had already put out several colorful evidence cards near trace evidence for him to photograph. One uniformed officer from the local police department was already hard at work under Alice Jones's direction, putting down wooden stakes around the crime scene, with a ball of twine standing by to attach to them. Another officer was stationed a few yards away to preserve the integrity of the primary crime scene. Alice herself approached with a flat-mouthed shovel and a bag of other smaller tools, such as trowels, brushes, and tweezers. She looked wan and half-out of humor.

"Where's the rest of the team?" Cortez asked, stunned. "I only see one other FBI agent."

"It's Thanksgiving Day, didn't you notice?" she muttered, putting down her shovel. "Everybody has families except me and Tanner. But his specialty is photography, not forensic medicine. So here I am, all alone, except for Officer Dane over there keeping potential visitors away, and Officer Parker here, who isn't even the homicide detective. He's robbery."

"He's all they gave you?" Cortez asked, aghast.

"His department celebrates Thanksgiving, too, Cortez, so he and Officer Dane were all they could spare," she drawled. "Lucky you, that I don't have a husband or a lover or somebody I could claim to get me a day off!"

"Point taken," he said on a sigh.

Jones relented. "Sorry," she murmured sheepishly. "I'm just overwhelmed, that's all. I'm used to having at least one trained criminologist to work with me. This is going to take time and expertise."

"Pity we don't have a forensic anthropologist," Cortez murmured.

Alice Jones gave him a smug grin. "I'm taking internet courses in forensic dentition," she said helpfully.

"Jones!" he exclaimed, brightening. "You're a wonder!"

She chuckled. "Nice to be appreciated, boss. Tanner and Parker and I will get busy." She hesitated. "But, you know, if you could get that anthropologist friend of yours back out here, it would be a help," she said seriously. "She said she'd done forensics, and she probably knows more about excavating than I'll have time to learn. This is a big job for just one technician." She glanced at him. "Is she squeamish?"

"I'll go ask her," Cortez said.

"I'll recommend you for a raise," she promised.

"It won't do any good," he said with a heartfelt sigh. "Our budget's already showing bone."

"It was just a hopeful thought," she said. "Pay no mind to the fact that I'm wearing four-year-old shoes and I can't afford to replace my glasses."

"Tell the SAC," he advised, meaning the special agent in charge of their unit. "But don't expect much. He just said that his son was applying for a second scholarship because their college fund had to be spent to make mortgage payments."

Jones stood up straight. "We don't need to know if monkeys sweat!" she announced belligerently.

He and Tanner, Parker and Officer Dane turned and stared at her.

She scowled. "Well, that's where our bureau budget's going, along with lots of other departments' budgets, on grants like that for studies that nobody cares about except a few researchers," she muttered. "Congress has no sense of proportion."

"I nominate you to do collective bargaining for our unit," Cortez said after a minute. "Hands?" he called loudly.

Tanner raised his. But so did the local police officers.

"Hey, you're not FBI," he called to the nonunit personnel.

"Are you sure?" Officer Parker asked wistfully. "I could check with my chief and see if he'd lie for me. I haven't had a raise for two years!"

Cortez shook his head. He gave the victim one last glance, scowling, as his mind returned to the gravity of the situation. You had to have a sense of humor in forensic work, he thought absently, or you'd go mad at the things you had to see. "I wonder who he is?" he asked aloud.

"He's victim number two in case file 45728," Jones offered helpfully.

He gave her a speaking glance and went to get Phoebe.

ALTHOUGH IT WAS THANKSGIVING, Phoebe had taken pity on foreign tourists who wanted to tour the museum. Phoebe was gathering her things and Marie was just finishing their tour when Cortez walked into the office.

The shock of seeing him after what had happened, after the way they'd parted, was like a body-blow. She couldn't quite get her breath. Little ripples of pleasure worked along her nerve endings just at the sight of him.

He was having similar problems, but he was able to hide his reaction. He'd spent a lifetime learning to conceal his deeper feelings. It helped in situations like this.

He rammed his hands into his pockets. "Are you squeamish?" he asked without preamble.

"Define squeamish," she invited.

"Can you look at a man who's missing the front of his face and a small area behind the cerebellum and help Alice Jones excavate around the body to procure trace evidence?"

"You want me to look at a dead body?" she asked, wide-eyed.

"Well...yes," he began hesitantly.

She was out of her desk, with her purse on her shoulder, headed out the door while he was catching his breath.

"Come on!" she called to him. "The trail will get cold!"

He followed her out to her car, past a curious Marie.

"Marie, you'll have to take care of business," Phoebe told her, grinning. "I'm going to be a consultant for the FBI!"

"Can't I come along and consult, too?" Marie asked, glancing miserably toward a special group of tourists who were muttering about the labeling of one of the exhibits.

"Sorry, only one escape per staff member per day," Phoebe murmured, grinning. "Close up as soon as our guests leave. I'll call you later."

She got in on the passenger side of Cortez's car and fastened her seat belt.

He slid in under the wheel and did the same, with a wry glance at her. "And I thought I'd have to coax you."

"Are you kidding? I've always been fascinated by forensics," she replied. "I did several courses of it in college and I've been an occasional consultant for local law enforcement when they found skeletal remains. I've even watched an autopsy."

He ground his teeth together. "I have, too, but not with much enthusiasm."

"Do you know who the dead man is?" she asked.

"No, but if you ask Jones anything about him, she'll tell you that he's male and dead."

She shook her head, smiling. "That's our Alice."

"He's not pretty, Phoebe," he told her.

She glanced at him. "Death never is," she said. "A GBI senior agent from Georgia told me once that how he gets through the grisly parts is remembering that he's the last advocate for the deceased. It's up to him to make sure the perpetrator is caught and punished for his crime. I like to think of it like that."

"So do I," he replied gently.

THEY DIDN'T TALK MUCH on the way to the crime scene. Phoebe was remarkably shy with him. He was feeling guilty about the way things had happened between them. He'd never meant to rush her into a physical relationship with him.

He pulled up near the crime scene and got out first, motioning for Phoebe to follow in his footsteps. He didn't want to contaminate evidence.

Leaving her purse in the car, Phoebe moved behind Cortez into the cave where the murder victim was lying. She hesitated, just for a second, at her first sight of the dead man. But just as quickly, she forced herself to move forward.

"Thanks for coming," Alice Jones said wearily, pausing in her slow excavation of the area around the body. It was called platforming, and each thin layer of soil had to be moved, sifted through a wire-mesh-bottomed box, and every bit and piece bagged and labeled. It was time-consuming work and, as the day began to heat up, sweaty work as well. "I really appreciate the rest of my team, now that I don't have them with me!"

"No problem," Phoebe replied. "Hand me a trowel and tell me how you want me to proceed."

"Take a look at the victim first, if you would," Alice said, directing her to the single point of entry they'd agreed on to protect the crime scene. "From the angle of the wound, I've assumed that he was shot from behind while he was bending over. There's blood splattered on the rocks about where his head would have been in a stooping posture. The wound is small behind, large in front, and the entry hole is small and precise."

"A handgun," Phoebe agreed, frowning as she studied the wound. "And he was shot from above and behind."

"More than likely," Alice agreed. "If we knew what caliber, we'd know the ejection pattern and where to look for the shell. It looks to me like one shot, with a high-caliber handgun at close range. I've got Officer Parker looking for the shell casing over there with a metal detector."

That would explain the odd humming sound Phoebe had heard when she entered the cave.

"Okay," Phoebe said, taking off her jacket. "I'm ready when you are."

Alice smiled grimly and handed her a trowel.

IT WAS ARDUOUS AND DRAWN-OUT, processing the crime scene. Phoebe had done excavations for years, but the dead body unnerved her. It was in the midrange of rigor mortis, and just beginning to bloat in the heat of the day. There was a faint, sickeningly sweet smell coming off the victim.

Alice was examining the body for PMI, or a rough estimate of time of death. "I'd say he's been out here from twelve to eighteen hours," she told Cortez absently, "considering the progress of rigor and internal body temperature. Once we autopsy him, we can be more precise, but I'd stand by that estimate."

"That means he was killed sometime yesterday," Cortez agreed.

"Probably last night," Alice added. "I've already checked his internal temperature," she murmured, glancing dryly at her colleagues, who'd looked away while she did it. "Considering that the body loses one to one and a half degrees of temperature for every hour after death, that fits the approximate time frame I've concocted. He died about 11:00 p.m. yesterday, give or take an hour or two considering the weather report for last night. It was about fifteen degrees below the present. I'll check with the weather guys at NOAA and get a graph and temperature readings for the area before I file my report."

"Pack him up and have the local funeral home send an ambulance out for him. They can hold him until he can be sent to the state crime lab for analysis," Cortez told her. "If we're lucky, the mortician will let you take some latent prints and DNA samples for our own lab, along with the local coroner."

"With the backup at HQ, it's not going to be easy to get immediate results," Alice reminded him.

"Now, I know you're on a first-name basis with the lab, Alice," Cortez coaxed. "And didn't you date one of the new assistants up there?"

She cleared her throat. "Actually, boss, I knocked him over a table in the cafeteria. I don't think mentioning my name will get us ahead of the queue."

Everybody looked at her.

She flushed. "It wasn't deliberate. He pulled out my chair

for me and I tripped over my own feet and he went flying into a dish of mashed potatoes and gravy."

"What did you do?" Phoebe asked, aghast.

"I got up and ran for my life," she confessed, blushing even more. "I don't think I'm cut out for romance."

"Good thing, because you're the best forensic scientist I've got," Cortez said with a smile.

She grinned. "About that raise…?"

"Get to work."

She saluted him, winked at Phoebe, and bent back to her task.

THERE WERE TWO PIECES of trace evidence that raised Cortez's eyebrows when Alice showed them to him. One was a long blond hair. Another was minute traces of face powder on the man's lapel when they turned him over in order to tuck him into a body bag.

"You think a woman was with him," Cortez mused.

Alice nodded. "I don't know that the trace evidence is going to give you a name, but it does indicate that there's a witness of some sort. At least, a person who was with him before he was killed."

"That's helpful," Cortez said. His eyes narrowed. He was remembering the photo of Bennett's sister—she had long blond hair. Her husband, Walks Far, was still in the hospital unconscious. There had to be a connection of some sort. But he didn't say it out loud.

The ambulance came and zipped the victim up in a body bag for transport. Alice went to her van to follow along to the funeral home, with a perfunctory wave toward Cortez and Phoebe. Tanner hitched a ride with her back to his motel. The policemen wrapped up and left as well. Phoebe had already phoned the museum and told Marie to let everyone go home and lock up. There wouldn't be anybody there on Thanksgiving Day anyway.

Cortez opened the passenger door of his car for Phoebe and waited until she was buckled up before he closed it.

She glanced at him uncomfortably as he got in and fastened his own seat belt. "Do you ever feel, well, dirty after you process a crime scene?"

He smiled gently. "Every time," he confessed. He lifted an eyebrow. "Not quite as blasé about it as you thought, are you?"

She returned the smile, a little sheepishly. "Not quite," she agreed. She folded her arms over her chest and stared through the windshield as Cortez drove down the highway back toward Chenocetah. "He looked so helpless."

"Victims always do," he replied. "That's why we work so hard to solve crimes. You never get the image of the victim out of your mind, but it eases the frustration when you can at least make an arrest."

"It's so complicated," she murmured. "First an anthropologist shows up and announces that he's found a Neanderthal skeleton. Then he's killed, and I'm shot at, and then that man at the construction company is knocked flat. Now here's another murder victim, who has a blond hair and face powder all over him." She looked at him. "How do you put that together?"

"With trace evidence and questioning." He stopped at a traffic light just as they reached the outskirts of town.

"You have a suspect," she mused.

He started, and then chuckled. "You're perceptive."

"That woman who came to see me at the museum was

blond," she recalled. "I don't remember about face powder, but she had long blond hair and a mole."

He nodded, stepping on the gas when the light changed.

She studied him hungrily, enjoying his profile, her heart pounding as she remembered the feel of his mouth on hers.

That intense scrutiny caught his attention. He glanced at her with soft, quiet eyes. "Careful," he cautioned softly. "It's been a long, dry spell, but my memory can reach back to that afternoon at your cabin with painful ease."

Her face colored softly. "It was…incredible."

He nodded, his jaw tautening as he averted his face. "And we're in the middle of a murder investigation."

"No time for hanky-panky," she translated with a soulful sigh.

He laughed in spite of himself. "Besides, it's Thanksgiving Day."

She grimaced. "I forgot! I have a turkey. I was going to cook it and offer you and Tina and Drake dinner today."

His eyebrows arched. "What a nice idea." His dark eyes twinkled. "Should I bring some maize and venison?" he added deeply.

She glared at him. "We are not doing the Pilgrim play," she pointed out. "Besides, you're a member of a native Plains tribe, not of the Eastern tribes who mingled with the British immigrants." She frowned. "In fact, I seem to recall that a number of the early settlers couldn't grow crops so they stole food from the native people…"

"Point one," he began lazily, "Native people don't place much emphasis on possessions. We share everything, including food. Greed is a concept we don't embrace. Point two, the Comanche nation is an offshoot of the Shoshone nation. But we consider that any member of our various bands is family. Family is the most important concept we have."

"Family should be the most important," she murmured, smiling at him. "It defines who we are." She gave him a long, quiet scrutiny. "You've had to fight for your identity all your life, haven't you?"

He nodded. "Self-esteem comes hard to members of a minority race. The statistics speak for themselves. Education reinforces our sense of worth. It's why my father and many other members of our community fight so hard for programs that help defeat poverty."

She nodded. "Activism has brought native people a long way. Especially political activism."

He laughed. "Don't get me started. My father is forever hosting seminars on how to lobby for funds for community outreach programs. He's a master planner."

He paused at a stop sign outside town and turned to glance at her with warm affection. But his dark eyes were sad all at once.

"What's wrong?" she wondered aloud.

"I was thinking about family. About what I sacrificed for mine. I can't regret it, because Joseph's life was worth everything. But it was a long, lonely three years, Phoebe," he told her.

The same pain and loneliness and sadness in his eyes were reflected in her own. She leaned her head back against the headrest and stared openly at him. "I hated you for a long time," she said. "I never dreamed that you hadn't sold me out deliberately. I'm a little ashamed of that. I should have known that it would have taken something drastic to change your mind."

He reached out and caught her small hand in his big

one. "We didn't know each other well enough," he replied quietly. "A few conversations, a few kisses, and we went our separate ways. You couldn't have known how seriously I took those things. I wanted to tell you. But Isaac was already in trouble, and I knew a family crisis was looming. I had high hopes for us. Fate got in the way."

Her fingers tangled hungrily in his. "I would have waited forever, if I'd known—!" she began, but her voice broke on the painful memory.

He threw the car out of gear, slipped her seat belt, and pulled her close. His mouth ground into hers hungrily. He groaned with repressed passion, his mouth opening, demanding on hers.

She shivered as her arms closed around his neck. "I'm on fire," she choked.

"Yes." He crushed her against his chest, enveloping her, as his mouth slid down her hot throat. He shuddered.

"Take me home, Jeremiah," she whispered brokenly. "Right now."

He wanted to argue. It was a bad idea. But she reached up and kissed him with anguished passion. He didn't have the strength to resist her. With unsteady hands, he put the car back in gear and turned it around in the road, to head it back with speed toward her cabin.

He didn't let go of her hand the whole way.

Her heart ran away as she recalled the exquisite satisfaction his lean, powerful body had given her. He was every dream she'd ever had, come true.

He wasn't blind to the danger, however, and his eyes were intent on the road as he drove down the long dirt road that led to her cabin. There wasn't another vehicle in sight. So far, so good. He needed to be working on his investigation. But it was Thanksgiving, after all, and he'd worked all day. A little recreation was in order, although he couldn't bring himself to think of Phoebe in those terms. What he found with her in bed was almost sacred.

He pulled up behind her cabin and cut off the engine. His body was taut, but his mind was still working overtime.

She studied him hungrily. "I went back to that café in Charleston every day, hoping I'd see you again," she said huskily. "And then, the very last day, there you were."

His eyes flashed. "I did the same thing, totally against my will. There were so many reasons why I didn't need to get involved with you."

She smiled up at him. "I know. None of them seemed to matter, though, in the end."

His chest rose and fell heavily. "We still have obstacles," he stated.

"Everyone has obstacles, Jeremiah," she reminded him. "But considering what the last three years of my life have been like, I'd rather have the obstacles."

He reached out and traced her lips with his lean forefinger. "Yes. So would I." He hesitated. "But you still don't know much about men."

"You're in a perfect position to teach me everything I need to know," she pointed out.

He looked down at her blouse, where two hard little peaks were evident. She wanted him. He recalled without hesitation the way her breasts felt under his mouth, the way they looked when he'd almost had her in the bed in his motel room.

Her hands went to the buttons. She undid them, her breath rustling in her throat, and then slipped the front clasp of her bra. She pulled it open, baring her breasts to his eyes.

"God in heaven, Phoebe," he ground out.

She unfastened her seat belt and moved toward him, pulling his mouth down to the soft, scented flesh. His lips opened on the hard peak of one breast, his tongue rubbing hungrily against it. She arched up to the pleasure and moaned huskily.

His arms riveted her to him while he fed on the softness of her body. His mind barely worked at all.

"Inside," he said roughly. "Right now."

HE BARELY REMEMBERED closing and locking the door behind them as she led the way into the bathroom. He closed it and deftly undressed her between hot, hungry kisses. He guided her hands to his shirt and tie and kissed her while she returned the favor.

Torrid minutes later, he drew her into the shower with him, almost bursting as they soaped each other in a fever of desire. It was all he could do to rinse and dry them, before the kisses became overwhelming and the need near bursting in his overheated body.

He drew her into bed with him, their hair still damp, because he knew he'd never manage time to dry it.

She wrapped her long legs over the backs of his thighs and arched up to him as he penetrated her with one soft, tender thrust of his lean hips. He caught his breath at the ease of his passage.

So did she. The heat of the encounter was like a throb of delight. She gasped out loud as she lifted to him again, her body open to his eyes, her shivering need so evident that it made him wild.

He spread her legs farther apart, his eyes dark and glittering in the soft semidarkness of her bedroom. The only sounds that managed to be heard above their furious heart-beats and the glide of flesh against sheets was the creak of the bedsprings as he thrust quickly into her receptive body.

He groaned, shuddering as the pleasure began to demand satisfaction. His lean hands caught her wrists and slammed them to the mattress on either side of her thrashing head.

"You're…killing me!" she sobbed, her eyes as wild as her body.

"We'll die together," he ground out. "Look into my eyes. Don't close yours. Look. Look!"

Her mouth opened on a feverish cry as he drove deeply into her, his body taut as drawn rope, his lips a thin line in his anguished drive for fulfillment.

She arched up to him, sobbing, as the furious movements of his hips teased her body into an urgent demand for satisfaction. Her nails bit into his back, clawing, digging into his flesh. She cried out helplessly, her eyes widening while his body crushed down into hers again and again.

His lean hand caught her upper thigh and clasped it hard enough to bruise as he finally found the rhythm and the pressure that made the pleasure explode in both their bodies.

"Don't…stop…don't…stop…don't…stop!" she sobbed, clinging to him as sweat drowned her heated body in moisture.

He poised just above her, his eyes black with passion, and then he drove into her with the last of his strength, his eyes still biting into hers at point-blank range as she suddenly convulsed under him and cried out.

He stiffened, his powerful body buckled over her. He groaned harshly and fell on her, crushing her into the mattress as he shuddered uncontrollably.

"Phoebe," he cried out at her ear, his voice deep and throbbing, like his body inside hers. "Phoebe…baby…baby!"

Her legs curled over his and she shuddered again as the pleasure bit into her, almost painful in its satiation.

Her arms wound around his damp back and she clung to him as they shivered deliciously in the aftermath of ecstasy, in a throbbing, sweet, hungry silence.

He shivered again and started to lift himself, but she pulled him back down.

"No," she sobbed at his ear, moving helplessly. "Please don't…please…I'm not…through…!"

He caught his weight on his forearms and lifted his head, looking into her wide, frantic eyes as he moved on her, smiling even through the exhaustion as he watched her experience pleasure in endless little spasms.

"Yes, it's good, isn't it?" he whispered, his eyes drinking in her satisfaction. "A woman's body is capable of endless climax," he added, shifting his hips suddenly so that she stiffened and sobbed. "But I can give you more than that. I can give you another orgasm…."

He shifted again, roughly, his body suddenly an instrument that he played like a priceless treasure. He lifted her to a level of pleasure that she had never experienced. She was rigid, her mouth open, her eyes open almost in horror as he took her right up the spiral into ecstasy. She cried out in a voice she didn't even recognize, and then cried endlessly when the shattering delight fell away in seconds.

She sobbed into his throat and he held her, comforted her, in the heavy silence.

"It wasn't like this before," she tried to put it into words. "I was scared!"

He kissed her wet eyelids closed. "And this is only the beginning," he whispered. "We've barely begun."

She drew back, her eyes seeking his. She was still shivering. "Really?"

"Really." He bent and kissed her tenderly. "But we have to stop for now."

"Why?" she asked, anguished.

He smiled indulgently. "When I pull out of you, it will become immediately clear," he mused wickedly.

His hips lifted, and she ground her teeth together.

"Too much of even a good thing," he said when they were lying side by side, "can be overkill. See what I mean?"

She grimaced. "I didn't realize."

He sighed. "There's something else you didn't realize."

She lifted both eyebrows.

He indicated his body.

It took her a minute to realize why she was looking at him. "Oops," she said.

"Oops is not a name I'd like to give our first child," he informed her with black humor.

12

PHOEBE SAT UP ALONGSIDE him, her body still throbbing faintly with the aftereffects of pleasure. She was shivering, and her hair was still wet. Now, her body was, too, from the incredible heat of their coming together.

He sprawled back on the pillows, his dark eyes possessive and affectionate as he studied her.

"There wasn't time," she began defensively.

His lean hand spread along her soft thigh. He smiled quizzically. "Have I lodged a complaint?" he asked softly. "I only said that I didn't want to call our baby 'Oops.'"

Her heart ran wild. "Are we having one right away, then?"

His eyebrow arched and his expression was purely wicked. "If we keep this up, undoubtedly. I actually had something in my wallet, too."

She made a face. "I was too busy trying to get my clothes off to ask."

He chuckled. "That makes two of us."

She searched over his lean, powerful body with hungry, soft eyes. "It felt…like it."

He lifted an eyebrow.

"Like…making a baby must feel," she faltered, coloring. "I thought, last time, that it couldn't get any better."

His eyes darkened. "I thought that, myself. But we reached a level I've never been to."

"Really?" she whispered, fascinated, because he was far more experienced than she was.

He drew in a long, slow breath as he studied her intensely. "Phoebe…" He paused, looking worried. "It's hard to find the right words…"

"It's all right," she interrupted, anxious in case he was feeling guilty again and trying to back away from commitment. "You don't have to say anything."

His hand caught hers and pulled her down into his arms. But he didn't kiss her. He wrapped her up against him and just held her, his breathing steady and comforting in the minutes that followed.

"When I wrap up this case," he said huskily, "we'll talk."

She nuzzled her cheek against his hair-roughened chest. It was a reprieve, of sorts. He wasn't promising anything. But she knew that he felt something for her, even if it was only desire. Perhaps it was more. "Okay."

His hand smoothed her damp hair. He was feeling things so profound that he couldn't manage to voice them. He hoped she understood. He was almost certain that she did. He felt at peace for the first time in recent years. He stared at the ceiling, unseeing, as the soft weight of her body against him triggered a painful arousal. He groaned.

She felt the tension and sat up, her eyes homing to that part of him that betrayed his innermost thoughts.

Her eyes met his. "I would let you," she said gently.

He sat up and kissed her, fiercely. "Lovers don't inflict deliberate pain on each other," he whispered. He smiled at her. "Thank you. But it's just a reflex." He leaned toward her conspiratorially. "I'm sore, too."

Her eyes widened, brightened. She laughed. "You are?"

"I am." He got up and pulled her up with him, his eyes enjoying her nudity. "So suppose we have another quick shower, put our clothes back on and see if Drake would like to bring Tina and Joseph out here for Thanksgiving dinner?"

She studied him hungrily. "That would be nice."

He bent and kissed her eyelids tenderly. "We're both spent, for the time being. Maybe that isn't a bad thing," he added, his eyes twinkling. "I need to concentrate on business for a few days, instead of your breasts." He glanced at them and groaned. "Do you have any idea how beautiful they are?"

Her eyes laughed. "They're small."

"Bull." He bent and drew his lips over them. "They're perfect. I ache every time I look at them." He laughed suddenly.

"What's funny?"

"I was trying to picture you, three years ago, stripping off your blouse for me."

She flushed. "I was a little prudish back then."

"Not anymore," he said with a grin.

She laughed. "Not anymore." She traced his lips with

her fingertips. Her eyes, as they met his, were dark with remembered pain. "I wanted so badly to lure you up to my motel room after the graduation exercises," she murmured.

"I wanted that, too. But I had a premonition," he added quietly. "No, I don't have my father's gift of precognition. But I had a feeling of utter doom. As it turned out, I was right. I'm sorry that I hurt you so badly," he ground out. "When Drake told me that you'd been suicidal…"

"He said that?" she exclaimed.

"He heard it from Marie," he replied.

"But, I wasn't," she corrected him at once. "Before I came to North Carolina, I took too many pills for a headache and scared Aunt Derrie to death," she added. "But I didn't want to die." She smiled ruefully. "Actually I wanted to live so that I could get even with you," she chuckled. "Revenge kept me going. And then you walked into my office like a stranger."

"It was a bad day," he said.

"For me, too." Her eyes adored him then she grimaced. "If I lost you again…!"

He caught her up in his arms and the sentence died under the hard, hungry pressure of his mouth. "I'll never let you go," he whispered. "Never! When they lay me down in the dark, I'll still be whispering your name…!"

She sobbed, clinging to him, as the kiss grew and grew and finally climaxed, leaving them both weak and shivery. They held each other close, unspeaking, for long minutes until they were finally able to draw apart.

She wiped at the tears in her eyes. He bent and kissed them away. "Don't cry," he whispered tenderly. "I won't ever leave you again. I swear it."

"Don't you get shot and die," she said firmly.

He smiled. “No. I won’t do that, either.”

She smiled back, a little wetly.

He sighed. “I could eat if you feel like cooking. You do the turkey and dressing, and I’ll open all the cans.” He grinned.

“And I thought you were going to offer to make bread.”

He pursed his lips. “I made bread once. My father tried to feed his to the dog, and the dog ran away. I haven’t made bread since.”

“In that case,” she said sweetly, “I’ll get out some cans for you to open!”

DRAKE SHOWED UP WITH Tina and Joseph barely two hours later. Alice Jones arrived at the same time they did, having accepted Cortez’s phoned invitation. He knew she had no family or close friends and she was good company.

That was, until Phoebe invited her into the kitchen to help with the turkey. Cortez sat in the living room with Tina and Joseph and Drake, while the two men exchanged the latest results of their interrogations.

Phoebe had the naked turkey in an aluminum-foil-lined roasting pan, breast side up. She was just putting together the dressing from a messy mixture of biscuits, corn bread, sage and onions in a big bowl, when she happened to glance at her guest.

There was Alice, bent over the turkey, frowning. She had her magnifying glass out and was looking pointedly at the breast area.

“Alice?” Phoebe began slowly.

“Blunt-force trauma to the sternum,” Alice was murmuring to herself. “Entrance wound right here. Bruising. Some tissue loss…”

"Alice, for God's sake, it's a dead turkey!" Phoebe burst out.

Alice gave her a blank stare. "Of course it's dead. I just want to know how it died. I mean, if there was fowl play…" She grinned.

Phoebe groaned aloud and threw a dishcloth at her.

"What's going on in there?" Cortez called from the living room.

"Alice is conducting a postmortem on the turkey!" Phoebe yelled back.

"You're not invited to Christmas dinner, Alice," he threatened.

"Can I help it if there's a dead body in the kitchen?" Alice wailed. "I have to keep my skills honed! Besides," she muttered, scowling at the bird, "I think this bird is a murder victim."

There were louder groans from the living room. Phoebe just laughed as she went back to her dressing.

IT WAS LIKE A BIG FAMILY, Phoebe thought, looking around the table at her guests. Drake was talking nonstop to Cortez, but he seemed to be ignoring Tina. In fact, Tina seemed to be ignoring him, too. She had Joseph in her lap because Phoebe didn't have a high chair, and she was ladeling little bits of cranberry sauce and turkey into his mouth and washing it down with milk.

After dinner, Drake went out onto the front porch. Phoebe followed him, noting that two of the other three adults were in a heated argument over forensic blood-spatter patterns while Tina cuddled Joseph and looked angry.

Drake stood at the end of the porch, glaring at the distant mountains.

"Hey. What's wrong with you?" Phoebe asked gently.

He glanced at her and grimaced. "Tina and I had an argument."

"Why?"

His dark eyes slid over Phoebe quietly. "I just mentioned how much fun you were to be around at the museum, how much you knew about the history of my people. How intelligent you were."

"And?"

"Tina's only got a high-school education," he murmured, "like me, and she doesn't know a lot about history. She's temperamental, too. She'll laugh at something I say one minute, and get her back up the next." His lips made a thin line. "Maybe she should go back to Asheville and marry Mr. Perfect Police Officer. To hear her tell it, he can wrestle sharks and chew up nails."

"Maybe she's trying to make you jealous," she suggested.

He laughed hollowly. "I thought we were on the verge of something good," he said, almost talking to himself. "But she's jealous of you." His eyes narrowed. "Are she and the FBI in there—" he indicated the living room "—close cousins? Or are they distantly related and she's got a flaming crush on him?"

"Why...I don't know," she faltered. "He just said they were cousins." Phoebe's heart jumped uncomfortably. "Why would you think she's got a crush on him?" she hedged.

"Well, she doesn't talk about anybody else, even the policeman in Asheville," he said irritably. "It's Jeremiah this, Jeremiah that. She thinks he's perfect. Whatever I do, he could do it better. That includes driving, talking, making conversation and breathing."

She went closer to him, smiling. "Listen, first days are always hard. Maybe she's feeling you out, you know?"

He reached out and toyed with a strand of her blond hair. "You're a nice woman," he said solemnly. "And I mean that in a nice way. I honestly like you."

She grinned. "I like you, too, Drake."

He smiled back at her. They stood close together on the porch, commiserating.

It was innocent. But to two pair of dark eyes looking through the living-room window, it didn't look innocent at all.

IT GOT WORSE WHEN Cortez received a call from Bennett about Walks Far's condition in the hospital. The Bennett Construction Company foreman was conscious.

"I'll have to go and talk to him," Cortez told Tina after speaking with the man. "We'll need to leave."

"I can't go!" Phoebe said at once, waving her arms at the table and dirty dishes. "I have to clean up here and put the food away."

"I'll wait and drive you back," Drake said easily. "I'm not on call until seven."

"Thanks, Drake," Phoebe said, smiling at him.

Two pair of eyes glared at him. He didn't notice.

Alice Jones saw trouble brewing and gathered up her purse and jacket. "Well, I appreciate lunch, but I'm going, too. I have a report to write about our dead body."

"You're going to write a report on our turkey?" Phoebe exclaimed.

Alice gave her a condescending look. "The murder victim in the cave, Phoebe. It's senseless to write a report on the turkey." She raised an eyebrow. "We just ate all the evidence." She grinned.

Phoebe laughed, shaking her head. "How I've missed you, Alice."

"I know, I have that effect on people," Alice agreed. "There's a medical examiner back in Texas who's crying his eyes out as we speak because I resigned to take this job."

"He has my full sympathy. But you could take the rest of the day off, you know," Phoebe advised. "It's still Thanksgiving."

"I live for my work," Alice said with a grin. "My van's right outside."

"You drove the evidence van here?" Cortez asked, wide-eyed.

"In case I find a dead body, I don't have to go back to the motel for my tools," Alice reminded him. "At the rate we're finding dead bodies lately, that's not really far-fetched," she added with a scowl.

"I'm glad you came, Alice," Phoebe said with a smile. "It was like old times."

"I enjoyed it, too."

"It was nice to meet you," Tina told the woman. She picked up Joseph, who was being cranky. "We'll go, then. Thanks for dinner, Phoebe," she muttered, but without looking at Phoebe.

"You're welcome," Phoebe said, frowning as she looked after the younger woman. She didn't understand Tina's sudden coolness. Drake noticed it and gave Tina a cold look. That only made things worse. She stalked out the door with Joseph fidgeting in her arms. She didn't waste a word on Drake.

Cortez started out behind them. He glanced at Phoebe, and he, too, looked unusually distant.

"Drake, leave her at the motel when you come back into town," he instructed quietly. "We've still got a killer on the loose."

"I'll remember." Drake hesitated. "If you find out anything from Bennett, how about giving me a heads up?" he asked.

"If I find out anything useful," Cortez agreed.

He went out behind Tina and Joseph, fingering his car keys, without a word of goodbye for either of them. He didn't look back.

Phoebe felt sick at her stomach. It was just like last time. In the bedroom, he was every woman's dream of tenderness. But the minute his clothes went back on, he was all business again. She felt as if there was an incredible distance between them.

Drake was feeling something similar.

"Did we just miss something?" he asked as he heard the car and the van start up outside.

"I wonder," Phoebe murmured as she started clearing the table.

CORTEZ WAS BROODING. Only a few hours before, he and Phoebe had been closer than many couples. Their physical attraction only grew. Every time he touched her, it was like starting over again. She was in his blood, in his heart, in his brain. She was part of him. But he'd lost ground, suddenly, and he didn't know why. Phoebe had looked odd when she and Drake came back inside, and the way she'd stared at him had made him feel empty. Had she suddenly discovered feelings for Drake? Had Cortez pushed her into a physical relationship too soon, and now she was regretting it?

"I can't believe I was attracted to that guy," Tina was muttering from the passenger seat. She turned to glance at Joseph in his car seat behind her. "If there's not something going on there, I'm a turnip."

Cortez wasn't paying attention. His eyes were on the road. He didn't like the way Phoebe had looked at Drake. The other man was younger and he'd been around for a while, taking Phoebe to lunch and teaching her to shoot a gun. Just how close were they? And if Phoebe felt something—anything—for Cortez, why was she spending so much time with Drake all of a sudden? Was she regretting her relationship with Cortez? Was she trying to back away and using Drake as a blind? She'd been a virgin. She had principles. He'd seduced her, thinking she was experienced. Did she blame him for that?

"You're very quiet," Tina said.

He shifted in the driver's seat. "I was thinking about the murder victim," he lied. "I still need more background information on Bennett."

"Work, work, work," she grumbled.

"You keep the doors locked," Cortez replied without acknowledging her comment. He stopped the car just in front of their motel rooms. "Don't open them for anyone," he added firmly. "Two people are dead. I don't want to put either of you at risk," he said, watching her lift Joseph from the car seat.

"I'll be careful," she replied. "You be careful, too," she instructed. "You aren't bulletproof."

"I'll see you later."

He waited until they were inside the room before he put the car in gear and drove away.

THE HOSPITAL WAS CROWDED. November was a cold month and viruses and flu were already going around the mountains.

Walks Far was in a room on the second floor. He'd briefly regained consciousness, but only to groan in pain. He wasn't able to answer questions. When Cortez walked in, he startled two people having a whispered, serious conversation. Jeb Bennett of Bennett Construction, and a blond woman with a mole on her cheek. Cortez recognized her immediately as Bennett's sister, Claudia, from the photograph he'd seen in Bennett's office.

Bennett got to his feet, looking oddly guilty. "Cortez, isn't it?" he blurted out, extending his hand. It was cold and clammy when Cortez shook it. "Uh, how are you progressing on the case?"

"We've got a new dead body," Cortez replied. The blond woman, he noted, still sat in her chair, twisting her purse in her well-manicured hands.

"Another...one?" Bennett exclaimed.

"Yes. We found him in a cave with a number of artifacts which we believe are stolen property. I've got a member of my unit checking them out now," Cortez said carefully.

"It's Thanksgiving," Bennett laughed. "You'll never get anybody to work today."

"I've already had a team checking and collecting forensic evidence at the primary crime scene," Cortez said. "In fact, we had an anthropologist at the scene."

"Where did you get one of those on a holiday?" Bennett wanted to know.

"She's curator at the local museum," he was told.

The blond woman stifled a gasp.

"In fact," Cortez added slowly, "I've just come from her house. She made Thanksgiving dinner for us."

"You think the dead man might have stolen the artifacts?" Bennett asked.

"Anybody's guess, until the forensics are processed."

"What sort of artifacts?" the blond woman asked with deliberate carelessness.

Cortez, who was a veteran of interrogation, noted that the woman was unusually nervous and that she wouldn't meet his eyes. "There was a Neanderthal skeleton, for one thing," he said. "And an effigy figure very much like the one in Phoebe Keller's museum." He hesitated. "You're Bennett's sister, aren't you?"

"That's right," Bennett confirmed. "This is Claudia Bennett…my sister. And Walks Far's wife," he added with visible reluctance. He noticed that Cortez didn't seem surprised by the information. The man was in law enforcement, after all. It wouldn't take much digging to turn up Walks Far's criminal past, and his marriage to Claudia. He was suddenly recalling with anguish that he'd told Cortez earlier that he didn't know much about Walks Far. Yet the man was married to his sister. He hadn't mentioned that, either.

"Yes," Claudia replied at once. "My husband was attacked. Have there been any arrests so far?" she added with belligerence.

"I don't work assault cases," Cortez told her. "My assignment is a murder on an Indian reservation. I'm assigned to the FBI's new Indian Country Crime Unit. We assist in homicides and federal crimes on various reservations.

We also teach local law enforcement how to use the latest investigative techniques."

Claudia swallowed, hard. "So that's why the FBI was called in," she said uneasily. "But they said the murder victim was on a dirt road just outside town!"

"The reservation sign was knocked over. We're speculating that the murderer dumped the anthropologist's body after dark and didn't realize where he was."

"Oh. I see." She gave Cortez a cautious scrutiny. "There was an effigy figure, you said?"

"Yes." He pursed his lips. "Miss Keller had an odd visitor last week who mentioned the theft of similar relics at a museum in New York. She said she'd recognize not only the art dealer who sold her the effigy figure, but the woman who came to the museum later under a false identity."

"Would she?" The woman's face paled. Her fingers clenched on her purse. "You mentioned an…art dealer?" she faltered.

"A bogus one," Cortez added. "We checked him out. He even hired on at one of the local construction sites. Maybe he was trying to keep an eye on his stash until he could find buyers for it. Now we're looking for a black SUV which we speculate was used to move the first murder victim to another site." He paused, eyeing both of them as they grew paler by the minute. His plan was working. By revealing what he knew about the case, they were shaking in their boots…just like he'd expected. Claudia was paler. "Now we have a second murder victim. Trace evidence links Walks Far to him."

Bennett looked as anxious as his sister. "But Walks Far is unconscious," he pointed out. "He was a victim himself. He couldn't have killed anyone!"

"I didn't say that he did," Cortez replied.

"The second murder victim, was it a man or a woman?" Bennett's sister asked.

"A man."

"Do you know who he is?" she persisted.

He shook his head. "He'll have to be identified through fingerprints and/or dental records," he replied. "His face is missing. He was shot in the back of the head."

Bennett looked sick. His sister looked like she was going to faint.

Cortez's eyes narrowed. "If either of you know anything about this case, things will go better for you if you tell me now."

They looked at each other. Bennett's sister composed herself and smiled vacantly. "What in the world would we know about murder?" she asked simply. She moved to her unconscious husband's bedside and took his big hand in hers. "I hope you can find the person who did this to my husband," she added. "I'm so glad he's going to be all right!" She sniffed and wiped at her eyes. They were dry as bone, Cortez noticed.

"We'll certainly let you know if we can think of anything that will help the case," Bennett said firmly. "Meanwhile, if you need anything, anything at all..."

Cortez played his hole card. He wouldn't have dared except he knew that Phoebe would be at the motel with Tina and perfectly safe from reprisals.

"I want to talk with Miss Keller again, at her house. She spoke to the first murder victim. She said she'd remembered something about the art dealer that could help us. She also saw a black SUV at the end of her driveway, which we think is involved with the murders. She'll be a material witness."

Bennett's sister's eyes narrowed, but she didn't say anything. She turned back to her husband and made a production of straightening the sheet over his broad chest.

"Anything I can do, let me know," Bennett repeated, forcing a smile.

"I'll do that," Cortez told him. "But under the circumstances, I'm sure you'll understand that I'm going to place a man here to keep watch over Walks Far. Until I find someone better, he's a prime suspect in this case," he added curtly, watching their reactions closely. Bennett looked worried. Claudia actually relaxed. Now he knew he was onto something.

He went out to his car, feeling smug. He'd stake out Phoebe's cabin, and with any luck at all, the perpetrator—or perpetrators—might fall right into his lap. He was certain that the Bennetts knew more than they wanted to tell him. Claudia Bennett might very well know who the killer was. Or Bennett might. And there was that matter of the blond hair they'd found on the body... He was going to keep an eye on both of them.

PHOEBE FINISHED PUTTING up the rest of dinner and then washed dishes, with Drake's help. She was trying to be cheerful, but she had a bad feeling about Tina's attitude. The woman had become an enemy for no reason that Phoebe could discern. Unless, Tina was really very distantly related to Cortez and she'd realized that she wanted him instead of Drake. Perhaps she saw Phoebe as a rival and meant to cut her out.

It was a disturbing thought. Tina was young and pretty,

but she was also Comanche. That would give her a definite edge with Cortez, especially if all he felt for Phoebe was physical.

"We'd better get moving," Drake reminded her. "I have to drop you off and get into my uniform. I go on duty pretty soon."

"I'll just get my jacket and purse, and I'm ready," she said with forced cheerfulness.

She locked up and they rode back into town together in a pleasant silence.

He pulled up in front of Tina's motel room and cut off the engine, turning to Phoebe with one arm across the back of her seat.

"If you get a chance, try to find out why Tina's mad at me, could you?" Drake asked her quietly. "I'd like to know what I've done to upset her."

She smiled at him. "I'll do what I can."

He touched her hair gently. "You're a nice woman, Phoebe Keller," he said quietly. He bent and kissed her forehead. "If you weren't hung up on the FBI guy, I'd be in there swinging to get a chance with you."

"You're a nice man," she replied. "But it's been Cortez for three years. I suppose he's a habit I can't break."

"Just my luck," he said, chuckling. "Well, we'd better get out before we start more gossip. I see the curtains moving." He indicated the room Tina was staying in.

Phoebe got out and knocked at the door. Tina let her in, but she looked angry. Joseph was lying on the second of the two double beds, sound asleep. Tina's eyes were red and swollen. She'd seen that tender kiss, and she was devastated.

"It was a great dinner, Phoebe," Drake said at the doorway, smiling at her. "Thanks."

"You're very welcome."

"You went to a lot of trouble," Drake added, staring pointedly at Tina. "But I'm the only person who even had the manners to say thanks."

Tina glared at him. "I don't need lessons in courtesy from you!"

His eyebrows arched. "Did I say you did?"

"I need to find my suitcase," Phoebe murmured, looking around. "I've got some notes in it about that art dealer..." She hesitated when she saw all her things piled in a heap on the floor, including her clothes that had been hanging in the closet and all her toiletries. Her suitcase was there, too, askew.

"This room is way too small for two grown women and a baby," Tina muttered, without looking at Phoebe. "I'm going to ask Jeremiah to get another room for you. It's too crowded in here."

Phoebe felt sick at the anger in Tina's dark eyes. She flushed, feeling like an intruder. It was obvious that she wasn't wanted here. She thought of her own little cabin, with her own things around her. At least she wouldn't have to put up with this sort of treatment on her own. Apparently Tina really was crazy about Cortez and furious at the competition. Maybe Cortez felt the same way. Well, Phoebe wasn't going to be used for a scapegoat.

She knelt by her things. "Drake, would you help me carry these out to the car, please? Then I'll get you to drop me by the museum to pick up my car."

Tina was remembering what Jeremiah had said about Phoebe being a potential target. It was why she was at the motel in the first place. Jealousy wasn't enough of an excuse to risk the older woman's life.

"Listen, I didn't…I didn't mean that," Tina said slowly.

Phoebe didn't look at her. She was quick and efficient. In a matter of minutes she transferred all her things to Drake's car and climbed into the passenger seat.

Drake glared at Tina. "Tell Cortez I'll take care of her," he said coldly. "She'll be safer with me than she is with you, and that's a fact, you heartless little brat!"

He turned on his heel and went back to the car.

Tina ran outside to the passenger side, her face frantic. "Phoebe, don't go," she began.

Phoebe looked at her with furious blue eyes. "I'm going home. I've had it with you and your so-called cousin and your mood swings! I've got a pistol and I know how to shoot it. You tell Cortez I'll take care of myself." She glanced at Drake who was just getting in the car. "Let's go," she said curtly, snapping her seat belt into place.

Tina was still calling to her when they drove away. Phoebe didn't even glance her way. She didn't want Tina to see how hurt she was.

13

Drake protested all the way to the museum, but Phoebe was upset and refused to listen. She took out her car keys, unlocked her vehicle, and transferred her belongings to it in a tense silence.

"This is nuts!" Drake fumed, waving his arms. "It's getting dark. And it's still threatening to snow! You can't stay out there all alone with a murderer running loose. He's already killed two people, Phoebe!"

"You taught me to shoot a pistol," she pointed out. "I can protect myself."

"Well, I can't," he bit off. "Cortez will skin me alive if anything happens to you! And Tina won't survive me by five minutes!"

"Something's going on between him and Tina," she said coldly. "And it's obvious that she's possessive of him," she added. "They can't be really related, or she wouldn't be so anxious to get rid of me. Maybe he's having second thoughts, too. He hardly spoke to me."

Drake grimaced. "Listen, I agree something's going on here that we don't understand. But it's not worth your life."

She looked up at him. "I'll be okay."

He drew in a long breath. He reached into his billfold and took out a card. "This is my number at work. You call and they'll call me. I can have somebody at your place in minutes."

She smiled. "You're a nice man. I really mean that."

"You just be careful. I don't like the idea of your being out there alone. You could get a room at the motel…"

"I don't want to be anywhere near Tina or Jeremiah right now, thanks," she bit off.

"Look, maybe we could call Alice. She can shoot, too…"

"Oh, no, you don't. I'm not having Alice and her microscope in my house." She laughed. "Anyway, I expect to get a good night's sleep. I'm working tomorrow, myself. We have a tour group coming in from Highlands, elderly Floridians on a holiday."

"They may get snowed in on the way."

"There are scrapers and sand trucks standing by, even this early in the season," she reminded him. "Thanks again, Drake." She opened the door.

"What do I tell Cortez when he comes after me with a skinning knife?" he wondered miserably.

"Tell him I held a gun on you and forced my way out of your car."

He shook his head. He had a bad feeling as he watched her drive away. On a whim, he took out his cell phone and tried to call Cortez. But the man must be in a dead spot, or had his phone turned off. He couldn't reach him and his voice mail wasn't working, either. Defeatedly, he got into his own car and went toward his apartment to change for work.

But the minute he got into his uniform, he drove to the sheriff's office to have a word with his boss.

PHOEBE DROVE UP AT HER cabin, carefully checking around before she even opened the door. She wondered if the killer was going to be after her next, but even danger was preferable to any more of Tina's cold shoulder.

The first thing she did, after locking all the doors and checking the windows, was to strip her bed and throw all the linen into the washing machine. She hated her bedroom for the memories that haunted her now.

It was crazy. She and Cortez had been closer than she'd ever dreamed they would be one day, yet in a matter of hours they were enemies. He'd said he cared about her, or at least he'd made her believe he did. But why was Tina so antagonistic? Tina had been going around with Drake and Marie had even seen a hot kiss between them. So why was Tina suddenly drawn to her cousin Cortez and treating Drake like dirt? Could Drake be right? Was Tina not closely related to Cortez, and now she decided that she wanted him? It was a puzzle she couldn't quite solve.

Her heart was breaking. Three years ago it hadn't been quite this bad, because she and Cortez hadn't been intimate. Her memories tormented her. Worst of all of them was Cortez walking away from her without a single word or a backward glance.

She went into the living room and turned on the television just as the phone rang. She went to answer it, hoping it would be Cortez with an explanation.

"It's Drake," came the immediate reply. "I've just spoken with my boss. I'm going to sleep on your sofa at night and work during the day when you're at the museum," he said firmly. "The sheriff and I agree that you're going to be the person most at risk with a murderer on the loose. He's agreed to change my schedule so that I can look out for you."

"That's very kind of you both, Drake," she said, and meant it. Now she wouldn't have to go back to the motel, which Cortez would certainly have tried to make her do. His sense of responsibility was enormous, even if he was full of regrets for becoming intimate with her.

"Since we're both out of favor with our respective partners," he murmured dryly, "I figure we can look out for each other."

She smiled. "That suits me. I have a guest room that you can use. Thanks, Drake."

"What are friends for?" he replied. "I'll see you about seven," he added.

"I'll fix the guest room for you."

She hung up and went to work.

CORTEZ DIDN'T LIKE THE look of Bennett's sister, or her wide-eyed innocent appearance. Why had Bennett hidden her relationship to Walks Far? And who had attacked Walks Far? Was there yet another person involved in the murders? Did Claudia Bennett know who it was?

There were a lot of unanswered questions here. The anthropologist who'd found the Neanderthal skeleton was dead. So was another, unidentified man. Was Walks Far involved in some museum theft, and the loot in that cave? Or had Walks Far discovered the man with the loot in the cave and someone had knocked him out and killed the other man? But why take Walks Far back to the work trailer—why not kill him? Surely he would be a material witness against the perpetrator. On the other hand, who was the other man? What was his connection to the hidden relics?

It was going to take a lot of forensic work to answer those questions, and meanwhile, Phoebe would be in more danger than ever before. He'd already asked the local police department to assign a man to keep watch outside Walks Far's room, to insure that nothing happened to him until he could be questioned. He'd keep Phoebe close at the motel, where she'd be out of danger.

Phoebe. He was still fuming about her little tête-à-tête with Drake at her house. The two of them were too cozy. He didn't like it. Neither did Tina, who was obviously jealous of Phoebe over Drake. It wasn't going to be a pleasant evening.

He pulled up in front of the motel. Before he could get out of the car, Tina had her door open and was motioning him inside.

His first thought was that something had happened to Joseph, but the little boy was sitting in the middle of the second double bed playing with toy action figures.

Tina had been crying. Her eyes were red and swollen and she looked miserable.

"What's wrong with you?" he asked. His eyes went around the room. "And where's Phoebe?"

"At her house," she said miserably.

"You let her go?" he exploded. He jerked out his cell phone and started dialing.

Tina started to speak, but she couldn't bring herself to say what had really happened. She felt guilty.

The phone rang and rang before it was answered.

"Hello?"

Cortez froze. That wasn't Phoebe. That was…Drake!

"What the hell is Phoebe doing there, and why are you there, too?" Cortez demanded.

"Ask Tina," Drake said icily. "As for what I'm doing here, I'm staying with Phoebe at night until we catch the killer… or killers."

Cortez scowled, glancing at Tina, who flushed.

"I'll come and bring Phoebe back here," Cortez began at once.

"She won't go," Drake said curtly. "Tina threw her out of the room. No way is she going to sink her pride enough to walk back in there. You can tell your cousin for me that I'm through competing with you. She's welcome to you and vice versa."

"What the hell is going on?" Cortez demanded.

"I told you. Ask Tina. I'm not on duty until tomorrow morning. You can contact the sheriff's office if you need backup."

The line went dead.

Cortez turned to Tina after he closed the flip phone, his eyes narrow and cold. "All right," he murmured coldly. "Spill it!"

Tina bit her lower lip. Tears were threatening again. "Drake and Phoebe were just sitting in the car for the longest time, laughing and talking…I just lost my temper. I piled her stuff on the floor and I said something like we needed more rooms." Her face fell, ashamed. "She packed and left, and Drake said he'd drive her to the museum to pick up her car. I tried to stop her," she added quickly. "But Drake was just hateful!"

Cortez stared at her uncomprehendingly. "Tina, there's a killer on the loose," he said slowly. "Phoebe's going to be the main target. Drake is a good lawman, but he's young and he hasn't had a lot of experience with murder cases. With the best of intentions, he could cost Phoebe her life."

She started crying again. "I know. I'm sorry!"

With a long, rough sigh, he pulled her into his arms and rocked her. "Damn!"

"I love him," she choked. "But all he ever talks about is Phoebe this, Phoebe that. He's infatuated with her. I think maybe she feels the same way about him. They're really chummy for people who are just friends. When they were sitting in the car, he kissed her. They were wrapped up like lovers!"

He'd noticed that they were friendly, but a kiss was something else again. He felt wounded. It was more painful for him than Tina might imagine, because she didn't realize he'd rekindled his romance with Phoebe. He couldn't tell her, either, not now, when Drake was going to be staying under the same roof with her. It would kill his pride to admit what a fool he'd been.

"What are we going to do?" she wailed.

"We're going to get some sleep," he replied. "Then, tomorrow, we'll see."

She wiped her eyes. "If anything happens to her, I'll never forgive myself."

His heart skipped, painfully. "If Drake's there at night, he can protect her," he replied, as much as he hated saying it aloud.

"What about during the day?" she groaned.

"She'll be at work six days out of seven. On Sundays, I'll talk with Drake and see what we can arrange."

Tina looked up at him through tears. "You could ask her to come back. I'd promise not to make any more trouble." Her lips made a thin line. "It's not her fault that Drake likes her more than me, after all."

He didn't reply. He had enough trouble without borrowing more. "Phoebe will be all right," he said.

"Sure she will," she agreed.

Neither of them believed it.

PHOEBE COOKED SUPPER for Drake and they watched television until almost midnight. Neither of them was in the mood for sleep, but fatigue eventually, caught up with them.

The next morning, Phoebe woke to the delicious aroma of scrambled eggs and bacon that Drake had whipped up for them.

She smiled as they ate breakfast, thinking how considerate her new roommate was. Then she dressed and drove in to work, pulling into the parking lot precisely at eight-thirty. She was comforted by the knowledge that Drake had followed her in his own car to ensure that she arrived safely. After personally escorting her into the museum, he departed for his police shift.

It had been a little disappointing that Cortez hadn't even phoned to check on her the night before. She hadn't really expected it, though. They hadn't parted as friends, and God knew what Tina had said about their argument. Then she remembered that Drake had kissed her forehead in the car. She grimaced. It might have looked much more ardent than it really was, and Tina would probably have told Cortez about it. Maybe they laughed about it and decided that they were better off together. She shut off the memory. It was like a closed chapter of her life. She'd better start thinking of it that way. Even more, she'd better start watching her back. There was still a killer on the loose, and she could identify the bogus art dealer.

Marie had obviously heard something, because she was very careful to be upbeat around Phoebe. So was her assistant, Harriett White.

The senior-citizens' group arrived promptly at ten, and Phoebe took them around the museum herself, just to avoid being in her office. It reminded her too well of the passionate kiss she'd shared with Cortez. The problem was, everything reminded her of Cortez.

CORTEZ HAD DELIBERATELY stayed away from the museum. Tina's talk about the kiss Phoebe and Drake had shared had hurt his pride. He was spoiling for a fight, and he didn't want to make things any worse than they already were.

He drove to the hospital after he got up to check on Walks Far. The man was still unconscious, but there was nobody at his bedside. Perhaps Bennett and his sister had been up all night. That was a charitable estimate, he decided.

He checked with the officer he'd requested to remain outside the door, and nobody had been in Walks Far's room all night. Curious, he thought as he went back to his car, that the family wasn't keeping a vigil. If that had been Tina or Joseph or any member of his family, he'd never have left the hospital.

He phoned Alice Jones from a public phone in the lobby. "Have you got anything new?" he asked.

"A tentative ID on the fingerprints of the second dead man," she replied excitedly. "I pulled a string or two," she chuckled, sensing his surprise. "The man's name is Fred Norton. He was listed as an art dealer, although our investigators can't find anybody who would admit he ever worked for them. Apparently he worked for a construction boss named Paul Corland for a few days earlier in the month. Norton's got a rap sheet the length of my leg, everything from petty theft to armed robbery and assault. And, get this, he was in prison with Bennett's foreman. I called Phoebe and she told me that was the name of the art dealer who sold her the effigy figure in her museum, the one that blond woman made such a fuss about possibly being stolen."

Cortez felt his pulse leap. Bingo! "That's the connection. It has to be. Bennett never mentioned that Walks Far was his brother-in-law, or that he had a prison record, when I first questioned him," he said, thinking aloud. "In fact, he pretended that he hardly knew the man."

"Well, well, the plot thickens!" Alice exclaimed. "But that doesn't explain the blond hair and face powder..."

"Bennett's sister is married to Walks Far," he added. "She's blond."

"Another revelation!"

"If we ran a DNA test on that hair, I'd bet that we'd have a perfect match to Claudia Bennett." His eyes narrowed as he stared at the opposing wall. "Suppose," he began, "that Walks Far and his wife knew the art dealer had those items stashed, and they looked around and found them in that cave. They discovered the stolen artifacts and the art dealer saw them. There was a struggle. Walks Far shot the other man."

"How'd he get back to the trailer? And how did he shoot

another man, if he'd already been assaulted and was in a coma?" Alice persisted.

He grimaced. "Stop messing up my theories."

"They won't hold water. Suppose Walks Far and his wife were making a bid for the stolen art and the thief happened on them. Then Walks Far and the other man struggled, there was a blow to Walks Far's head, but Walks Far shot the other guy before he passed out. His wife drags him back to whatever she's driving, takes him back to the work trailer, pulls him inside and leaves lights on so the police will investigate."

"Not bad," he murmured thoughtfully.

"Which makes Walks Far at the least an eyewitness to murder, if not a suspect."

"I've got a guard on him at the hospital, but he hasn't regained consciousness again." He frowned. "I'm going to put a tail on Bennett's sister, just in case. I've got a hunch she's up to her eyebrows in this. Phoebe said the woman who came to her office was tall, blond, expensively dressed and had a mole. Bennett's sister matches the description."

"A husband and a lover and an accomplice, maybe?" Alice was fishing.

"Maybe."

Cortez searched his memory for what Corland had said about the man who came and worked for a couple of days and then just walked off the job. Things were beginning to come together. "What did the dead man drive?" he asked immediately. "Was it a late-model SUV?"

"I'm not psychic, Cortez!" Alice exclaimed. "You're lucky I could get the ID from his prints," she added. "By the way, I just spoke to Phoebe on the phone a few minutes ago. She's really somber today. You guys have a fight or something?"

"Or something," he said tightly. "Keep digging. See if you can connect him with a black SUV of any age or model."

"I'll do it, even though half the offices are closed today. Some people get long holidays…of course, nobody cares about my time off—"

He hung up.

ON A HUNCH, CORTEZ WENT back to the motel and phoned the Department of Motor Vehicles, barely taking time to kiss Joseph and speak to Tina, who was still brooding and miserable. He gave his ID and the man's name, and hoped for a miracle.

None was forthcoming. The man drove a sedan. He thanked the employee and hung up.

He was doing nothing but running into dead ends. It might not be a bad idea to put some more pressure on Bennett and see what he could come up with.

But meanwhile, he and the local police, sheriff's department and his own unit started checking for owners of black SUV models locally.

Cortez still missed Phoebe and wanted to talk to her, but the case took precedence. The art dealer was dead, but whoever killed him might still have a reason to go after Phoebe to tie up loose ends. He had to catch the killer before she ended up in the line of fire. Somehow, he'd work things out with her. Despite the evidence of that kiss Tina had seen her share with Drake, deep down he didn't believe she could have been intimate with him and in love with another man. It was completely out of character. She was remarkably old-fashioned. He thought about that, and it lightened his heart. He was going to work things out with her. He'd never been more certain of anything. Now, he had to catch the murderer, and quickly.

SUNDAY WAS A STUMBLING block, because all the state and federal offices were closed. He endured Tina's watery, bitter mood and played with Joseph, wishing all the while that he could go and patch things up with Phoebe.

But Monday, Cortez did some further checking and finally found the identity of the dead anthropologist. He was from Oklahoma all right, but was temporarily teaching at a North Carolina university. By checking with the staff there, he discovered that the man's name was Professor Dan Morgan, who taught anthropology at the college. He'd been missing for some time. But he had no relatives, certainly no daughter. Phoebe had recalled that the man told someone waiting for him that he was speaking to his daughter. Perhaps it had been a ruse, to distract the person from knowing who he was talking to on the phone.

Then an assistant of the professor's, mastering her tears on learning of his death, recalled that he'd gone to Chenocetah to see a relative of his, a cousin, who worked for a man named Bennett. The cousin's name was Walks Far.

Cortez was elated. Finally a connection! He thanked the assistant, gave his condolences and hung up. Then he cursed silently, because Walks Far had known the first murder victim and had lied about it. He should have seen through the lie.

"I'll be back when I can," he told Tina after he'd kissed Joseph and cuddled him for a minute. "I've got a lead. I have to get to the hospital and see about a comatose suspect."

"Have you spoken to Drake at all?" she asked with downcast eyes.

He stared down at her until she looked at him. "Why do you think she's mixed up with Drake?"

"She's always laughing with him, talking to him. He admires her," she muttered. "They're so…friendly! And she's been walking around in a daze lately, like a woman deeply in love." She frowned. "She has to be involved with him."

He lifted an eyebrow. "She's involved, all right, but not with Drake."

Her eyes widened. So she hadn't been wrong at first, when she'd teased Phoebe about being crazy about Cortez. "Oh, no. I couldn't have been that wrong!"

"You really are in love with Drake, aren't you?"

She bit her lip. "He started talking about Phoebe all the time."

"Why?"

She shifted. "Well, I hated the way he praised her, and I sort of started praising you. A lot. He got quiet and remote, and then he just didn't call or come around at all. I figured it was Phoebe."

"Maybe he thought we were distant cousins," he murmured, thinking aloud.

Her eyebrows arched. "But I said we were cousins."

"You didn't say we were first cousins, did you?" he added.

She thought back. "Well, no."

He patted her cheek, smiling. "It will all come right. We jumped to the wrong conclusion before, but now that

I really think about it, I can guarantee that Phoebe isn't messing around with Drake."

Her face became radiant. "Then there's a chance…" She stopped. "I've ruined everything! She'll never forgive me. Neither will Drake!"

"It will all work out. I promise it will. But right now, I've got to catch a killer. You keep Joseph in here and the door locked. Got that?"

She nodded. "You be careful," she added. "I've gotten used to you."

He smiled. "I'm bulletproof. Honest. See you."

"See you."

He went out the door, and closed it firmly behind him.

WALKS FAR WAS AWAKE. He'd been talking to Bennett, who was standing close beside his bed. The men looked worn out and guilty. When they saw Cortez, both of them seemed to go pale.

Cortez came in and closed the door behind him. He approached the bed, bristling with bad temper.

"Where's your sister?" he asked at once, his dark eyes lancing into Bennett's blue ones.

Bennett let out a harsh breath. "I don't know," he said curtly.

"Running for the border, unless I miss my guess," Walks Far said in a diminished, groggy tone. He stared up at Cortez. "You've figured it all out, haven't you?"

"I've figured out that you and your entourage are up to your necks in this double murder investigation." His eyes narrowed. "Why don't you both make it easy on yourselves and fill in the missing blanks for me? You know it's all going to come out eventually."

Walks Far let out a defeated breath and Bennett gave him the grim nod to cooperate. "My wife was running around on me with the art dealer, Fred Norton, whom I met in prison. He robbed a museum in New York, with her help, and hid the loot in a cave on Yardley's property. He got a job with Corland so that he could keep an eye on the cave, but from a safe distance, so it wouldn't look as if he were that interested in Yardley's site. Although he did try to get a job at Yardley's operation when Corland fired him."

"Did you know about the stolen stuff all along?" Cortez inquired.

Walks Far grimaced, holding his head. "Not this time. Fred stayed with us after we got out of prison. She started going off places alone, or supposedly alone, after Fred moved out and we came up here to work on this job. She'd kept free of crime for several years, or so I thought."

"She'd kept free of what?" Cortez exclaimed.

Bennett and Walks Far exchanged glances. "Might as well come clean with all of it," Bennett said in a resigned tone. He sat down beside Walks Far's bed. "My sister was first arrested for theft at the age of sixteen. I paid the owner for the merchandise so he wouldn't prosecute. But it didn't stop. She took a priceless figurine and a jade necklace, equally rare, out of an exhibit of Chinese art. I couldn't afford that payoff, so Walks Far took the rap for her, to make sure she wouldn't have to go to prison."

"Which explains the theft on your record," Cortez told the other Native American.

Walks Far nodded. "She'd married me just before the theft. I thought she really cared. She did, until she met Fred. He stayed with us for a couple of months, since we both got out of prison at the same time."

"In between she took another piece of jewelry from a museum," Bennett said. "I turned her in that time. She got probation, but she dumped toxic chemicals into a local stream and made sure the authorities came after me. I got probation, too, and a hefty fine."

"We've both made sacrifices for her," Walks Far said miserably. "But it was never enough. She wanted designer clothes and expensive jewelry and flashy cars. She liked the thrill she got from stealing. I couldn't give her what she needed. Fred obviously could."

"He sold an effigy figure to Phoebe at the local museum," Cortez said. "That must have been the serpent that undid paradise. It was risky, a sale so soon after a notorious theft of easily recognized artifacts."

"Especially when I discovered the loot and called my cousin to come and look at it. I didn't let on that I thought it was stolen so Dan truly believed the artifacts were a genuine discovery. He initially thought the danger came from the developers not wanting the discovery of the artifacts to halt the construction project. He had no idea what was really going on…until it was too late." Walks Far added quietly, "He's dead because of me. I had no idea my wife was connected to the robbery. I was scouting the caves on the back of all three construction sites and I came across the stash in the cave on Yardley's construction project. I saw Fred's car there," he muttered. "I suspected the artifacts were stolen, so I had Dan come down and identify them, to confirm it. I didn't think he'd get in any trouble. Obviously he was checking the stolen merchandise and figured out what was really going on when he was discovered. Fred must have caught him in the act and killed him."

"Actually, we believe Fred killed him at his motel. Fred

obviously knew that he'd seen the stash, though. He murdered Dan, then the killer planted the body on a dirt road," Cortez said. "But he didn't know it was on Indian land and that the FBI would be called in on the case. That must have hit him hard.

"How did Fred die? And who hit you?" Cortez persisted.

Walks Far gave him a long, sad look. "I don't know who hit me, or how I got back to the trailer. I had a strange phone call, about some artifacts in a cave on Yardley's property. They said it was being moved. I rushed out there, alone, to check it out. I walked into the cave with a flashlight. The next thing I knew, I was here. Least of all do I know who killed Fred."

"But we have a suspicion. A terrible one," Bennett said heavily.

"I think it was Fred who knocked me out when I walked into the cave. I was just going to see if the loot was still there, and then I was going to call the police," Walks Far continued. "The lights went out when I was barely inside the cave. I woke up in here," he added, looking around the hospital room ruefully.

"You think your sister may have killed Fred," Cortez said to Bennett.

The other man nodded slowly. "It's the only thing that makes sense. She made a comment about men not being trustworthy and that if she wanted anything done right, she had to do the job herself." He met Cortez's eyes. "I hope you're having Miss Keller watched," he added. "Claudia let slip that she'd been to the museum and saw an effigy figure there and told Miss Keller about it being stolen. She said Miss Keller could identify Fred. It didn't make sense at the time, but it does now. Miss Keller can positively identify Fred, but she can also identify Claudia as the one who made those suspicious inquiries about the effigy figure. If she killed Fred, what's one more death to get rid of the witnesses who could tie her to Fred?"

Cortez felt sick. He'd made that remark himself, about Phoebe and the effigy figure, right in front of Bennett's sister in the hope of luring the real killer to the cabin. But that was when he'd assumed Phoebe would be safe and sound at the motel!

"I'll testify against her," Bennett said solemnly, "if you can catch her before she does anything more tragic."

"How was Fred killed?" Walks Far asked curiously.

"He was shot in the back of the head at close range," Cortez told him. "I'd speculate that your wife had him stoop down to look at something and then shot him."

Walks Far had to agree. "She'd do anything to stay out of prison. She's terrified of it. Not that it's ever stopped her from taking what she wanted." He shook his head and winced at the pain. "I never should have taken the rap for her the first time. If she'd had to face the consequences of her actions, perhaps it would never have gone this far. Two men are dead."

"I'm afraid it will take more than a false confession to get her out of this," he said, turning. "I'm sorry. I've got probable cause and I'm going to take out a warrant for her arrest as quickly as I can."

"It's the only thing left to do," Bennett agreed. "I'm sorry I didn't level with you sooner. She's the only living relative I have left," he added curtly.

Cortez remembered his own brother, Isaac, and the boy's brushes with the law until the final one that took his life. "I understand better than you realize."

"And I'm sorry. I didn't let on about the professor being my cousin when you first showed me his picture," Walks Far said sheepishly. "I was afraid it would incriminate me, and I wanted to do some digging myself before I went to the authorities."

Cortez nodded. "Thanks for clearing everything up. I'll be in touch."

CORTEZ WENT TO THE SUPERIOR court judge's office and spoke to the man, laying out his evidence. The judge was convinced that arresting Miss Bennett was the next logical step to take.

He walked out of the courthouse with the warrant and called the sheriff's office, asking for Drake.

"You need to watch Phoebe as carefully as you can," Cortez told him when they were connected. "I've just taken out a warrant for the arrest of Bennett's sister for the murder of Fred Norton, the so-called art dealer who sold Phoebe the effigy figure. She's the only person who can positively identify the art dealer and Miss Bennett and tie them together with the murders. Her life is going to be in danger until I have Miss Bennett in custody."

"I've been trying to get in touch with you. I've got some more news," Drake said quietly. "Miss Bennett drives a black SUV with a worn tread."

Cortez's heart jumped. "Phoebe's at the museum, isn't she?"

Drake groaned. "That's why I was trying to find you!"

"Tell me!" Cortez said at once.

"Phoebe left a message for me about thirty minutes ago. I

was away from the radio on a call and I just got it. She took off an hour early to do some pruning in her rose garden. She's at her house, alone!"

14

CORTEZ FELT HIS HEART SINK. "She's alone?" he repeated it as if he couldn't believe it.

"I'm on my way out there right now," Drake promised. "You go and get the Bennett woman. Trust me. I won't let anything happen to Phoebe!"

"All right," Cortez said heavily.

"Listen, Phoebe and I are friends," Drake added curtly. "That's all we've ever been. We thought maybe Tina had something going with you..."

"Tina's my first cousin," Cortez interrupted grimly. "Her father and my father are brothers."

Drake felt sick. "She was rude to Phoebe, hateful. Phoebe and I talked about it. It didn't make sense unless she was jealous of the time you were spending with Phoebe. She started talking about you constantly, how great you were.

We didn't know you were first cousins. We thought she'd decided she wanted you instead of me."

"She was jealous, you idiot!" Cortez shot back. "She's in love with you!"

There was an audible intake of breath. "She…she is? She loves me?"

Cortez smiled in spite of himself. "That kiss she saw you share with Phoebe tore her up."

"Well!" Drake felt elated. "And it was only a little kiss on the forehead, too!"

Cortez felt better. It was all a misunderstanding. He could get Phoebe back, and could explain it to her. But first, they had to make sure she was protected. "Get out there and keep Phoebe safe! I'm going to work."

"You bet!" Drake said at once.

"And get a BOLO out on that SUV, just in case," he added, meaning a "be on the lookout for" radio alert. "I'll swing by the local police department and have an officer go to Bennett's house with me to serve the warrant. I'll be on my way to Bennett's. His sister and Walks Far were staying with him."

"Will do."

He hung up, got into his car, and broke speed limits getting out of town.

PHOEBE WAS GLAD TO HAVE a little time to herself. The breakup with Cortez, the argument with Tina and the pressures of her job had combined to make her miserable. She'd planned to do some long-needed pruning in her rose garden. But she couldn't do it in her flimsy gray slacks and white shell blouse under the suit coat she was wearing with flat dress shoes. She'd have to change first. She still had the pistol Drake had loaned her and she was fairly certain the killer or killers wouldn't be crazy enough to go after her in broad daylight.

But when she walked into her house, after shedding her jacket and purse, she heard an ominous click as she walked past the hallway into the kitchen.

"Just hold it right there," a woman's voice said from behind her.

Phoebe didn't have to be told who it was. She recognized the voice. She started to turn.

"Don't do it," the woman said, sounding cold and calculating. "I've killed before, I can do it again. You just head right out the back door. Don't stop."

"My jacket," Phoebe said, hesitating.

"You won't need it where you're going," came the sarcastic reply. "Open the door."

Phoebe did, with her heart racing, trying to be alert so that she could take advantage of any opportunity she got to escape. She couldn't outrun a bullet, though. She ground her teeth together. Maybe, once they were underway…

There was a black SUV out of sight behind the corner of the house. The blond woman jerked open the back door and stood too far away for Phoebe to grab at the gun.

"Get in," she said, motioning with the pistol. A .45 caliber one, Phoebe noticed, and the woman held it with a very professional grip.

Phoebe turned her back to climb up into the SUV when she felt a sudden hard blow, and the lights went out.

SHE CAME TO VERY SLOWLY. She felt the vehicle slow down and stop. Her eyes opened. There were trees. Fir trees. They were in a forest. There was a mountain nearby.

Claudia Bennett Walks Far jerked open the back door. The .45 was clenched tightly in her hand. "Get out," she rasped.

Phoebe's head was splitting. She felt sick at her stomach. But she knew the woman was going to kill her. She had to think of a way to save herself in time.

"Get out!" Claudia raged, jerking at her foot violently. "You've ruined everything, you and your FBI boyfriend! I had to kill Fred because of you, damn you! He was going to leave me and take the artifacts for himself! He'd already killed that archaeologist. I told him not to move that stash for a year, but he got greedy and sold you an effigy figure. I got scared and thought maybe I could get you to point him out and get him arrested. But it backfired. He knew you could identify him and he lost his nerve! He was going to take the stash and run for it and leave me holding the bag. He was going to tell everybody I killed that archaeologist," she sneered. "Well, I wasn't about to go to prison. Now he's dead, thanks to you, and you're the last witness who can connect me to anybody. So you have to be got out of the way. I'm not going to prison. I'm getting out of here!"

Phoebe was thinking as she slid out of the big SUV. She leaned against the side of it, as if she could barely stand up.

"Get moving!" Claudia raged, poking her in the back with the gun.

If she could turn, whip around and hit that gun...

Claudia moved back and cocked the pistol.

Phoebe pushed herself drowsily away from the big vehicle and started walking down a dirt road.

"That way, down the path," Claudia motioned her into a grove of oak and hemlock trees.

It was getting dark. Snow was blowing around them.

It was freezing cold and the frigid winds seeped right through Phoebe's sleeveless blouse. She rubbed her arms and shivered.

"You won't be cold for long," Claudia laughed with black humor. "Keep walking."

"What good will it do to kill me?" Phoebe tried reasoning with her. "You can get away!"

"You can identify me. Nobody else can."

"You're insane," Phoebe muttered. "By now, they'll probably have connected you to the murder and traced this SUV to you. It's all over. You just haven't realized it yet."

"I'll get away. They'll be too busy looking for you to look for me," she said with chilling certainty.

"I'll be missed…"

"Not right away. You're home early, aren't you? I called the museum to see where you were. Your assistant was so helpful," she added, laughing.

They were under a big oak tree now. There was a series of slight ridges that fell down a hill that seemed to go on forever, from one leaf-blanketed level to another. There were holly bushes and scrub pine and fallen trees all around. Phoebe's heart was racing madly. Maybe if she ran…

"Stop!" Claudia called at once.

Phoebe felt the woman close behind. She had to be quick. She had to be accurate. She couldn't afford to hesitate even for a second.

"Get down on your knees," Claudia said firmly.

Phoebe's head turned toward her bravely. "Haven't you got the guts to look me in the eyes while you kill me?" she taunted.

Claudia's eyes darkened with fury. "Get on your knees!" she screamed, fumbling the pistol to a higher position.

"Right now there's a chance you might escape the death penalty," Phoebe said as she got down to her knees. Her heart was raging in her chest. It might be her last few seconds of life. She was keenly aware of the danger. "If you give yourself up…"

"I've already killed one person!" Claudia said angrily. "What's one more? They can't kill you twice, can they?"

She played her last card. "Listen, my fiancé is with the FBI." She felt herself shivering with mingled fear and cold. "If you kill me, he'll hunt you down if it's the last thing he ever does in this life." As she said it, she realized it was the truth. She'd been stupid to believe he could go from her to any other woman. He loved her. She loved him. If only she'd had time to tell him one last time…

"I don't care" came the cold reply. Claudia took a long, steadying breath and lowered the barrel of the pistol until the back of Phoebe's head filled her frame of vision.

Phoebe heard that telltale breath. She knew what was coming. It was now or never, the last chance she'd get to save herself. If she hesitated, her life was gone. She spared one last thought for the consequences, because she was likely to die no matter what she did. Her life didn't flash before her, though. She didn't have time for memories. She didn't have time for anything.

With a silent prayer for help, all at once, she pivoted and threw her arm up as hard as she could, twisting her upper body at the same time. Her forearm connected sharply with Claudia's forearm. Claudia cried out with surprise and pain as the heavy pistol went flying through the air, over the ridge and down into the detritus and leaf mounds below.

While Claudia was momentarily shocked speechless, Phoebe took off at a dead run, throwing her body over the ridge and tucking her head as she rolled and rolled and rolled. Her head was really throbbing and she couldn't see as well as normal. But at least she'd escaped for the moment. If only Claudia didn't have another gun hidden in that big SUV, she might get away.

"No!" Claudia screamed. "You bitch!"

Phoebe tucked her head and flattened her body, ignoring her throbbing head and the nausea that welled in her throat. She closed her eyes and thought about Cortez, about the day they met, about his strength and comforting arms. She would love him forever…

"I'll get you!" Claudia raged. She struggled down the first shallow bank and looked around for the pistol. She kicked at the leaves, trying to find it, but she couldn't see it. The clouds were getting thicker now, the sky was darkening. It was spitting snow.

"Come back here!" Claudia screamed furiously. She stopped, panting from her exertions, and looked around her wildly. She looked a little more, but she was wearing high heels and a neat gray suit, hardly the outfit for the forest.

"What the hell!" she spat. "You'll freeze to death out here, anyway. You don't even know where you are! Rot in hell, you bitch!"

She ran back to the SUV, climbed in, started the engine and roared off with a blaze of dust lifting behind her.

Phoebe was tempted to get right up and follow the SUV out of the forest. But she wasn't certain that Claudia wouldn't come back, just to check and see if she'd peeked out and made herself a target. There was every possibility that the woman would come back, just in case Phoebe got brave enough to stick her head up.

Sure enough, not five minutes later, the SUV roared back

down the dirt road and screeched to a halt just above where Phoebe was lying perfectly still, not moving.

The SUV sat there, the engine idling, for another five minutes. Then, all at once, it turned and roared away.

But Phoebe still gave it another few minutes before she moved. The snow was really coming down now, and the heat of adrenaline had left her. She was freezing. Being out in the elements all night might kill her. Hypothermia was deadly. She didn't have anything to cover herself with. Her arms were bare and the slacks were lightweight. She'd probably freeze to death. She didn't know where she was. Neither did anybody else. Surely Cortez and Drake would search for her, but there wasn't much chance that they'd find her out here in the wilderness in time.

She sat up, listening, as the sky slowly began to darken. But the SUV didn't come back. The other woman didn't return this time.

Now it was a question of whether to stay put or try to walk out. Nobody had any idea where she was. If she stayed in the forest, she might die there. It was deep in the woods, she knew that already. Probably it was in the national forest. There were black bears at this altitude. Cougars had been seen. There were bobcats and even coyotes and wolves in the deserted places.

On the other hand, it was rapidly getting dark. She had no flashlight, no candle, no matches. And there was no moon, because the sky was overcast. Her only hope would be to feel the ruts and keep in them, to follow the track the SUV had left.

She considered taking off her shoes, but she might get frostbite in her feet if she did that. It had to be freezing for it to snow. She pulled dead limbs off a small tree, which were long enough to let her "feel" the height of the vegetation around the ruts. There was a chance, only a very small one, that she might be able to walk out of the forest. It was that, or do nothing. Staying in one place would be immediately fatal. She'd freeze to death waiting for someone to look for her here. If she could reach a road, any sort of road, she might get help. That was also going to be something of a long shot, because not a lot of people traveled the back roads of these mountains on a snowy night unless they lived in them. But there might be a sheriff's car patrolling. She had to hope there might be.

She moved as quickly as she could along the ruts through the forest. It was so quiet, she thought. Nothing was stirring. There wasn't even a bird song. The only noise was the creaking of tree limbs in the heavy wind as snow blew all around. It peppered Phoebe's uncovered face, and the sting of it made her realize that snow wasn't her only problem. It was now sleeting as well.

She put one foot in front of the other and tried as hard as she could to think only of each step as she made it. She had to concentrate on getting out of the forest as quickly as possible.

She came to a fork in the road and hesitated, grinding her teeth together. But while she debated which way to go, she heard that odd, distant, faraway singing. It sounded like Cherokee. It was coming from the right fork. She smiled to herself and turned to the right without a single hesitation. Maybe, she thought, there was just a little chance of escape.

CONVINCED THAT DRAKE was looking after Phoebe for him, Cortez walked up to the front door of an elegant mansion just inside the city limits of Chenocetah. He had Officer

Parker with him to serve the warrant, which was local. This house was rented by Walks Far, although Bennett was paying for it.

Cortez rang the doorbell three times, but there was no answer. He and Officer Parker went around the side of the house to the backyard. The garage door was open. The SUV registered to Claudia was missing.

It only took a second for Cortez to connect the missing SUV and the desperate woman whose first thought would be to get Phoebe before she could testify against her.

Cortez whipped out his phone and started to call Drake, but before he could punch in the number, the phone rang noisily.

"Yes?" he answered at once.

"It's Drake" came the terse reply. "Phoebe's not here."

It was a nightmare. His heart raced, although it didn't show on his hard face. "Have you searched the house?"

"Everywhere. Her purse and car keys are still here."

Which meant, quite obviously, that she'd left without them. Probably at gunpoint.

"Do you have any idea where the Bennett woman might take Phoebe?" Cortez asked at once. "It would be somewhere deserted, off the beaten path."

"Everywhere is off the beaten path this far back in the mountains," Drake said miserably. "I put out a BOLO, but we've had no contact."

Cortez drew in a short breath. "I'm going to see Bennett," he said. "He might have some ideas. It's a long shot, but it's all we've got. I'll be in touch the minute I know anything. Have you got a helicopter?"

"Sure, it's in the Batcave, right alongside the amphibious vehicles," Drake muttered sarcastically.

"Sorry," Cortez said sheepishly. "I'll phone DEA. They usually have aircraft."

"They may have it, but they're not going up at night in a sleet and snowstorm," Drake replied. "No pilot is going to risk that."

"Damn!"

"I'll talk to the sheriff," Drake added. "We've got a mounted Sheriff's Posse in our county—horses can go where vehicles can't. And we've got a top-notch Emergency Management Agency locally. The director is one great guy. I'll call him, too."

"Thanks, Drake," Cortez said stiffly. "I'll get back to you."

He hung up, explained the situation to Officer Parker, and the two of them rushed back to town.

BENNETT WAS AT HIS construction company trailer, with a glass of whiskey at his fingertips. Nobody was working tonight. Not even him. He looked up as Cortez came barreling in the door.

He raised his glass. "I'm going down as an accessory after the fact, right? Are you here to arrest me?"

Cortez paused at the front of the desk. "Your sister has Phoebe," he said at once.

The other man scowled. "Are you sure?"

"Your sister's SUV has been seen at her house before. The police found a witness who saw it pass by this afternoon, just before Phoebe disappeared. Her car keys and driver's license are still in her purse, at the house, but she's gone. It won't take rocket science to put those facts together and draw a conclusion."

Bennett closed his eyes. "Oh, God!"

Cortez leaned against the desk, his dark eyes blazing. "Listen to me, there may be a chance that I can help your sister escape the death penalty. She's obviously unbalanced. But you have to help me!"

"What can I do? I don't know where she is!"

"Think," Cortez said firmly. "If your sister planned to do harm to Phoebe, she'd more than likely take her to a place she was familiar with! Someplace deserted, off the beaten path. But she'd have to know such an area to go there. She'd want someplace where she wouldn't likely be disturbed or discovered."

Bennett stared at the desk, frowning. "Well…there was a place she talked about, the only place she really liked up here. She hated the country. I think it's part of the reason she got involved with Fred in the first place. We're going to be here for months."

"She could have gone back to Atlanta without you," Cortez pointed out.

"Not likely. There wasn't any excitement there." Bennett grimaced. "Today, I refused to give her any money unless she stayed here with Walks Far while he was in the hospital. She was furious. She said she didn't care if he died. That was when I knew she'd done something. She'd gone to see him that day you stopped by only because I'd threatened her. After that, she went wild. I couldn't even talk to her."

"Where did she talk about? What spot did she like?" Cortez pressed.

"The Yonah National Forest," he said. "A roadside park deep in the woods, where they said gold had been found once. There were cabins to rent near the little picnic area." He scowled. "Maybe Fred was staying there. I know he wasn't in town, because Walks Far checked all the motels looking for him when Claudia let slip that he was in the area."

Cortez's heart leaped. It was a big area, but better than trying to search the whole state. "Thanks," he told Bennett. "I'll do what I can for you. And for her. If Phoebe's unharmed," he added coldly.

Bennett watched him leave with grave misgivings. If Phoebe was dead, he'd have no peace for the rest of his life. Cortez would make a deadly enemy.

PHOEBE HEARD THE HOWL of a cat and she stiffened. She listened. It was very quiet, except for the sleet hitting the ground. She was so cold. She walked in place, waving her arms, trying to coax heat from her body. It wouldn't take long for hypothermia to set in. Then she'd fall into a deep sleep, from which she'd never awaken. She had to keep moving or die.

She felt for plant growth with the keen switch, following the ruts. She couldn't go very fast because she couldn't see her feet. But ironically, as the snow began to cover the ground, it made it easier to see the ruts. An advantage in a disadvantage. But it gave her a little hope. She might yet be able to make it out of the forest, at least to a more public road. If only her feet weren't freezing in her knee-high hose and flat shoes. If only she wasn't shivering so!

She pictured a roaring fire in her cozy fireplace at home, and soft music playing. She pictured herself lying across Cortez's lap, dreaming. She listened for the sound of those singing voices, but she didn't hear them anymore.

She put one foot in front of the other and moved on.

DRAKE ANSWERED THE PHONE the minute it rang. "Stewart," he said abruptly.

"It's me," Cortez replied. "Bennett said his sister talked about a little roadside park in the Yonah National Forest, near the cabins. Know any enforcement guys out that way?"

"Yes, I do," he said. "The forest service has an enforcement officer who's a friend of mine, and there's also state game and fish enforcement. They'd be glad to lend us a hand with the search. I've put out the word to a local tracker as well. I'll organize it."

"I'll be there as quickly as I can."

"You'll need chains," Drake said. "We're getting sleet and snow mixed. It won't take long for it to stick on the roads. You'll never make it on regular tires."

Cortez groaned. Another delay!

"Listen," Drake added, "go by the sheriff's department and get the sheriff to come out here with you. He's got a four-wheel-drive vehicle and it's already got chains."

"Thanks, Drake! See you soon." He hung up and started toward the sheriff's office.

THE SHERIFF OF YONAH County, Bob Steele, was a big man, tall with curly silver hair and black eyebrows. He was a pleasant man, but he inspired respect. He heard Cortez out, scowling.

"It's sleeting," the sheriff said at once. "You think the Bennett woman left Miss Keller out in this weather?"

"Yes," Cortez said tightly, "unless she's already killed her," he added, voicing a thought he didn't want to acknowledge.

The sheriff got up from his desk and took his pistol out

of the drawer, sticking it into the holster at his belt. He was somber. "We'll hope for the best," he said.

"I appreciate the help you've already given us, letting Drake shift his hours so that he could watch Phoebe."

"How the hell did the Bennett woman get to her?" the sheriff asked.

"Phoebe took off early from work to prune her damned roses," Cortez muttered on his way out the door. "Without letting anyone know."

"Not a good idea, with a killer running loose," was the reply.

"Damned straight, and when we catch up with her, she's going to get it rubbed in for the next half century!"

The sheriff only smiled. He knew, as Cortez did, that the first twenty-four hours were crucial in a hostage case. If they didn't find Miss Keller in that time, she was likely to be dead—of a bullet, or exposure. He unlocked the four-wheel-drive SUV and climbed in with Cortez.

THE GROUND WAS WHITE. Phoebe tossed aside the sticks, because she could see the ruts quite well now. She stopped periodically to listen for the sound of an approaching vehicle, because the Bennett woman might still come back gunning for her. She couldn't take any chances.

Her hands felt frozen and her arms were getting numb. She'd never really experienced cold on this scale. She could hardly feel her feet. They were numb, too, and she worried about frostbite. That amused her, because she was likely to die out here, so what did it matter? She rubbed her arms furiously. If only she'd hit that Bennett woman harder, she muttered to herself. Running might have been a mistake.

But the other woman was taller than she was, and Phoebe had the disadvantage of having been hit over the head.

Her head still hurt, but the nausea had abated just a little bit. The cold helped keep it at bay. She looked around. The woods were everywhere. She couldn't see anything that looked like a main road. There was no telling how far back in the forest she was. If it was several miles, she doubted her chances of making it out alive.

She stopped again, listening, but there wasn't anything to hear. The sleet had stopped and now it was snowing, big, fluffy flakes that drifted in front of her face as they fluttered to the ground. It was beautiful, quiet, and almost surreal. It was also deadly. If she didn't keep moving, she would freeze to death.

She put one foot in front of the other and kept walking. There was no longer any chance of seeing the tire tracks of the Bennett woman's SUV, because they were covered up by the snow. But the ruts were still visible, because the grass had been beaten down and crushed by the weight of the big vehicle. She followed them doggedly, her arms wrapped tight around her chest to hold in what little warmth was still left in her body. She cursed the thin blouse and flimsy slacks. Why hadn't she worn something warmer? If only she had a jacket, a blanket, anything to keep her warm!

Once, she thought she heard something in the distance. She stopped, turning her head toward the direction from which it came. She stood very still, waiting, hoping. But the sound vanished quickly. Perhaps, she thought, it was a car going along the highway. She might be closer to it than she'd realized. Her heart lifted, and she began to walk faster. Hope, she thought, was the last thing a person in danger lost. There was always hope.

She remembered her last sight of Cortez's broad back, walking away. She wondered if he regretted their parting as much as she did. She knew he'd feel guilty if she died. It was the way he was made. She'd had a lot of time to consider his attitude, and Tina's, since she'd been out in the wilds. She realized, finally, that it was jealousy. She'd been on the porch talking to Drake. It hadn't been any sort of intimate conversation, but it might have seemed like one to people who were already insecure with their own feelings. She knew Cortez cared for her. He'd talked about children a lot. She loved him. If she got out of this, she promised herself, she was going to sit on him and make him listen to her. She was going to convince him—and Tina—that there was nothing going on between her and Drake Stewart. She wasn't about to let Cortez get away a second time. She walked faster.

MEANWHILE, THE SHERIFF and Cortez were driving along the roads in the national forest while the snow continued to fall.

"It's like trying to find a straw in a haystack," Cortez said tersely as he stared intently ahead.

"It's a big forest," the sheriff agreed. "But you're right in concluding that Miss Bennett would likely take Miss Keller to a place she knew. Since she's not a native, thank God, that narrows the search area a bit."

"I wish we could get in the air," Cortez said fervently. "We'd stand a better chance of finding her."

"She seems like a very sharp woman," came the quiet reply.

"She is," Cortez said, "and she's got a great background in anthropology and archaeology. She's no stranger to back roads and wilderness." His eyes narrowed. "She'd try to walk out, if she could. She'd be on a path."

"You don't think she'd stay put?"

"It's unlikely," Cortez replied. "It's too wet to make a fire and there's the risk of exposure. She'd keep moving. I'm sure of it."

"At first light, I'll get a plane out here if I have to commandeer one, and a pilot to go with it," the sheriff promised. "One way or another, we'll find her."

"It wouldn't hurt to check with the posse and see if they've found any sign."

The sheriff already had the mike in his hand. He grinned at Cortez. "Just what I thought myself."

BUT THE POSSE HAD NOTHING. Neither did the forestry people. It was difficult to search at night, even with the snow making it light enough to see. The forest was immense, and a lone person would just blend in with it.

A call came in from the dispatcher. The sheriff answered it, while Cortez's heart leaped with hope.

"We've had contact from one of your units," the dispatcher said. "One of the guests in a cabin saw a four-wheel-drive vehicle go by twice, headed for the dead end past the picnic area about three hours ago."

"On my way," the sheriff said, stopping to wheel the vehicle around.

Cortez grinned. Finally a break! Now if only they found Phoebe alive…

15

PHOEBE WAS BEGINNING to tire. She was in good health and her legs were strong, but the combination of exertion, exposure and lack of food was telling on her. She'd had breakfast, but she hadn't been hungry at lunch. She'd used up her reserve energy. She stopped, at a sudden crossroad where the road split into four different directions. Looking ahead at the incredible expanse of snow and forest, she felt despair. There were no obvious tracks, and this time there was no distant singing to point the way. For the first time since the ordeal began, she felt that it was going to be impossible to walk to safety.

If she'd had more strength, if she knew where she was going, even the direction, there might have been a chance. She didn't know where she was, so she didn't know in which direction to go. If she made the wrong choice, she was going to die. If she stayed here, she was going to die. If she went into the woods and covered herself up with leaves and pine tree limbs to try and keep warm, they'd never find her and she was still going to die.

She was soaked to the skin from the falling snow. Her hair was wet as well. Her feet were totally numb, her hose soaked. As she took one more step, she became aware that she couldn't feel her feet.

It was too much. She had no more hope. It was going to end, because she couldn't walk anymore. She was so tired. She seemed to have been walking forever. She was cold and hungry and her feet were frozen. She looked up and felt the sleet and snow hit her in the face. She closed her eyes. It was all over.

She sat down in the middle of the crossroads with a long sigh, and then curled herself into a ball and closed her eyes. They said freezing to death wasn't painful. She hoped that was true. She hoped that Cortez would remember how wonderful their brief time together had been, before Tina and Drake complicated everything. Before she complicated everything. She should have gone to Cortez and made him listen. He would have to live with the guilt of walking away from her, and that hurt her, too. She loved him. She whispered his name and her breath sighed out in a weak, final little burst.

IN THE SHERIFF'S CAR, Cortez was grinding his teeth. The road had four forks just past the cabins. What had seemed like pinpointing a location was now another puzzle.

"Stop," he told the sheriff. He got out of the car and walked to the crossroads, narrowing his eyes as he bent down to look carefully at the ground. The snow had covered up everything, but surely there would be a trace of tire tracks if the Bennett woman had come this way!

The sheriff got out and stooped as well, searching. He brushed at snow-covered leaves gently.

"You hunt, don't you?" Cortez asked him.

"Since I was a teen. You're looking for ruts, right?"

"Right. It's the only chance we have."

They bent to the task with flashlights. It didn't take long. The dirt roads weren't well-traveled this time of year, so there were no old tracks to confuse them.

"Found it!" Cortez called, motioning to the sheriff, who stooped beside him.

There, just under the snow, was a firm tire track in the soft dirt—missing one vertical tread! He explained it to the sheriff, who'd been following the case.

"Good thing she didn't realize that tread was so easily identifiable," Sheriff Steele said.

"Absolutely. Let's go!" Cortez jumped up, running for the car.

The sheriff got in under the wheel, started the engine, and turned down the path from which the four-wheel-drive vehicle had come. He called on his radio for reinforcements, in case they had more crossroads to check. Considering how long Phoebe had been missing, she'd be near dead of exposure by now. Another few hours and it wouldn't matter if they found her—because it wouldn't be in time.

Cortez knew that. He also knew that there was every possibility that Claudia Bennett had killed Phoebe. She could be lying in the snow, her soft eyes closed forever in death. His jaw clenched so tight that his teeth hurt. As the car sped along the snow-covered trail, he was praying for all he was worth.

The rutted path seemed to go on forever, down and down, around curves and turns, toward a valley below. There was still a chance that the Bennett woman had killed Phoebe, just as she'd killed her accomplice. Unarmed, Phoebe wouldn't have stood a chance. Cortez couldn't think about that possibility. He'd been cold to her at their parting. It would haunt him forever if she died.

The snow was still coming down, heavier now. The sheriff was slowing for the turns. Both men were intent on the road ahead as it leveled out and ran in a straight line toward the horizon.

The radio buzzed and the sheriff answered it. He stopped the car in the middle of the road and listened, his eyes wide and stunned. Cortez was listening, too. He only smiled.

"We have a message from a Mr. Redhawk in Oklahoma to relay to you," the dispatcher had said. "He says it concerns this case, and it's important."

"Okay," the sheriff replied, puzzled by Cortez's fixed gaze. "Let's have it."

"He says you should look for a fork in the road where two huge hemlock trees are placed, one across from the other, and there's a dead log lying halfway in the road. She'll be there. He also says—" she hesitated, clearing her throat "—that the young lady is pregnant."

Cortez groaned out loud. "Is she alive? Ask him if she's alive!" he demanded.

The sheriff gave him a curious look, but he relayed the question.

There was a brief pause. "Yes. He says she is."

"Thank God!" Cortez ground out, averting his face, which would show a suspicious wetness in his dark eyes.

The sheriff thanked the dispatcher and gave Cortez

a glance. He barely noticed. Phoebe was pregnant? He couldn't believe it! But his father was almost never wrong. If he hit the nail on the head this time, he might have just saved Phoebe.

The sheriff's expression was elegant. "You don't believe in this psychic business, I hope," he scoffed. Just as the last word left his lips, they parted and he gaped as he stopped the car suddenly.

There, in front of them, the road forked. At the left fork, there were two hemlock trees and a dead log just halfway in the road. "My God!" he exclaimed. "Who is that Redhawk guy?"

"My father," Cortez murmured dryly. "He's a shaman." He didn't add that among the Comanche there was no organized group of medicine men, or shaman, that visions were individual and private. His father's gift wasn't because of any status in the culture he belonged to. It was as individual as Charles Redhawk himself was.

The sheriff glanced at him. "I'd like to meet that gentleman," he said sincerely, wheeling the car down the rutted road.

Cortez leaned as far forward as his seat belt would allow, his narrowed eyes intent on the road ahead. Please, he prayed silently, please don't let me lose her. Nothing in life would ever matter again if Phoebe wasn't in the world.

The sheriff slowed as they rounded a curve and then accelerated on the straightaway, where the surroundings widened into clearings on both sides of the road. There were huge oaks and pines and hemlock trees along the road. Snow blanketed the surroundings. In the rear view mirror, he could see his own tire tracks growing deeper.

"Stop!" Cortez yelled suddenly.

Instinctively the sheriff hit the brakes and stopped about a foot from a curled-up figure right in the middle of the road.

Cortez jumped out and ran to Phoebe. He caught her up in his arms, horrified that it might be too late, despite his father's assurances. His arms crushed her to his chest. "Phoebe…sweetheart, can you hear me?" he grated at her ear.

Incredibly, after seconds of anguish, he suddenly felt her breath against his throat. "Thank God, thank God, thank God!" He groaned into her hair. "Phoebe. Baby, can you hear me? Phoebe! Phoebe!"

She heard a voice. She felt warm, strong arms around her. Had she died? She took a painful breath and coughed, shivering as her eyes slowly opened. She looked up into Cortez's drawn, contorted, beloved face. "Jeremiah?" she murmured. She smiled as her cold fingers reached up to touch his cheek. "Am I dead and gone to heaven?" she whispered fervently.

"Not dead," he groaned. "But it feels like heaven. Thank God we found you in time…!" His mouth ground down into hers fervently, with all his fear behind its pressure. Under it, her lips were cold, but responsive. He wanted to kiss her until she warmed, but there was no time for it now. He had to force himself to stop. His face pushed into her throat as he held her. He let her go for a minute and wrenched off his jacket and stuffed her into it.

"Oh, that's so warm," she whispered delightedly, shivering.

"You're half-frozen!" he groaned, wrapping her up tight.

"I never thought you'd find me," she whispered, clinging

to him. "My feet were numb. I couldn't walk anymore. I was so afraid…!"

His mouth stopped the words. "You're safe. You're safe now! I'll never let you go again! Not until I die. I swear it!" He pulled her up gently, hesitating when she cried out as she put pressure on her feet. He turned her so that he could lift her with his right arm, so that his left only had to support her legs. He carried her to the car, ignoring the twinge of pain in his shoulder.

"You'll hurt your shoulder! You mustn't lift me…!" she protested.

"Be quiet." It was painful to know that even now, she was more concerned for him than for herself. She loved him. He could feel it. He loved her, with every cell in his body. He wrapped her up tighter.

Even though he felt the pain with every step, he carried her all the way to the car. He had the sheriff open the door from the inside, and he put her into the back seat. He pulled off her shoes and rubbed her stockinged feet roughly with his big hands, until feeling came back into them. "Have you got a blanket?" he asked the sheriff.

"No, but I've got a sleeping bag in the boot," the sheriff replied, popping the trunk button on the dash. He went to fetch it, handing it in to Cortez, who wrapped it quickly around Phoebe's legs.

"We have to get her to the hospital at once," Cortez said to the sheriff. Only then did he recall the other thing his father had said. He looked at her with wide, curious eyes, wondering if the old man could possibly be right. He had a high percentage of accuracy. Could she be carrying his child? It seemed almost too much to hope for, on top of the miracle that put her, alive, in his arms after the terror of the past few hours.

"We can't go to the hospital," Phoebe said in a croaky tone. "I know where the pistol landed. We have to find it. I'm sure it's the murder weapon."

"Phoebe," Cortez protested.

"I knocked it out of her hands at the last minute," she added. "She was going to shoot me in the back. I thought if I could turn fast enough and knock the pistol out of her hands, I might be able to get away. I was scared to death, but it worked. She has small hands and it was a big .45 automatic."

Cortez shivered at the thought of what could have happened, at point-blank range with a gun of that caliber. He could still see the last murder victim, most of his face missing. He wrapped Phoebe up tighter, his face anguished. "You need treatment," he argued.

"It can wait. I'm all right. If we don't go now," she said gently, "I'll forget. She can't be allowed to get away because you don't have the gun that will convict her." She glanced past him at Sheriff Steele, who was trying to be invisible. "Tell him I'm right," she pleaded.

The sheriff grimaced. "He knows you're right," he replied.

Cortez lifted his head. His eyes were warm and soft in the interior light of the sheriff's car. "Okay, we'll look for the gun. That's my girl," he added softly, and with pride.

She smiled and touched his mouth with her fingertips.

"We'll look," he said, getting out of the car. He closed her door. "Let's go," he told the sheriff. "If she can point out that weapon, we'll have a good case."

"You bet we will," Steele said with a chuckle.

THEY DROVE TO THE SPOT where the Bennett woman had almost killed Phoebe. Incredibly, she'd walked almost three miles from the site.

"Pull right in there," she pointed over the front seats. "It was just in front of that big oak tree."

The sheriff stopped the car. Phoebe, warm now, got out and handed Cortez back his jacket. She was wrapped up in the sleeping bag, wearing it like a shawl.

"It's this way," she said, gritting her teeth as she recalled the terror of her last visit to the spot.

She led the two men to the edge of the small ridge that sloped down to yet another, and then another. She closed her eyes, remembering her position and Claudia Bennett's position. For an instant, she felt sick. Then she caught herself and straightened. A lot depended on her memory. She couldn't let a killer get away.

She looked toward the ridge. "It went in that direction," she pointed past the big oak tree. "It was very heavy, so it couldn't have gone too far. She tried to search for it when I ran and hid, but she couldn't find it. Snow was falling and it was getting dark. I guess she thought I might attack her from behind if she stayed," she added with a wan smile.

Cortez was looking around with a guarded expression. He could picture Phoebe with a gun at her back held by a desperate woman. If she hadn't had good reflexes... He couldn't bear to think about it.

The sheriff gathered a few sticks and made an arrow with them, pointing in the direction Phoebe had indicated.

"Great idea," Cortez said with a smile. "I'll get my forensic team out here with a metal detector. We'll find the gun in no time," he assured the sheriff. He turned to Phoebe. "Right now, we've got to get you to a hospital."

Even as he spoke, a deputy sheriff's car came down the road behind them, followed by a green forestry-service vehicle.

"Talk about great timing," the sheriff chuckled as Drake Stewart got out of his car and approached them, the forest ranger following suit. "Drake, you need to take Phoebe to the emergency room and get her checked out."

She turned to Cortez. "You aren't coming?" she asked suddenly, worried.

He hesitated for a second, torn between duty and concern.

"It doesn't take rocket science to process a crime scene," the sheriff told Cortez. "Too many cooks spoil the soup, anyway. I'll stay out here with your forensic team. We'll find the gun and I'll show them where to get impressions of the tire tracks," the sheriff assured Cortez.

"I'll call Alice Jones right now and bring her out here with her van and equipment," Cortez compromised.

"I'll drop Phoebe and Cortez at the hospital, then I'll go by the motel where Alice Jones is staying and lead her out here," Drake volunteered.

"Good man," Steele said, smiling. "You do that." He glanced at Cortez with a somber expression. "The perp is still on the loose, and she's already tried to kill Miss Keller once. You're needed more at the hospital than here."

"Thanks," Cortez told him.

The sheriff shrugged his big shoulders. "We're all on the same side."

"Indeed we are," Cortez added, with a grin. "You'd make a great addition to our Indian Country Crime Unit. We value local law enforcement."

"Consider me appropriated," Steele told him, smiling. "You'd better get going."

"I'll get your sleeping bag back to you," Phoebe told the sheriff. "Thanks a million!"

"You're welcome," he said gently. "I'm sorry this happened to you. But I'm very glad you're going to be all right."

"Me, too," she murmured, smiling as she caught Cortez's big hand in hers and held tight.

REACTION BEGAN TO SET IN when Phoebe was in a cubicle in the emergency room, waiting for the resident on duty to examine her. She couldn't let go of Cortez's hand.

"How in the world did you find me?" she asked. "I didn't know where I was or how to get out of the forest. I heard strange singing in the distance and went the right way. But when I got to the crossroads, I was too tired and numb to go on. How in the world did you find me?"

"My father led me to you," he murmured enigmatically. He linked her fingers into his, searching her wan face intently. His hair was down, as he usually wore it when he tracked. She reached out and touched a long, thick strand of it.

"I've always loved your hair," she commented softly.

He caught her hand and drew it, palm up, to his mouth. His eyes closed as he savored the soft scent of it, her own special scent. "This has been the longest day of my life," he said huskily.

"Mine, too," she replied.

"Thank God you were desperate enough to try getting that gun out of her hands, or you'd be a case number," he murmured.

"I don't want to die," she said simply. She looked into his dark eyes. "Not until you do."

He nodded solemnly. "Not until I do, sweetheart," he whispered huskily. His eyes were so tender and dark that she felt like crying.

The resident came in while they were still looking at each other. "What's the problem?" he asked pleasantly. He looked at his notes and added, "Miss Keller?"

"I was kidnapped at gunpoint and carried off to be assassinated," she said quietly. "She hit me over the head with something first, I don't know what. I have headache and I had some nausea at first. But my biggest complaint is exposure. I had to walk out of the national forest to get help, and all I had on were a sleeveless blouse, thin slacks and flat shoes with stockings. I'm freezing."

The resident was giving her a tongue-in-cheek look. It lasted just until Cortez pulled out his ID and flashed it under the student doctor's nose.

"She's not making it up," Cortez said. "We've got a BOLO out for the perp. A woman, and she's already killed once."

The resident looked interested. "The guy in the cave, right?"

"I'm impressed," Cortez said, grinning.

"That's why your name looked familiar," he told Phoebe. "You're the anthropologist everybody's talking about. You're the curator at the local Native American museum."

"Yes, I am," Phoebe confessed.

The doctor pulled his stethoscope from around his neck, plugged it into his ears and listened to her chest. He did a standard examination, careful to look for any signs of concussion.

"We won't know until we do an MRI, of course," he said, "but considering that you were unconscious for a few minutes, I think it's concussion. Any dizziness, light sensitivity, nausea?"

"Nausea, just at first. No light sensitivity. Heck of a headache," she added with a weak laugh.

"Well, I think we should keep you tonight," the resident said. "I'll need to run more tests..."

"Can you do a blood test? We think she may be pregnant," Cortez added with breathless tenderness, combined with a glance at Phoebe's shocked face that was as intense as a confession of love.

"You can't know that!" she exclaimed.

"I didn't. When my father called and told us where to look for you, he said you're pregnant."

"Is your father a doctor?" the resident asked curiously.

Cortez cleared his throat. "He's a shaman."

The resident's eyebrows arched. He clasped the chart to his chest. "Let me guess. He told you to put two large silver coins in your pocket just before you were shot," he murmured to Phoebe. He nodded when she laughed self-consciously and Cortez arched both eyebrows. "He's become a local legend among the medical staff here. Considering his batting average, I'd say the blood test is a pretty good idea." He gave Cortez a measuring glance.

Cortez clutched Phoebe's hand and smiled. "It's mine," he said proudly. "And we're getting married next week, whether she wants to or not."

The resident chuckled and went to arrange for a room for her. Phoebe gaped at Cortez. Her heart was racing wildly.

"You want to marry me?" she whispered, shocked.

"Of course," he said simply.

"But you never said...you always talked about...I didn't think..." she faltered, unable to formulate even one single coherent thought.

He touched her mouth gently with his. "I love you with my very soul," he whispered, his eyes dark and soft and solemn. "With my heart, with my mind, with my body. I want to share my life with you. I'll love you all the way to the grave, Phoebe," he whispered. "Until I close my eyes forever. And the memory of you will go with me into the darkness."

She was fighting tears. She drew her long fingers against his cheek. Tears were stinging her eyelids. "I've loved you since the day we met," she whispered back. "I never stopped. Not even when I thought you tossed me aside for some other woman who was closer to your own culture."

"Now you know why I did it," he replied. "Why I had to do it."

She smiled. "I love Joseph, too."

"We'll have children of our own," he said. "Starting with this one," he added, tracing her belly lightly. He smiled. "What a delight!"

Her fingers rested atop his and she smiled with wonder. "Yes."

They looked into each other's eyes and dreamed of the future.

BUT REALITY INTRUDED when Phoebe was settled down in a private room. Cortez's cell phone rang noisily. He answered it.

"We found the pistol and got impressions of the tire tracks. We've got her on the run," Sheriff Steele told Cortez. "Every unit in the county is on the road looking for her and she's been spotted just outside town. Do you have any idea where she might go underground?"

Cortez thought for a moment. "Where's the last place you'd think to look for her?"

The sheriff paused. "Miss Keller's house."

"My guess, too. I'm on my way. I'll meet you at the end of Phoebe's driveway."

"Post a man at the door of her room, just in case," the older man suggested.

"No argument there," Cortez replied.

He hung up and went to the bed, where Phoebe, although sedated, was still awake enough to worry.

"Don't you go out there and get yourself killed," she said firmly. "If I really am pregnant—and God knows how they could tell this quickly from a blood test—our baby is going to need a father!"

He smiled down at her. "And a mother," he pointed out. He bent and kissed her tenderly. "I'm going to call the local police and have them send an officer over to take care of you while I'm gone."

"Okay."

"I'll be careful," he promised. "We can't let her get away," he added grimly.

"No, we can't. I'll just hang around here. I love gourmet food."

He winked, and left her reluctantly.

THE RESIDENT CAME IN a few minutes later, looking whimsical. "I have two announcements," he said.

She held out her hand, palm up.

"You're pregnant."

She grinned from ear to ear and propped her hands on her stomach. "Gosh, I didn't get you anything!"

He grinned back.

"Second announcement?" she prompted.

"It seems that you have a visitor." He stood aside. A tall, slim, elegant silver-haired man in a vested gray suit walked in. He had dark eyes and high cheekbones. He looked vaguely Spanish.

Phoebe was puzzled. She stared at the newcomer intently. The resident smiled and walked out the door to finish his rounds.

"So you're Phoebe," the man said in a cultured voice. He smiled warmly. "I'm impressed, and not only with your credentials. You have courage."

She blinked. "I'm sorry, I don't know you, do I?"

He waved the question away, moving forward to stand over her. "That isn't important. I'm glad you're safe. I had worried that I wouldn't be in time."

She was more confused by the second. Perhaps the drugs had her hallucinating.

"I was already in Atlanta. The problem was getting a commuter flight up here, with the weather being so bad," he said. "But just in case they had too much trouble finding you, I was going to volunteer for the search party. God knows how I'll explain this to my boss," he added wistfully.

"Your boss?"

"I teach history at our local community college in Oklahoma. Final exams are in four days."

Her lower jaw fell. "You're…!"

"Jeremiah's father, yes," he confirmed. He grinned from ear to ear. "See, no rattles, no bells, no beads and I actually did courses in anthropology. Think what a handy grandfather I'm going to make!"

CORTEZ HAD MADE IT TO his own car, still parked at the motel. Tina came running out with Joseph in her arms.

"Is she all right? Did you find her?" she exclaimed.

"She's fine. They've got her at the hospital, and they're keeping her overnight."

"She was hurt?" Tina exclaimed, crushed with guilt.

"A little, but they're keeping her for further precautionary tests. We think she's pregnant." He grinned wickedly. "You're going to be an aunt again!"

Tina's eyes widened like saucers. "It's…yours?"

He glared at her. "Of course it's mine!"

"How could I have been so wrong about Drake and Phoebe?" she groaned.

"Love makes us do crazy things, I suppose," he said gently. "Drake knows everything now, I might add. He's walking on clouds because you care about him."

Her eyes opened wide. "He is? He is?" She cleared her throat. "About Phoebe. I'll apologize to her on my knees, I swear I will. Where are you going?"

"To catch the perp. Stay inside with the door locked."

"I will. Oh, did you get the call?"

He paused. "What call? From whom?"

"From your father," she replied with a wicked grin. "He's on his way to the hospital!"

16

CORTEZ LAUGHED. "DIDN'T he think we could handle this by ourselves?" he asked.

"You know Uncle Charles," she said brightly. "He's already fond of Phoebe. He said he couldn't wait to see her. He also said that he wanted to be at the wedding. He hoped he was in time."

Cortez, from a lifetime of living with his father's uncanny gift, only shook his head. "We're getting married in five days, God knows how he knew."

"Can I come?" Tina asked wanly.

"Of course you can. Phoebe doesn't hold grudges."

"Thank goodness."

He kissed Joseph and then Tina, and got into the car. "I'll see you later. Lock the door!"

"You got it!" Tina ran back inside, her face radiant with delight.

Cortez burned rubber getting out to Phoebe's house. At the end of her driveway, he found Sheriff Steele, Drake, and a recently-arrived special agent from a nearby field office, Special Agent Jack Norris.

"The same neighbor who saw her leave here yesterday just confirmed that she came back a few minutes ago," Sheriff Steele told Cortez. "We're debating tactics."

"Rush her," Cortez said coldly. "I won't risk letting her get away."

"She can't," the sheriff assured him. "This is the only road out. The snow's getting pretty deep. She slid around just getting to Phoebe's house."

"Waiting her out is going to use up manpower and time," Cortez replied. "She's got nothing to lose. She won't mind killing again. Homicide, or even suicide, would make no difference now."

"We can draw straws to see who doesn't have to go first," Drake mused.

Cortez stalked back to his car. "There's no need for straws. I'm going. Norris, you're backup. You drive. Go slow, because I'm diving out at the old well in the front yard. You continue around back, but keep your head down." He glanced toward the sheriff. "I'm counting on you two to stop her if she gets this far."

They nodded solemnly. "It's your show," Sheriff Steele said. "Good luck."

Cortez threw up his hand in acknowledgment. Norris, a new agent, dark-haired and tall, climbed in under the wheel and Cortez got in on the passenger side.

They eased closer to the house. Cortez expected a shoot-out, but there were no shots fired at them from the house.

"Here, when you turn at the pine trees just at the side

of the house, slow down and I'll get out. They'll provide cover," he told Norris.

"Yes, sir. Then what do I do?"

"Park in front of her SUV so she can't move it forward," Cortez told him. "The only alternative then would be for her to back into the trees. There's a sheer drop of about a hundred feet down that foot path. I checked it out one day when Phoebe was at work. She didn't even know about it."

"That's a long fall," Norris agreed.

"A fatal one, in a vehicle. Okay. Here goes. Stop!"

Norris stopped, Cortez jumped out and pulled his service revolver. He'd like to take Claudia Bennett alive, but she'd already killed once. He wasn't taking chances.

He eased to the front porch and peered in through the windows while Norris was making noise backing in the snow-covered driveway.

Under the cover of the noise, he tried the door and found it unlocked. He eased in, glad he was wearing crepe-soled shoes, so that he made no noise. He hoped the boards didn't creak.

He stopped, closed his eyes, and listened. Norris had stopped the car and cut off the engine. It was quiet, except for the sound of the wind outside. The snow had stopped, but the wind hadn't.

There was a faint scuffing sound in the kitchen. Holding the automatic firmly in both hands, Cortez moved past the dining room and to the doorway of the kitchen. He saw the stove and refrigerator and the tile floor. He saw a shoe, barely moving.

He darted into the room with the pistol leveled and grimaced. Claudia Bennett was lying on the floor. Beside her, on the tile, was the pistol Phoebe had learned to shoot. The blond woman had a spreading red stain on the front of her skirt. She looked up at Cortez through dazed, cold eyes.

He knelt beside her, yelling for Norris. The other agent opened the back door, which was unlocked, and moved into the room. He had his service revolver out as well, but he put it away when he saw the woman on the floor.

"Were you shot?" Cortez asked her.

She swallowed. "It doesn't hurt much, isn't that strange?" She swallowed again. "Fred was supposed to keep the artifacts for a year…before he sold them. The fool went straight to the museum here…and sold one to that Keller…woman." She tried to breathe and winced. The stain was spreading even more.

Cortez reached onto the counter and pulled down a dish towel. He folded it quickly and pressed it hard to the woman's wound. She groaned.

"Call 911," Cortez told Norris.

"It's no good," she told Cortez. "I've been lying here… several minutes. I aimed for…my heart but I fumbled and shot myself in the stomach." She laughed and then choked, coughing and wincing even more. "My husband…called that archaeologist, his cousin. I panicked. I told Fred. We called the man and told him we were in law enforcement and that we knew about the artifacts. He told us to come get him and he'd show us where they were. We went to his motel. He was on the phone. We didn't know who he'd called. As soon as he hung up, Fred shot him. He'd taped an empty soft drink liter-sized bottle to the end of the pistol to make a silencer. Nobody heard. We loaded him in the car and dumped him on a dirt road…out of town. We had no idea…it was on Cherokee land," she added miserably. "The last thing we wanted…was to involve the feds."

Praying that the EMTs would get to her in time, Cortez listened intently as she struggled to get the words out.

She swallowed hard again before continuing. "Fred said he wasn't going back to prison, no matter what. He scared me. I figured he'd turn me in, and I've got…a record. So I posed as a teacher to get to Miss Keller. It was a stroke of good luck on my part—I found the name of a real teacher from an article in the local paper about the woman winning some fancy teacher's award. Anyway, I hoped Phoebe would remember Fred and tell the police, so he'd get put away real fast. But it had the opposite effect." She caught her breath. Her voice was getting weaker. "Fred said he was taking the artifacts and he was going to pin the murder on me.

"I wasn't about to let that happen. So I lured Walks Far to the cave so he could catch Fred red-handed and turn him into the authorities. But Fred was too smart. He knocked out Walks Far and was going to kill him. I had a pistol of my own in my pocket, a .45 automatic. I told Fred to check my husband's pockets to make sure he wasn't wearing a wire. I knew he wasn't—I just needed Fred…to bend down. He did, and I shot him in the back of the head."

"You could have pleaded self-defense," Cortez said curtly, acknowledging Norris's nod that the medics and police were on the way. "How did you move the body?"

"After I killed Fred, it was just a matter of time until they found me. I was so scared that I could have moved a stove by myself! I dragged Walks Far to the truck, drove him back to the construction trailer and turned on the lights. I thought that would buy me some time. Maybe they'd think Walks Far killed Fred and managed to get out of there to the construction site somehow. But Miss Keller was a wild card, you see. I had to kill her so she couldn't identify me as the woman from the museum. She could connect me to Fred."

Cortez stiffened in anger.

"But Miss Keller knocked my pistol out of my hand and it got lost. I couldn't find it and she ran where I couldn't take the SUV. I took off, but before I could get packed I heard on the radio that Miss Keller had been found. I knew that it was all over. I came here, because I thought I'd be safe while I decided what to do. She had a pistol of her own—I found it by the bedside table."

Despite all the misery Claudia had caused, Cortez couldn't help but feel a pang of sympathy for her final act of desperation. He squeezed her hand, urging her to continue.

She laughed pathetically. "Suddenly it just didn't seem worth all the trouble, to run and hide. And I couldn't go to prison. Walks Far used to talk about how horrible it was..." She grimaced. "I'm sorry," she whispered, looking up at Cortez with glazed eyes. "Tell my brother...and my husband...I love them, and I'm sorry!"

"I'll tell them," Cortez said quietly. "Just one more thing...how did you arrange the museum heist?"

"Fred impersonated a guard so that we could get into the museum in New York at night. I helped him steal the artifacts," she added sadly. Claudia closed her eyes. "It was all for the excitement. Walks Far was so boring and normal. I wanted adventure, money...power." She sighed slowly and she opened her eyes one last time. "I was...so close... to making it. Tell my husband...he should have turned me in...years ago. I let him take the rap for me when I stole those jewels from the museum. He's got a record, and he never did anything wrong…except love me. What a… fool…what a sweet, sweet fool…"

Claudia's eyes closed. Her breath sighed out and she went still. Cortez felt for a pulse. She'd bled to death internally, he was sure of it. But he tried to revive her, all the same. He was still trying when the EMTs roared up and took over for him.

He locked the house to preserve the crime scene and he and Norris followed the ambulance to the hospital. But Claudia Bennett was pronounced dead on arrival.

Cortez stopped by Walks Far's room to tell him what had happened. His brother-in-law, Bennett, came in a few minutes later. He repeated the story for the other man as well.

"Norris and I heard her confession," Cortez told the Cherokee man somberly. "A deathbed confession is as good as a written, notarized one. You can hire a lawyer and apply to the governor for a full pardon for the crime you were convicted of. We'll back you up." He glanced at Bennett. "You could get the dumping charge off your record as well. For what it's worth, I'm sorry. I had a brother who was in trouble with the law all his life," he added. "Sometimes all the love and care in the world won't save another person from prison."

"I suppose not," Bennett said. He shook hands with Cortez. "Thank you, for not letting her die without trying to save her. She did shoot herself?"

He nodded. "With Phoebe's gun—the one our deputy sheriff gave her to protect herself with."

"You can't win when Fate starts calling in bets," Walks Far said solemnly. "I loved her. But she didn't know what love was."

"She said to tell you both that she loved you, and that she was sorry," he replied. He leaned forward, his eyes intent on Walks Far's sad face. "She saved you from being shot by the killer. She didn't have to. She was already an accessory to murder. One more wouldn't have mattered. But she killed him to save you."

Walks Far managed a smile. "Thanks."

Cortez shrugged. "Give it time," he advised both men. "It does heal."

Bennett only nodded. "I'd better call the funeral home…" He hesitated.

"We'll have to have an autopsy first," Cortez replied. "No coroner is going to take my word for how she died. You can still have her taken to the local funeral home, though. The state crime lab will take it from there."

Bennett grimaced. "I'll never stop wondering if I could have saved her, if I'd let her take the rap for the first felony she committed. I was so concerned with our family name. Now look at it."

"You can't second-guess the past. You just have to live with it and go on. I'll be in touch," he added. "I have to see about Phoebe."

"You found her?" Bennett asked abruptly. "She's alive?"

"She's going to be fine." He smiled. "So one good thing came out of an otherwise rotten situation."

"Thank God," Bennett said. "That's one death I won't have on my conscience."

"I'm glad she's going to be all right," Walks Far said. "Be well."

"You, too," Cortez said as he left.

His father was sitting in the chair beside Phoebe's bed, beaming. He looked up when his son walked in the door.

They exchanged greetings in Comanche and embraced heartily.

"I approve of your choice," Mr. Redhawk told his son. He glanced wickedly at Phoebe. "But I do wonder what you told her about me. She was shocked when she saw me."

"Oh, she was just expecting you in a loincloth and a war-bonnet, riding a painted pony," Cortez teased, watching Phoebe color furiously.

"I was not!" she argued at once.

Both men chuckled.

"So, do I get to be best man?" he asked Cortez. "I can't stay long. I've got final exams next week, and nobody to sub for me."

"We'll be comfortably on our honeymoon by then," Cortez assured him. He bent and kissed Phoebe tenderly, his dark eyes possessive and loving as they met hers.

"Where are you going to live?" he asked Cortez.

"Oh, dear," Phoebe murmured, having grown attached to her little community over the years.

Cortez pursed his lips. "Well, I can live anywhere I like," he told her. "As long as there's an airport nearby. And I'm rather fond of Chenocetah. These Cherokee people aren't bad."

Her eyes lit up. "Really? You mean it?"

"It would be a good place to raise our kids," he replied. "Joseph will have plenty of opportunities to learn how to speak the local language, too."

"I can always come to visit in the summers," Cortez's father added, smiling.

"I'm a good cook," Phoebe said. "I'll feed you up."

"I must look undernourished," he told his son.

"You're a bit lean," Cortez mused.

"That's a deal, then. What are you going to name my grandson?"

They both looked at him, stunned.

"Sorry," he said with a sheepish grin. "I guess you didn't want to know what you were getting until the delivery, huh?"

Phoebe cleared her throat. "You saved my life. Twice. I guess that entitles you to say anything you like. And thank you!"

He chuckled. "Just a gift. I like to think I use it wisely. You're welcome."

"What about that Bennett woman?" she asked Cortez suddenly.

"Suicide," he said. "We'll talk about it later," he added, not wanting to tell her where the woman had died. They still had to work the crime scene.

"We mustn't have secrets," she pointed out.

"And we won't," he assured her, smiling. "Just this one. And only for today."

"Tina called," his father said. "She wants to come and apologize to Phoebe. Is it okay?"

"Of course," Phoebe said at once. "I don't hold grudges."

"Good thing," Cortez murmured. "Tina's worn herself out crying."

"Jealousy is hell," Phoebe murmured, searching his eyes quietly. And she should know, she thought. She'd hated Cortez's wife when she knew he had one.

His eyes darkened. "Yes," he had to agree, because he'd had his own problems over Drake.

"They can both come to the wedding," she told him complacently.

He just smiled.

THEY WERE MARRIED THE next week. Alice Jones and the rest of the unit had gone back to D.C. Cortez had checked with his old boss and made arrangements to live in Chenocetah and be on call whenever he was needed. His new assignment was to teach Sheriff Steele, Drake, and Officer Parker the basics of investigations on Indian Reservations, so that they could officially be part of the FBI's Indian Country Crime Unit.

Tina and Drake made up so publicly, at the hospital, that people gossiped about it for a week. Tina made up with Phoebe, as well, crying all over the older woman incoherently until she was certain she'd been forgiven. Phoebe grew closer to Joseph with every passing day, and also to her future father-in-law. His specialty was colonial American history, primarily the French and Indian War of the 1750s. Many sites around North Carolina were linked to this period. As Mr. Redhawk told Phoebe, he'd have plenty of places to explore when he came to visit them.

Bennett and Yardley and Cortland continued with their respective projects. Walks Far was on his way to a pardon. Bennett himself was cleared of the dumping charges.

Phoebe brought her chow, Jock, back home and Cortez and Joseph moved in with her. Christmas was a wonderful celebration, with the museum staff and their families turning out for the celebration, as well as Tina and Drake and Sheriff Steele, a bachelor. They included several police officers in the festivities as well. Phoebe decorated a huge tree in the living room. The Native Americans only grinned at her enthusiasm for the custom, and helped wrap gifts.

On Christmas Eve, Cortez presented Phoebe with a diamond wedding band surrounded by rubies.

She touched the sparkling stones with wonder. "It's beautiful," she whispered.

"It's the color of the sky, just before sunrise," he told her gently, and he smiled as he bent to kiss her. "It's to remind you that even the most frightening nights do end in morning."

"Hope never dies," she agreed. She looked up at him with wonder. "It was all worth it, you know."

"What was?"

"All the years of pain and grief," she replied. "There really is a rainbow at the end of the storm. I'm living in it."

He kissed her tenderly again. "Me, too." He wrapped her up close and tucked her against his broad chest. His eyes closed. "Merry Christmas."

She snuggled closer. "It's the merriest one I've ever had. Maybe we'll have dozens and dozens more."

Joseph came wandering into the living room, grinning at the tree and at the two adults. "Santa Claus up the chimney now?" he wondered, looking worriedly at the fire in the fireplace. "Santa Claus burn up?" he added, looking ready to cry. "Joseph won't have toys!" He wailed.

Cortez got up and went to the youngster, picking him up to hug him while Phoebe collapsed in laughter.

"Listen, young man," he said to the child, "that red suit Santa wears is fireproof. I swear!"

Joseph blinked and then he smiled. "Okay, Daddy!"

"So you rush right back to bed, if you want presents! Santa won't come until you're asleep."

"Going right now!" Joseph agreed. He looked at the corner where Jock was curled up asleep. "Jock not bite Santa?" he added worriedly.

"Jock loves Santa," Cortez assured him.

"Jock not chase reindeer?" the child persisted.

"Jock loves reindeer," Phoebe agreed. "A lot!"

"Okay." Joseph kissed Cortez, and then Phoebe, and waddled back off to his room down the hall. The door closed behind him.

"Fireproof, are you?" Phoebe mused, giving him a speaking glance. "Come here and let's see!"

He went down into her arms on the sofa with a hungry groan, crushing her mouth under his.

It seemed he wasn't fireproof, after all.

★ ★ ★ ★ ★